# Born to Hustle

## A Novel

# Born to Hustle

## A Novel

Edward A. Dreyfus

Enchanted Villa Press

Pacific Palisades, CA

**Enchanted Villa Press**
**16901 Enchanted Place**
**Pacific Palisades, CA 90272**
**www.edwarddreyfusbooks.com**

Publisher's Note: This is a work of fiction. Names, characters, places, and incidents are a product of the author's imagination. Locales and public names are sometimes used for atmospheric purposes. Any resemblance to actual people, living or dead, or to businesses, companies, events, institutions, or locales is completely coincidental.

**Born to Hustle/Edward A. Dreyfus**
ISBN 978-0692192436

## DEDICATION

This book is dedicated to the many people who shared their stories and struggles with me as they searched to find their unique identity amidst the dysfunction of their family.

I especially dedicate this work to identical twins who have unique challenges in defining their own individuality and sense of self as separate from their look-alike twin.

# ACKNOWLEDGEMENTS

While writing is a solitary activity, much like raising a child, it takes a community to produce a book. I thank my family and friends who listened as I struggled with various challenges. They shared their thoughts, suggestions, and ideas to help me break through impasses in plot and character development. I particularly thank my editor, Rita Hubbard, who constantly pushed me, challenged me, questioned me, and with her incisive comments and suggestions helped me become a better writer. I thank Kristen Bryant who produced the cover of this and several other of my books. And lastly, I want to thank "the bad-assed boys-in-black" who inspired me to write this work of fiction.

# TABLE OF CONTENTS

Dedication

Acknowledgements

CHAPTER ONE

# In the Beginning

## *1982*

"Here they come!" announced the obstetrician as she extracted the first baby from the womb of 19-year-old Martina Suarez. Fourteen minutes later, the second twin arrived on the scene. "Identical boys!" exclaimed the doctor.

The infants were four weeks premature; each weighed in at exactly four pounds and nineteen inches long. This was about average for thirty-two-week preemies.

Martina was married for only one year, and now she was a mother—and of twins, no less. On the one hand, she was excited, as most new mothers would be. On the other hand, she was overwhelmed by the responsibilities caring for two babies would bring. A sense of foreboding enveloped her as she thought about how her husband, Lucas, had reacted when he had heard she was pregnant with twins. Her initial excitement at having delivered twins quickly dissipated. Rather than feeling happy, she felt dread.

She and Lucas had learned that she was carrying twins only when she was admitted to the emergency room after her water broke. They were so tiny, and positioned in her uterus in such a way, that the ultrasounds taken during Martina's pregnancy had not picked up that there were twins. The twins' hearts had beat in unison during the ultrasound, and the obstetrician had assumed that there was only one very small fetus. Once Martina's water broke, the fetuses shifted their positions, and the ultrasound taken in the ER revealed that she was carrying twins.

On hearing the news from the ER nurse that there were two fetuses instead of one, Lucas had become irate.

"What the fuck! How the fuck are we going to support and take care of twins! I'm fuckin' out of here!"

With that outburst, Lucas raced out of the ER and headed for the nearest pub. It was apparent to Martina that Lucas resented the idea that as a husband and father he would have to give up spending his time and his inheritance solely on himself. Sharing was not Lucas's strong suit. He was all about himself.

Lucas was only twenty years old and totally unprepared for fatherhood. He was the only child of indulgent parents who travelled extensively for the family business. They had little interest in being hands-on parents. His own mother's pregnancy had been an accident. His parents' real "baby" was their business; it took all of their time. Hence, Lucas was left in the care of various nannies and other employed caregivers who indulged him for fear of losing their jobs. They took no responsibility for disciplining him. He never had to control his anger; there were no limits placed upon him, no controls. Therefore, he developed into a demanding child with a violent temper, intimidating his caregivers, and often getting into fights with other children.

As he reached adolescence, he hung out with a wild, affluent crowd that loved to drink. His temper got worse when he drank. His maternal grandfather, who had started the family business, left Lucas a modest trust fund, making working for a living unnecessary as long as he was responsible in his spending. Lucas always expected things to just land in his lap.

When the nurse placed the twin boys on her chest, Martina couldn't help but smile. "They're so little," she whispered.

"No worries," replied the nurse with a knowing smile. "They're healthy and will grow like weeds."

Martina was just the opposite of Lucas. With a predisposition for shyness, she grew into an anxious child, lacking in self-confidence. Her parents were financially comfortable—not as wealthy as her in-laws—but nevertheless, they pampered and coddled her. She was, and continued to be, her daddy's little girl and her mother's baby. She grew up with few responsibilities other than to be sweet and pretty. She never had to learn to fend for herself.

Martina had met Lucas when they were both attending college. She was attracted to his bad-boy look and devil-may-care attitude. He appeared to have enough self-confidence for the two of them. At the time, she hadn't realized that what she thought was confidence was mostly bravado. And what she thought was strength was mostly an angry, troubled, immature, spoiled adolescent.

Martina was very attractive, with green eyes and long, black, wavy hair that hung loosely on her shoulders. Though Argentinian, she looked more European. She was slim, even now after having delivered twins. She never thought of herself as beautiful, but most people found her striking, especially men. When her parents first met Lucas, they both had serious reservations about him. He had developed a reputation within the Argentinian community for being impulsive and spoiled by his parents who were known to have a jet-set lifestyle. Martina had been kept on a short leash, whereas Lucas had had no leash at all.

Lucas had pursued her and had been quite charming. He could make her laugh with his devil-may-care attitude and his playful behavior. She had been far less adventurous and prone to avoid taking chances. Where she was afraid to jaywalk, Lucas would halt traffic by walking across the street raising his arm like a traffic cop stopping traffic. Nothing seemed to frighten or worry him. Martina worried about everything: parking tickets, passing tests with less than a perfect score, and how she looked in the mirror.

Lucas had been attracted to her looks and docility; he had basked in her admiration of his brashness. Like a teenager, he loved showing off for her. Lucas had introduced her to a more playful and exciting life than she had previously known. When she became pregnant, Martina's immediate reaction had been guilt and anxiety. Lucas, however, simply took it in stride. He even seemed excited by the prospect of being a father and did the right thing: he married her. But shortly after the wedding, things changed. Martina recognized that despite his initial excitement about becoming a parent, Lucas was not ready for the responsibilities of being a husband—much less a father. He just wanted to listen to music with his friends, play cards, go to parties, and get drunk.

During her pregnancy, Martina came to realize that she had married an overgrown child prone to temper tantrums. Whenever she refused him sex, Lucas would sulk and throw a fit. If she asked for help with the housework, he would leave, yelling, *"Ese es el trabajo de las mujeres!* (that's women's work!)"*, slamming the door behind him. Lucas expected Martina to take care of him, the house, and now the babies. The babies rivaled his need to always be the center of attention. Being a father did not fit the life he wanted.

*Now I will be the mother of three children*, thought Martina, *and two of them preemies. How am I going to manage?*

She knew her parents would help, at least with money, but they had a very active life in both Los Angeles and Buenos Aires, where they had a home and business. In addition, they had an active social life. They would not be available for daily emotional support. And Lucas's parents, though they had indulged him all of his life, practically disowned him when they learned he had impregnated Martina and planned to get married without even having a job. He had dropped out of college as a junior and spent his time carousing around, drinking, and blowing through the modest inheritance he had received from his grandfather. His parents were quite conservative and devout Catholics. They attended mass regularly, went to confession every week, and took communion every Sunday. They viewed Martina as having sinned; she would always be seen as a fallen woman.

Martina knew that she couldn't count on her in-laws for any form of emotional support. Martina and Lucas were going to be on their own raising these children. Other than financially, they were going to have to learn how to be parents without help from their parents. Emotionally, they were children themselves, and now they had two kids.

Martina continued to look from one to the other of the tiny babies lying on either side of her chest. Her eyes filled with tears of love.

Suddenly, Lucas burst into the room. He was drunk.

"Lemme see my babies!" he yelled. He looked frenzied. Lucas was a wiry, slim man who stood about five-ten with dark eyes and unruly, curly hair. When drunk, he could look particularly menacing. He was loud and glassy eyed, with a pronounced sneer on his lips; over all, he appeared crazed.

His tone alone frightened Martina. The younger nurse was totally taken aback, but the older nurse was calm and fearless. Her glare alone showed Lucas she was in charge.

"Mr. Suarez, you are not going to come near these babies, much less touch them until you are sober, you hear me? And when you are sober, washed, and wearing a hospital gown, then and only then will you get to be near these beautiful babies. Do you understand what I'm sayin'?" She continued to glare at him.

Lucas froze, wide-eyed, like a deer caught in the headlights. He wasn't used to anyone, especially a woman, giving him orders. But then he suddenly lunged toward the nurse, stumbled over the food tray, and fell. The younger nurse was already calling for hospital security. By the time Lucas picked himself up, two beefy, armed security guards arrived. They grabbed him by the arms and ushered him out of the room and out of the hospital.

"Fuck you, bitch!" he yelled over his shoulder as they dragged him off. "I'll be back!"

Martina was in tears.

The nurses held the babies in their arms. The older nurse turned to Martina and said, "Now don't you worry, honey. It's gonna be okay. We're gonna take these beautiful boys to the NICU—that's the Neonatal Intensive Care Unit—and make sure they are taken care of, and then I'll be back. In the meantime, why don't you get some sleep? You did good work delivering these sweeties, and now you should rest."

And so began the first day in the lives of twins Brian and Alan Suarez with their timid mother and abusive, alcoholic father.

Martina was discharged about three days after the delivery, but the twins remained in the NICU for another three weeks. They were then placed in the neonatal maternity ward for another week before they were discharged.

On the day of her leaving the hospital, Lucas picked up Martina and drove her home. During the ride, he apologized for how he had been behaving and promised to do better. He told Martina that he was looking forward to becoming a father and would be a better husband. Martina wanted to believe him, but even within their short courtship and marriage, she had already accumulated a closetful of promises. That was Lucas's way; he'd promise, be contrite, and then just as quickly forget the promises when they interfered with what he wanted to do.

Martina returned every day to visit her babies—without Lucas.

The couple lived in a two-bedroom condo that Lucas's parents had bought as an investment property. Despite their disapproval of the marriage, his parents had allowed the young couple to stay in the condo as a wedding gift, with the idea that once Lucas found a job he would begin paying rent. Now that he was a father and husband, they were no longer willing to indulge him. He had to learn to pay his own way. And just as they never had any desire to be parents, they did not have any particular interest in being grandparents.

One bedroom was set up like a nursery for the twins. Martina's parents had furnished it as a gift while Martina was in the hospital. Her parents also hired a nanny to help care for the boys. When Martina walked into the apartment and saw the sky-blue nursery with the twin cribs with mobiles hanging over them, her eyes misted over. She gazed about and smiled. Then her eyes landed on a bookcase filled with trucks and other typical boy's toys.

"Those must have been your doing," she said, turning to Lucas. "Don't you think they're a little young for trucks?"

"Maybe now," Lucas replied, smiling, "but they'll grow. I want them to know they are real boys."

Martina just shook her head. She knew better than to say anything aloud.

*Like you?* she thought. *Not if I can help it.*

The day Brian and Alan arrived home, friends and family crowded into the condo to give them a proper Argentinian welcome, complete with music and lots of food. Lucas had invited all his friends to see his two sons. By this time, the boys had grown to over seven pounds. Despite having almost doubled their birth weight, the twins were still essentially newborns. The noise in the house, especially after the newborns having spent three weeks in the quiet confines of the NICU, was overwhelming for the twins as well as Martina. The infants cried constantly. Though tiny, their shrill screams, especially when combined, were louder than a stuck pig. They seemed to feed off one another as though they were competing for a "who can cry the loudest medal."

Martina and the nanny picked them up, humming softly in an attempt to comfort them. The laughter, music, and loud voices coming from the living room made it even more difficult for either of them to quiet the infants.

Each time the infants did settle down a bit, Lucas would barge into the nursery, disrupting the temporary quiet. Not caring about anyone else, he kept wanting to show them off. He joined in one toast after the other until he could hardly walk without stumbling. Being intoxicated was getting to be his customary state, and when drunk, he became even more irritable and impatient than normal. The crying finally got to him.

"Can't you shut these damn kids up?" he demanded of Martina. "Don't they ever sleep!"

"How can they sleep with all the noise you and your friends are creating," replied an exasperated Martina. "They need quiet."

"They're gonna have to get used to noise," yelled Lucas. "This ain't no hospital!"

This was the way things went. The nanny learned that when Lucas was around, there wasn't going to be peace and quiet. She tried to give him a wide berth, avoiding interacting with him and staying clear of both his temper and his attempts to back her into a corner where he would try to grope her. He was constantly making sexual comments and leering at her in a lascivious way.

Despite it being a small apartment, she managed to leave any room just as he entered it. By maintaining her vigilance, keeping an eye on where Lucas might be at any given moment, she was able to avoid being alone with him in the same room. Lucas knew that as an undocumented immigrant she wouldn't report him to the police, and he took full advantage of it.

It wasn't long before the nanny discovered that when she placed the twins in a single crib together, they both would stop crying. They would cuddle up with one another, falling asleep as one bundle. Even before they were able to crawl, they managed to snuggle up to one another, replicating their position as it was in the womb. They became inseparable. They were more like clones—mirror images of one another— emulating each other's sounds and movements. Martina thought of them as womb-mates.

Lucas was constantly in a state of heightened irritability. He yelled about everything. He criticized Martina, he criticized the nanny, and he continued to drink. So much for his promises of being a good husband and father. Thankfully, he spent most of his days out of the home, but when there, he created chaos. He would come home and hit the ground running with his yelling and temper tantrums, disrupting whatever peace and quiet there was. He kicked things, threw and knocked items off tables, and punched walls. It was like a cyclone had torn through the front door. His temper frightened Martina to the point that she feared he would hurt either her or the twins—or both. He would lean over their cribs and scream at them to shut up. Martina was afraid that he would hit them.

The first nanny quit, fearful for her safety. By the time Brian and Alan were three months old, they had had three different nannies. And by the time they were three years old, there were too many to count. They lived in a war zone. The constant tumult and Martina's ever-increasing anxiety disrupted any form of secure attachment to their mother from developing. Similar to many preemies, after spending weeks in an incubator, the twins had difficulty attaching to their mother. And living with an anxious, frightened mother made a secure attachment virtually impossible. It had already reached the point that no adult could comfort them, including Martina. They never experienced their mother as their go-to source for comfort. They lived in a constant state of threat. Their only source of comfort was one another.

Martina had become increasingly anxious and depressed, causing her to sleep more and eat less. Headaches were constant. Lucas spent more time out of the home than in it. With her parents spending more of their time in Buenos Aires, she relied more and more upon the various nannies to care for the twins as well as for her own emotional support. Though she heard of women who sought psychological help for depression and marriage counseling, seeking help for herself was not part of her culture; and seeing a marriage counselor was totally out of the question.

On more than one occasion, Lucas would violently shake the twins, scaring Martina. Their little heads would snap back and forth like bobble dolls, causing them to scream even louder. Martina had read about *shaken baby syndrome* and feared that Lucas's constant shaking of the twins would cause them permanent brain damage. The more he yelled, the more frightened the boys became, and of course, the more they cried.

Friends advised Martina to call Child Protective Services and file a complaint against Lucas for child abuse. She refused. She didn't want the children to grow up without a father. She didn't think about the long-term effects on the twins of living in a house where no one protected them.

During one of Martina's follow-up visits to the pediatrician, the doctor, who had some familiarity with Lucas's erratic behavior from having read the obstetrician's medical records, suspected that things were not going well for Martina at home. He was concerned with the development of the twins and explained to her the potential developmental and psychological damage the boys could be undergoing by living in a chaotic home.

"An infant's brain is very susceptible to trauma, both physical and emotional," he explained. "Children growing up in war areas often experience problems in learning how to talk and walk, or they may develop learning disabilities."

Martina listened attentively, feeling increasingly guilty as the doctor spoke.

The doctor continued, "Living in a home filled with violence and strife can be like a war zone to an infant and can have a similar effect on an infant's brain."

Martina just sat with her hands folded in her lap. The doctor had the file from the hospital and had read the notation by the nurse who had witnessed Lucas's drunken outburst in the hospital.

"Mrs. Suarez, I noticed that your husband may have a drinking problem," said the doctor. "Is that causing a problem at home?"

Martina's eyes filled with tears. She could feel her face flush. She stared at her hands as she spoke. "No," she said shaking her head. "Everything is fine." She tried to smile without success.

"Are you sure?" asked the doctor, leaning toward her. "If something is going on at home, we can help you. If your husband is drinking and frightening the babies, that could affect their development. Does he hurt them?"

Martina remained quiet, continuing to look at her hands.

The doctor continued, "You know, children need a secure environment where they feel safe in order to thrive. Your children need it even more because they were preemies. They were separated from you early. Their attachment to you is very important. They need to feel comforted. If you're frightened or upset, they feel it. Do you understand?"

Tears rolled down Martina's face. She knew the doctor was right, but felt like a child being reprimanded. She nodded her head to indicate that she understood.

When the doctor finished examining the twins, Martina asked, "Are they okay?"

The doctor nodded. "They seem to be fine … physically. I can't say how they are emotionally or psychologically. That remains to be seen. However, if I suspect that they are being physically harmed by their father, you know I am required by law to report him to Child Protective Services."

Guilt-ridden, Martina left the doctor's office and pushed the stroller built for two toward the elevator. She felt confused and tormented. On the one hand, she knew that staying with Lucas was not good for herself or her children. On the other hand, she didn't want to have to rely upon her parents for complete financial support. Martina already felt guilty for relying so much on her parents. It was enough that they helped with their generosity toward the twins.

She also wondered what would happen to the condo that Lucas's parents had provided them. If she divorced Lucas, would his parents still permit her to stay there with the boys? She knew that Lucas's inheritance would soon run out. He was a spendthrift with no attempt to budget his money. She knew she had it easier than a lot of people, especially when it came to finances. Whatever Lucas gave her could be spent on food and clothing; the rent and nanny were covered by her parents and in-laws. Nevertheless, since Lucas wanted to spend all the money on himself, it felt like she couldn't survive without him. She also struggled with whether the children would be better off in a single-parent home, growing up with divorced parents. She blamed herself for not being stronger and for not being able to stand up to Lucas.

Over the next couple of years, Lucas's drinking increased. As did the shouting, shoving, occasional slapping of both Martina and the children. Martina fell into a deeper depression, lost her appetite, and could barely get out of bed. On the advice of her doctor, she finally sought counseling for her depression and continual weight loss.

The female psychiatrist to whom she had been referred prescribed antidepressant medication and recommended that she join a support group for spouses of alcoholics. After several months of listening to the stories of other people in circumstances similar to her own, and with the group's encouragement, Martina made the decision to file for a divorce.

Having witnessed Lucas's violent outbursts firsthand, Martina's parents supported her decision.

"You've got to think of your children," said her father. "They will be better off without their violent father in the house than growing up watching how he treats you."

"It's not good for the children to always be frightened, sweetheart," added her mother.

"I know," replied Martina. "That's what my doctor said. But what will you think of me? Pregnant before being married and now divorced with two children before I'm twenty-five." Tears welled.

Her father hugged her. "We will always love you, Martina. No matter what," he said. Her mother joined them in the hug.

Of course, Lucas was furious when he was served. He stormed through the apartment, knocked things off tables, punched holes in walls, and swore at the top of his lungs. While he didn't love Martina and had little interest in the children, he couldn't tolerate that any of his possessions—and that was all they were to him—would be taken away from him. And his parents, despite their disappointment in their son, sided with him.

"You will always be our son, Lucas," said his father. "No matter what our disagreements may be, we are still a family."

They also wanted their condo back. Neither Lucas nor his parents expressed any deep concern for the well-being of the twins. They were only concerned with money. Martina and the twins had to move, just as Martina had anticipated.

At first, Lucas considered fighting Martina for custody, not because he wanted to care for the twins, but because he wanted to avoid having to pay for child support. But once he learned about the allegations against him and the witnesses to his drinking and violence, including the incident in the hospital when the twins were born, he relented. He was especially concerned that Martina could file child and spousal abuse charges which could result in criminal prosecution. On the advice of his counsel, Lucas agreed to grant Martina both physical and legal custody of the children. He would have visitation rights on the condition that he would attend AA meetings, and all visitations would be supervised by a third party.

Martina, Brian, and Alan moved into a two-bedroom apartment near Martina's parents. Her parents continued to absorb the cost of hiring a nanny so that Martina could find employment to supplement the financial support ordered by the court. She enrolled in a cosmetology school which, with her parent's financial support, she was able to attend full-time. She completed the program in less than a year. The twins continued to be cared for by nannies, and occasionally by their grandmother when she was in Los Angeles.

Once their parents were divorced, they only saw their father one day a week. Their mother was preoccupied with going to school, and while they lived near their grandparents, they rarely saw them. Except for one another and the nannies, they were essentially alone.

Their visits with Lucas were dreaded. Even in the presence of the nanny who accompanied them on their visits with their father, Lucas was critical of everything they did. They would cry whenever he was with them. They would tremble in anticipation of his visit, especially Brian. They regularly had upset stomachs and began what became a lifelong battle with gastrointestinal problems.

Whenever they were in Lucas's presence, Brian's stomach problems increased to the point of vomiting. Alan seemed more able to tolerate Lucas's volatility; even at only three years of age, he seemed to be able to contain his emotions. Brian began to manifest an assortment of additional psychosomatic issues including bouts of shortness of breath, hand-sweating, and night terrors. People generally frightened him. It did not matter where they were—a supermarket or a restaurant—Lucas would explode. The boys lived in constant fear of the next tirade. Martina was helpless. But there was no legal way she could stop his visits.

"Unless there is physical abuse of the boys," the court-appointed social worker had explained, "there is nothing the court or I can do. Unfortunately, emotional abuse is not considered grounds for denying parental visits."

Martina beseeched the social worker, "But I am afraid of what he might to do them!"

"I'm sorry, Martina, but my hands are tied," said the social worker. "There's nothing I can do." The social worker looked at Martina with sadness in her eyes. Over the years, she'd had to say this to many women in similar positions. She felt for the children, but she too was helpless.

Both the boys showed varying signs of anxiety that always began the day before Lucas's visits. Alan became more withdrawn, as though steeling himself, and Brian became nauseous. Since the divorce from Lucas, Martina had begun making conscious efforts to soothe the boys and create a more secure attachment bond. Between her visits to the psychiatrist and her support group, she began to understand the importance of bonding with her children. She felt she owed them that much since she hadn't shielded them when Lucas lived with them. But on the day of Lucas's visits, she too was frightened. And the twins sensed it. She was unable to protect her children from their father's verbal abuse. It had taken every ounce of strength and courage for her to divorce him. That was the best she could do.

# CHAPTER TWO

# The Early Years

## *1986-1995*

With an alcoholic father given to rages and constant criticism and a timid and anxious, though well-meaning mother, Brian and Alan didn't get off to a flying start in this world. Quite the contrary. They were forced to rely on each other for survival in a dysfunctional family. One set of grandparents was busy jet-setting around the world and the other set, for all intents and purposes, had disowned them. The preemies became each other's security blanket and best friend. As toddlers, they quickly learned they could never trust anyone else except each other for comfort and protection.

From a health standpoint, they bordered on what the doctors called the "failure to thrive" syndrome, often due to a combination of biological and psychosocial factors. This meant that though they had made some improvement after their parents divorced, they remained short and slight in build. Alan was slightly more robust than Brian, but they were both small children. Other than that, they were so much alike physically that it became virtually impossible for anyone to tell them apart, including Martina. They were truly identical twins.

Martina did everything suggested by the magazine articles she read. She tried dressing them differently instead of exactly alike the way many parents of twins often do. She would dress them in different colors, or she would dress one in solid colors and the other in stripes. She also put nail polish on the soles of their feet to tell them apart. But eventually, the polish would get washed off.

As they matured, Brian and Alan figured out that they looked alike. And as their motor skills increased, the boys quickly learned how to outwit Martina by simply exchanging clothing with one another. As they matured, the game of trying to outwit their mother gave them considerable pleasure.

Lucas, however, did not find their antics amusing. When they tried to dupe him, he would become enraged. His shouts and threats kept them in a constant state of apprehension. Between their father's shouting, pounding the table, and kicking of furniture and their mother's timidity, they were left vulnerable and unprotected. They became fearful and distrusting. Even as youngsters, the seeds of distrust took hold. The natural joy and spontaneity common to children was squashed, especially when they were with their father. They weren't permitted to wrestle, laugh out loud, tease, or make any sort of noise common to children for fear of being scolded. Instead, they became wary, constantly looking over their shoulders, and fearful lest their father suddenly make an appearance. They never knew when he would grab or smack them for something they may have said or done, sometimes coming up from behind when they least expected it.

The boys figured out ways of distancing themselves from their father. They also figured out how to avoid behaving in ways that would upset him. They became very skillful at being little angels when they were around him: quiet and obedient. But internally their resentment toward him and all authority continued to grow.

In order to protect themselves from Lucas's outrages, they discovered that they could weather his tirades by imagining themselves to be other people and fantasizing about being in safe places. Sometimes the safe place was a fort, other times a cave.

The fort was their favorite. In it, they were fearless soldiers. Fantasy became a refuge. They practiced becoming like the action heroes they admired, steeling themselves against any attack. They envisioned themselves being able to endure any form of torture, often practicing on one another. They would yell directly in each other's face and practice not flinching. They would even threaten to strike one another; sometimes they would follow through and practice not reacting. They worked at being able to turn off their feelings and become impervious to all physical and verbal threats. One of their favorite exercises was practicing looking straight ahead as though in a trance as they verbally attacked one another. In these feigned attacks, they imitated Lucas. They even slammed their hands down a table just as their father did. These practice exercises helped them deal more effectively with the threats coming from Lucas. Like many children born into traumatic circumstances, they learned how to adapt.

By the time they were five years old, the boys had become quite adept at playing different roles. They behaved one way when they were with their father, another way with their mother, and still another way when in preschool. They became chameleons, changing their personas, depending on the circumstances, with one goal: survival.

\*\*\*

They grew to be quite handsome with black hair, green eyes, and olive skin. Though small in stature and slight of build, they learned how to use their looks to manipulate the adults, mostly women, in their world who fawned over them—women in the supermarket, teachers, and even the nannies who looked after them. They could turn on tears as needed, smile, and behave in a manner to endear themselves to others.

Not only did being identical twins endear them to adults, but they also learned how to use being idents to their advantage. When one of them got in trouble in school, each blamed the other. They had become quite practiced at swapping clothes and other potential forms of identification. Teachers were often flummoxed by not being sure which twin to punish when they misbehaved. When a classmate blamed Alan for doing something, neither the teacher nor the child could be certain that it wasn't Brian who did it. And vice versa.

In exasperation, the teachers finally resorted to punishing both twins. Alan and Brian protested that it wasn't fair, but there was nothing left for the teachers to do. Despite the twins having instigated the deception, they still thought it was unfair when the teachers punished both of them for the actions of one. This further augmented the twins' resentment of authority.

As time went on, Brian and Alan recognized that rather than conform to the expectations of others, they would have to become even more clever. It became a game—the twins against the rest of the world. Developing techniques for outwitting the adult world became their common mission. They defended themselves against what they perceived as a hostile world where no one could be counted upon to protect them. They could count only on one another and their wits, especially their ability to become a different character and turn off their feelings. As their confidence grew, their fears diminished—except when it came to their father. However, even with him, a growing anger began to take the place of fear.

By the time they reached first grade, Martina had learned to tell them apart. She found subtle differences between them, noticing, for example, that Brian tended to be more serious and far more sensitive than Alan. His customary facial expression leaned toward frowning, whereas Alan tended to smile more often. She also discovered a freckle on Brian's left ear.

By the time they were beginning school, there were other giveaways, whether slight mannerisms like Brian's tendency to scratch the back of his head when concentrating, or Alan's barely detectible lisp, and other nuances that made them different. She knew her boys. It always dismayed Brian and Alan how she could call them out even when they were trying to fool her. Lucas, on the other hand, could never tell them apart. He was too self-absorbed or too drunk to pay attention to subtleties. When he was with them, he would tie a ribbon around their necks, yellow for Brian and purple for Alan. God help them if they exchanged them with one another. They quickly learned that to do so would be at their own peril; the consequences were severe.

Martina worried about her boys for different reasons. She wondered about Alan's remote, somewhat detached, behavior around others and Brian's shyness. Though Brian had outgrown his early bouts of vomiting and most of the nausea, he still experienced stomach gurgling as well other symptoms of anxiety—most noticeably, excessive sweating especially when confronting new situations.

As they got older, their resentment had reached such proportions that they would spend hours developing strategies for exacting their revenge.

One of their major fantasies was to become rich. The rich people in their world, whether their grandparents or their wealthy friends or characters they saw on television, always seemed to have a better life; they seemed to get whatever they wanted, especially respect from others. Kids in school wearing the coolest clothes were the most popular; they got respect. Super heroes got respect because they were strong and powerful. Eventually, the twins came to believe that respect and power were connected to money.

They loved watching television programs where the hero was a loner taking on the world, developing skills of treachery and daring, and fooling everyone. They favored shows where the protagonist was so wealthy that he could command respect and have others do his bidding. They modeled themselves after such characters as James Bond, Harry Callahan aka *Dirty Harry*, and even Tony Soprano.

The twins thought getting away with wrongdoings was to be admired. They worked at developing a personality style that would be virtually without empathy and have no personal vulnerability. Rather than experiencing fear, *they* would be feared.

It seemed to Brian that it was easier for Alan to pull off their various capers without worrying, whereas Brian always had a tinge of anxiety. His hands would perspire, his stomach would growl. Sometimes his heart would pound so hard he could hear it. It just seemed to happen. Brian had to work at being fearless, whereas for Alan it came more naturally. Still, whatever fear Brian felt was not sufficient to stop him from acting. Thanks to his father, living in fear had become normal for Brian, just a part of life, disconnected from any particular behavior on his part. He thought similarly about his physiological symptoms: for him they were just normal.

Until they began middle school, the twins' lives mostly consisted of watching television, playing video games, and constructing strategies for making money. They had a very active fantasy life seeing themselves as all-powerful masters of the universe. But in truth, they were still short, slightly built kids with few friends. They spent most of their time in their room playing together, making up games and strategies for world domination. They loved video games with similar themes.

Martina worried about them. She tried to encourage them to play with other children, but the twins had no interest. They were satisfied with life in their fort, their fantasies, their video games, and their television shows. It was here that they felt safe.

Unbeknownst to Martina, in school, Brian and Alan were trying to adopt the personality styles of their heroes; they were experimenting. They experimented with being remote and serious like Jason Bourne and Harry Callahan or tough like Tony Soprano. They felt more of a kinship with Jason Bourne and Harry Callahan – "make my day," they would shout pointing at one another. They wanted to be clever like Angus MacGyver and shrewd like the conmen they saw portrayed in movies. They admired how they could be in dangerous situations without fear and how they could be tortured without reacting.

They were too slight to be a bully like Tony Soprano, but they were able to adopt Tony's disregard for right and wrong. For him, the ends always justified the means. Because of their slight stature and their general social awkwardness, when the twins enacted either of these roles, they became the butt of jokes by their classmates and were viewed as nerds or weirdoes. Undaunted, Alan and Brian worked on developing their persona. They had few friends and little desire for them. Their ultimate goal was to become clever, using their brains to gain power rather than brute strength, and to be unhampered by social conventions of right and wrong.

The summer before middle school was a turning point for the twins. They spent hours each day developing a strategy for their entrance into the new school. They beseeched their mother to allow them to redecorate their bedroom so that it resembled more of an office than a bedroom. They made their beds to look like couches and placed a large coffee table between them.

They asked Martina to buy them desks to be placed side by side against the wall between the beds and a single triple dresser on the opposite wall with a flatbed television screen above it. None of the furniture was very expensive, but it served its function. To others, their bedroom looked more like a well-appointed college dorm. To Brian and Alan, it was their *Situation Room* and their sanctuary; this was their fort, their cave. It was in this room where they hatched their first major plan to transform themselves and become the badass twins of Michael J. Clinton Middle School. In it, they felt safe.

Alan and Brian sat in their Situation Room. As was their custom, they had the stereo on, blasting out rock tunes as a form of soundproofing to prevent anyone from overhearing what was going on. They knew their mother was curious about what they were up to and most likely had stuck her head in their room from time to time. That was one of the reasons they took such precautions.

For her part, Martina was indeed curious about what they were doing. She would often stop by their door to listen. She had learned a long time ago that her boys were very secretive and would become upset with her anytime she asked questions or intruded. Wanting to keep the peace, she respected their wishes. But that didn't quell her curiosity. The music blocked her from hearing anything, and when she would peek in when the twins were not at home, she saw nothing unusual—other than that the room was neat as a pin, unlike the stories she had heard from other parents about how sloppy their sons were.

"As I see it, bro, we have two and a half months to do two things," Alan began. He spoke in a controlled and serious tone, almost angrily. "We have to brand ourselves so that no one ever sees us as a couple of nerds or wannabes. We gotta become supercool."

"Agreed," replied Brian, smiling at the thought. "And the second thing?"

"We gotta make some serious bucks," Alan continued. "Money is power. We need to come up with a scheme for putting dollars in our wallets."

"And chicks love guys with money," snickered Brian.

Puberty had brought on a new interest in girls. And now that they were about to enter middle school, learning how to talk with girls took on a new importance.

"Right," agreed Alan. "Becoming supercool would be easier if we had the money. To be cool, we need to dress the part. And to dress the part, we need money."

"And to get chicks, we need money and clothes. How much have we got now?" asked Brian. "We've been putting money away for a long time. Birthday money plus the money we've lifted out of Dad's wallet when he was too drunk to notice. What do we have?" He scratched the back of his head.

Alan stood up and opened the closet door. He fumbled around at the left rear of the closet, pulling out a twelve-inch square piece of drywall that revealed a metal box. He retrieved the box by its handle and placed it on the coffee table. He removed the key from its hiding place taped under the table and unlocked the box. It contained bills and coins. He counted it out.

"Five hundred and ten bucks," he said, nodding his head.

"It's not much," replied Brian. "So, we gotta figure out how to turn it into a lot more. If we spend the money to try to look cool, then we won't have any money left. And it takes money to make money."

They sat in silence. Alan sat at his desk and began surfing the internet on the big-screen computer, while Brian sat deep in the thought, scratching the back of his head.

"Hey, bro, I got an idea," said Alan. He spun enthusiastically in his desk chair to face his brother. "This could really make us some serious money."

Brian leaned back with his feet up on the coffee table and his hands behind his head. "Watcha got?"

"Ya know how stores sometimes don't refund cash when you try to return something?" asked Alan.

"Yeah, they give only store credit. So?" inquired Brian. "It's a pain in the butt."

"And ya know how much of the stuff these stores sell can be bought a lot cheaper online and in discount stores, right?" continued Alan.

Brian nodded. "It's a wonder they can stay in business."

The more Alan explained, the more excited he became. "Well, what if we could buy stuff cheap online and return it in a store for a full retail-store credit?"

"Okay. So, how does that make us money?" asked Brian.

Alan gave his brother a broad smile. "Well, what if we could sell the store credit at a discount, but still make a profit?"

Brian bolted upright as though he'd been struck by lightning. "Whoa!" he exclaimed, scratching the back of his head. "You mean, we go buy some stuff on the cheap, go to these other stores to return the merchandise—"

"Tell them we received it as a gift, so we don't have to show a receipt—"

"And then sell the store credits at school for a profit. Like if we buy something online for ten bucks, return it to the retail store for a twenty-dollar credit, and sell the credit for fifteen, we make five on the deal. Not too shabby." Brian nodded his head and smiled as the idea began to grow on him.

"We just have to find the best online prices and then find local stores that carry the same brands," explained Alan as he sat back in the chair and placed his feet on the desk. "The department stores would be best. The bigger, the better. We would have to be sure the stuff is not on sale 'cause stores only refund at current store prices."

"If we could buy closeout sales and return them for retail price, that would be perfect," said a gleeful Brian. He stood and paced as he talked. "I heard there are places downtown that sell the same stuff cheap. We should take a bus ride downtown and check it out."

Alan nodded. "We can use our savings to start the business and buy cool threads with the profits."

Brian stopped pacing and lost the smile. "Wait! Why would anyone want to buy our store credits when they can find stuff online themselves?" Brian, always the more cautious of the twins, attended to the details, very aware of everything that could go wrong. Alan was far more adventurous, even a bit impulsive.

Alan thought for a moment, placing his palms on either side of head. "Because these rich kids prefer to shop in a mall," said Alan. "They want to be seen; they want to be waited on. Like on those reality TV shows where we see rich people shopping in stores, not on the internet. Money is not a big deal when they're using daddy's credit card."

"I get it. You're right," said Brian with a smile. He sat back down.

This was the first venture for the entrepreneurial twins. They spent hours meticulously searching the internet for the best deals they could find. They used several different search engines rather than just the most popular ones to find deals. They went through page after page hoping to find both known and lesser known companies that would be willing to negotiate with them. They spent additional time on eBay and Craigslist. And they spent more hours looking up department stores that carried the same merchandise. This went on for days. They hardly slept. They were bleary-eyed. When Martina asked about their late hours and expressed concern for their health, they told her that they were working on homework and a school project.

They realized that in order to buy merchandise online they would have to have a credit card. And to have a credit card, they needed to be over eighteen and have a Social Security card. They had Social Security cards, but they were minors.

They decided to use their mother's card. Since she went to bed before them, they had easy access to her handbag which was always left on the kitchen counter. They found her Social Security card in her wallet and wrote down the number.

Once they had secured the number, they began applying for credit cards. The banks were quite accommodating. In fact, they seemed so willing to give cards away that the boys' biggest challenge was which bank to choose for their first account. They agreed that they needed a bank with a branch in their neighborhood or at least within easy biking distance from home and school. One other challenge was that they needed a physical address for receiving the credit cards because they definitely couldn't receive them at home. They got around this snag by renting a large mailbox in the local strip mall. They would make all their payments in person at the bank with cash, and they would have all their statements routed to the mailbox.

Through a series of small purchases over the course of several days, Brian and Alan tested out their scam. They bought some items on eBay, had them sent to their mailing address, and received them in a few days. They then went to the large malls to return the items, telling the cashiers that they received the items as gifts.

The first time they put their plan into action, they were nervous. Brian's stomach was gurgling and his hands were sweating. If Alan was anxious, there was no way to tell. He was able to contain his feelings and seemed to be totally confident.

The sales people in the department stores hardly looked at that them. They simply took the merchandise, wrote up the refund, and handed them the receipt. Much to Brian's surprise, they had no trouble getting the store credits. On their way home, Alan beamed. He walked with a swagger. Brian was mostly relieved and spent the first few minutes just wiping the perspiration off his hands and waiting for his stomach to settle. Only then was he able to break into a grin and join his brother in doing the happy-dance.

In the process of searching for items to sell, they learned about knockoffs and gray-market items, one being counterfeit, simply copied, and the other being legitimately manufactured abroad, only made to different specifications than those manufactured for the U.S. customer. Sizes ran smaller in some Asian countries like China, where people tended to be of slighter stature and shorter than people in western countries like the U.S. French brands tended to be cut slimmer. The same was true for colors; they could be called the same, but the shades were different depending on the specifications of the country.

The twins learned a lot about the fashion industry and how things were merchandised. They discovered it was a lot easier to buy quantity merchandise by going downtown to the garment district. Rather than relying upon deliveries sent to their apartment, they could simply put items in their back packs and sneak the stuff into their apartment when their mother was out. Most of the items they bought through eBay were manufactured in Asia, especially China; these were most often the counterfeit goods. The Chinese, they learned, were quite good at copying American designs.

Alan and Brian carefully recorded everything they did and learned. They went over every detail, creating a series of dos and don'ts along with a master to-do list dividing the responsibilities between them. The scam worked. They were even able to slip in a few gray-market items, keeping the originals for themselves. This was easy because store clerks in large department stores were minimum-wage earners and not much older than themselves. They didn't pay attention to the details; they simply wrote the store refunds.

The twins accumulated store refunds in several of the major department stores like Macy's and Nordstrom, and some smaller chain stores that had a liberal return policy. These stores relied on quantity sales and could easily absorb returns into their inventories. They avoided the boutique one-of-a-kind stores and the mom-and-pop-run stores where they could be easily recognized.

Chain stores were okay. They went to great lengths to avoid being recognized by the salespeople, often trying to disguise themselves by wearing baseball hats and dark glasses. Sometimes, they would have to leave a shop if they recognized a salesperson with whom they had done a previous transaction. It was easier in large department stores where they could return merchandise with any cashier. It wouldn't work for them to be spotted as constantly returning merchandise. Large stores had many sales people and were open long hours; the personnel changed depending on the day and shift. When it came to chain stores, there were enough of them to vary the location of the store and the personnel. The scam required a lot of focus and planning. It wasn't as easy as they first thought. But they made it work.

Back in the Situation Room, Brian and Alan planned their next steps.

"Okay," said Brian, "we have about eight hundred dollars' worth of store credits. Now we gotta plan how we're gonna sell them."

"Shouldn't be a problem," replied Alan. "The kids at Clinton Middle School are all brand conscious. Like I said, they shop in malls, not online. They think it's cool to buy retail. And they understand store credit. And that's why we did most of our business at the high-end department stores. That's where they shop."

"We'd better get busy," said Brian. "We gotta be able to pay off our credit card at the end of each month, or we'll lose it. We don't want the bank to have any excuse to contact Mom."

"I read online that banks like people to make payments rather than pay off the credit cards," replied Alan. "If we can make payments, they will see us as a good credit risk and may even increase our credit line."

Brian looked at his brother with raised eyebrows. "You're shittin' me, right?"

"I shit you not, bro," answered Alan. "That's the way the system works."

Brian chuckled. "Well, all right then," he said. "We're in business."

"And we need to buy some cool threads for ourselves," added Alan. "And we gotta do it now."

"Huh, now?" asked Brian. "And just how are we gonna buy cool stuff for ourselves and still have enough refunds to sell for cash?"

Alan gave him a sly smile. "We've got credit, bro, remember? And we don't have to spend much to look cool."

Brian looked at him curiously with one eyebrow raised. "What did you have in mind?"

"Black," replied Alan. "Black jeans, black tees, black socks, and black Converses."

Brian smiled. "Twins-in-black! I love it!"

"Bad-assed boys-in-black!" exclaimed Alan.

They high-fived.

"We can find that stuff cheap online," continued Alan. "Even knockoffs. What do we care if the labels are not genuine? We buy cheap. I bet we can do it for two hundred for the both of us."

"That will wipe us out," said Brian. "That's all we have— plus the eight hundred in credits."

"Not for long," replied Alan with a knowing smirk. "Not for long, bro."

CHAPTER THREE

# Middle School

## *1995–1997*

B
y the time school opened for the new year, Brian and
Alan had branded themselves Hip, Slick, and Cool—
HS&C. That was the name they gave their fledgling
business. Having a name made them feel more like adults,
more powerful, more in control. As co-founders of their own
company, they could hide their insecurities behind a brand, a
name.

They had spent years practicing how to adopt different
personality styles to suit the occasion and had spent hours
watching movies where the lead characters took on various
identities. They watched hours of grifter movies where the
protagonists were suave and cool, capable of conning people
while appearing friendly; people easily fell for the scam just
because the grifter appeared to be trustworthy. They
particularly liked Leonardo DiCaprio in *Catch Me If You Can*.
His ability to change into different characters appealed to
them. They tried to model the uber-cool moves of the
notorious conmen depicted in this genre of film.

They practiced walking like their action heroes such as
James Bond, and characters played by Steven Seagal, standing

ramrod straight and showing little facial emotion. Alan practiced smiling in front of a mirror, learning to turn it on and off at will. Brian practiced raising one eyebrow. They often critiqued one another as they practiced various movements with both their hands and their heads—a slight movement of the head signaling acknowledgement or indicating a direction, a finger movement or slight wave of a hand. They practiced a unique smile, and even developed a signature form of acknowledgement—a two-finger salute of sorts, but with only a wrist movement, more like a flick. Everything they did was to enhance the HS&C brand.

They used such movements with one another, a kind of sign language. They learned to read each other. In the process, they learned to give the impression of being in total control of their emotions, at least in terms of their appearance to others.

Unlike many identical twins who worked hard at differentiating themselves from one another, especially by adopting different styles of dress, Alan and Brian capitalized on looking as much alike as possible as part of their hustle. They worked hard at becoming identical to one another in every way, including emotionally. They wanted to be able to merge into one being at will, thereby being able to change places with one another and be in two places at the same time, each being able to substitute for the other.

It was beginning to pay off. They had learned how to turn off their emotions, detach themselves, and play a part like the characters in their television shows. They practiced playing the same character. Alan was always better at it than Brian. Alan would actually feel calm, while Brian could merely act it, giving the appearance of being calm, but inside was another story.

Like most actors, when Brian was in character, his stomach was quiet and his hands didn't sweat; he became someone else. But as soon as he came out of character, his feelings would re-emerge. Brian had to practice similar to the way he and Alan had practiced in their fort to steel themselves for their father's attacks. He would put himself into what Alan had once described as a trance, visualizing himself to be someone else—a state where he no longer felt like himself. When in the state, Alan could yell at him, even twist his arm without Brian even flinching. Brian then was able to step into the character he was playing. He was acting.

By contrast, Alan simply became more of what he was already becoming, a person who could detach himself from his emotions at will. Alan didn't have to work at it.

They had spent most of their grammar-school years practicing not to react to their father's verbal abuse and not to panic when other kids bullied them. Running the store-credit scam gave them more practice. They practiced showing no fear to the point that when in character they feared nothing. All it took was for them to become someone else. Middle school was going to be another training ground.

On the first day of school, they woke up early. Unlike most days when they pulled their pillows over their heads to catch a few minutes more sleep, they jumped out of bed as soon as their alarm went off; it was showtime! Just as any actor, they knew how important it was for them to get into character. They carefully dressed for their first performance of the new semester. They gelled and spiked their hair, donned tight-fitting, black Levi 510 jeans, Calvin Klein black tee shirts, and their knockoff Converse sneakers. Standing in front of the mirror, they saw the double image of two fashionably dressed, good-looking, slim thirteen-year-olds staring back at them. Their swarthy complexion, green eyes, and black hair gave them a European look. They put on their Ray-Ban sunglasses, picked up their black backpacks, and gave each other a high five. They had transformed themselves from weirdo-geeks to *their* version of uber-cool.

Just as they were about to leave the apartment, Martina popped her head through the kitchen door.

"Forgetting something," she said, turning her cheek in their direction. The supercool twins stopped, smiled, and one by one kissed their mother goodbye.

"Have a good first day, boys," she said with a smile as she watched them leave for their first day at middle school.

As they walked into William Clinton Middle School on that first day of school, all eyes were upon them. The boys gave the twins a once over with their eyes, admiring their outfits and feeling a bit of envy. A couple of them even sneered, feeling instantly competitive. The girls smiled in the coquettish way teenage girls smile when they look at boys.

The twins received nods and a few waves and fist bumps from those students they had met during the summer. A few gave them a high five. Alan and Brian returned the acknowledgement with their well-practiced two-finger salute, a smile, and a nod of their heads. They practiced the restraint of the uber-cool dudes they wanted to be. They swaggered down the school corridor, back packs slung over their shoulders, as they went to their first class of the new year.

Their store-credit scam took off. Within a short time, they became famous in their middle school for having all the hippest fashion styles—with their always-in-black style—and money to burn. They also created a buzz in the school for their uber-cool attitude in class as well and, of course, for their identical appearance. And as always, no one could tell them apart.

"This is working like a charm, bro," said Alan at one of the strategy sessions. "We've become walking advertisements for our biz." He gave Brian a self-satisfied smile.

"You're right," Brian replied, grinning. "It couldn't be going better. Even the guys who were jealous when we first got there are now our customers."

"We've got to keep our focus," said Alan. "And always be looking for the latest and greatest fashion styles. We gotta stay current."

Brian nodded. "You bet. And we gotta keep on the lookout for other products if we are going to stay on course for the big bucks."

"Yeah," replied Alan. "Never again will we be picked on or laughed at. Nobody bullies the badass twins-in-black."

Middle school was their training ground to prepare them for high school and beyond. They were always thinking ahead. They were on course to becoming rich and powerful. They wanted to be millionaires by the time they were twenty-five. They believed money was the way to overcome their insecurities. With money, they hoped to be able to buy popularity and be included in the in-groups. They wanted to turn the tables on all those who had picked on them. All of those who had teased them, called them names, or mocked them would have to look up to them when they were rich.

Their plan worked. By wearing the latest fashions and owning the latest gadgets, they soon found themselves the center of attention. Everyone wanted to include the hip twins in their group and invite them to their parties. Everyone wanted them on their A-list. The more popular they became, the more secure they felt. Even some of the kids who had bullied and teased them in grammar school, now wanted to be their friends.

They spent their out-of-school time developing new strategies for making money and learning the art of the hustle. They constantly were on the lookout for another way to hustle, another scam, so long as it made them money. Doing things that were not entirely legal didn't bother them. They had not developed a strong moral compass or a guilty conscience. They sought out opportunities to take advantage of any situation that would make money.

In grade school, they came up with several profitable hustles capitalizing on their identical appearance.

"Remember that TV show we saw where the kid puts a doll in a baby stroller and hangs out in the park with other moms so that she can steal their purses while they fuss over their babies?" asked Brian while lying in bed one Saturday morning.

"Yeah," replied Alan, "so?"

"We could do that," Brian replied. "Actually, I was thinking we could just go to the park and just swipe 'em. No need for a doll or stroller. Those bags sit in the strollers while the moms chat and watch the kids playing in the sandbox. One of us could show up just in case the other is spotted. These moms couldn't be sure which of us snagged the bag even if they wanted to report it."

Alan tapped a finger to his temple. "You're always thinking, bro. Always using the noodle."

Brian chuckled as he scratched his head.

"We could do the same thing in stores," added Brian.

"In stores? You mean shoplifting?" asked Alan.

And so it began. They tried their hand at shoplifting and snatching purses left in baby carriages at playgrounds. When Alan snatched the purse, Brian situated himself near where the mothers sat minding their children, reading a book. If a mother called the police and tried to describe the person who had snatched the purse, they would then notice Brian sitting on a bench and accuse him. But other mothers vouched for him, saying that he had been sitting there all the time, reading. Both the cops and the mother whose purse had been snatched were left uncertain. The cop ended up saying that she must have misidentified the thief.

Alan and Brian watched another TV show where a kid learned how to manipulate a deck of cards to hustle at poker games. This inspired them to go on YouTube where they found all sorts of tutorials on how to deal from various places in the deck, as well as tutorials on how to cheat at poker. They studied these tutorials carefully and spent many hours practicing. They learned how to deal from the bottom and elsewhere in the deck, how to mark cards with their fingernail, along with other card manipulations, cuts, and shuffles. In addition, they practiced feigning ignorance of the game to give the impression that they were an easy mark. Once proficient enough, they started hustling kids in poker games, but never in their own neighborhood.

As with the purse snatching, one brother would always provide the alibi for the other if they were caught. If one of them should get caught, there was no way of telling which one was running the scam. With their identical appearance, even when busted, no one could be certain which brother had lifted the purse or was dealing from the bottom of the deck. They set it up that way. One of them always had an alibi proving he was somewhere else at the time of the hustle.

The one thing they realized was that in order for the scam to work, the brother who got caught had to be able to get away from the scene to support the claim that they had caught the wrong person. If someone caught him red-handed and held onto him before he ran, he was doomed. And that was exactly what happened during one poker game.

Alan was playing with a bunch of older kids on the other side of town in the back room of a billiard parlor. Despite the room being dimly lit, Alan wore sunglasses and a baseball cap. There were four other players at the table, all in their twenties. It was Alan's deal. He was winning, but not too much. For this hand, the pot was larger than most. He shuffled and dealt the cards, giving himself a pat full house. Before the first play even began, one of the players suddenly reached across the table and grabbed Alan's wrist, calling him out.

"He's dealing from the bottom!" yelled the guy holding Alan's arm.

The rest of the players jumped Alan. They knocked him to the ground and piled on him. Alan could barely breathe. The punches landed solidly to his ribs and his back, knocking the breath out of him. The bodies on top of him blocked his attempts to scream.

Alan stopped moving. He lay perfectly still, not breathing.

"He's not moving," exclaimed one of the guys.

They all slowly began to get up off the lifeless body and backed off. Without waiting for them to stand completely upright, Alan jumped up and bolted toward the rear door. He stumbled at first, quickly regained his balance, and ran out the back door of the room at full speed. The others, realizing they had been duped, ran after him. Alan sped down the alley toward the street. He made a quick right turn at the corner. As he fled past, he noticed Brian sitting on a bench at the bus stop chatting with an older gentleman. Alan ducked into a building. The four card players turned the corner and spotted Brian.

"There he is," shouted one, "grab him!"

Brian acted startled. "Hey, what's going on?"

He tried to move away, holding his arms in front of his face for protection. His sunglasses fell to the ground.

"We saw you dealing from the bottom of the deck!" said the guy who had spotted Alan.

"I don't know what you're talking about," said Brian. "I've been sitting here for the last twenty minutes waiting for the bus!"

"That's right," said the older gentleman. "We've been just chatting, waiting for the bus. I'm afraid you boys must have him mixed up with someone else."

Not knowing what to do next, the boys left, muttering among themselves.

This was the last time the twins used the poker hustle. It took two weeks for Alan to heal from the beating he had taken. Martina couldn't help but notice Alan's bruises. The twins told her that Alan had accidently gotten hurt while fooling around with some kids in the park.

In addition to hustling in general, the twins continued to watch movies and read books about famous conmen and anything that had to do with getting rich, especially *Think and Grow Rich*. They also loved the Jason Bourne books. Their role models were all fictional, one-dimensional characters who showed limited depth of personality, empathy, or complexity. While the twins read their textbooks only enough to pass their tests, they did read the biographies of modern-day grifters, trying to learn the secrets of the con, such as Ponzi schemes. They used the internet incessantly, always searching for opportunities. Hustling had become a way of life. It was a life they felt born to be living.

After the store-credit business, one of their most successful scams was connecting with shopkeepers in the low-rent districts downtown, searching for bargains that they could resell at a profit. Whether the goods were real or copies of brands, legitimately acquired or not, none of this bothered them. The only thing that concerned them was whether they could make a profit.

At first, the business people in the area were reluctant to do business with a couple of kids. But they soon learned that these weren't two ordinary teenagers. And they did business in cash. It wasn't long before word spread in the community of these odd-lot merchandisers.

Many of the upper-middle-class kids in their neighborhood didn't care for making money or searching for bargains. Either they were trust-fund children, or their parents supplied them with enough cash and credit cards that they could buy whatever they wanted without regard for price.

Most of those rich kids didn't care about spending their parent's money at Saks or Neiman's. But there were many more kids who were not quite in that league. They received generous, but limited, allowances. They wanted the high-end stuff but couldn't quite afford it all. Even kids had to keep up with the Joneses, just like their parents.

This was the HS&C demographic. These were the kids that Brian and Alan targeted. They decided that their mission was to provide the latest in electronics, fashion, and watches to the middle-income students at prices they could afford. These kids had little concern for the authenticity of the item. It was the look that mattered. And the label. These label-conscious kids were the easiest to scam. Telling them it was genuine was good enough. As long as the merchandise looked authentic and was packaged correctly, they asked no questions. The twins found it amusing that these same kids wouldn't buy stuff from a street peddler, but had no problem buying the same stuff from them.

Packaging was everything, and the twins realized that this included themselves. It was how they looked that mattered. It was their credibility that made conning possible. That's why it was called a confidence game—the con. The kids and the vendors trusted the twins.

Alan and Brian were their own best advertising. Alan had a knack for putting together the latest styles in unique ways. He loved reading *GQ* magazine. They always wore the latest fashions and had the latest gadgets. They wore the labels and the watches like store mannequins or magazine models. However, they didn't wear them at home; they kept them stored in their backpacks. When around their mother, they dressed down, keeping a low profile. They did not want to raise her suspicion and have her ask questions about where and how they obtained the items.

"One thing I realize, bro, it doesn't take much money to look good," said Alan. "I read a magazine article that says the important thing is to have one really good item, like shoes for example. People notice the high-end item and assume everything else is high-end. Other stuff should just be good quality."

"That's pretty cool," replied Brian. "I'll leave that stuff to you. You're the guy with an eye."

When they were asked where they got their money to buy all the latest stuff, the twins simply used what they had read: "It doesn't take much money to have good stuff and look good." They left out the part about having one genuine, high-end item since they wanted to sell them everything. They told people they could get stuff cheap and were willing to get stuff for them as well.

While Brian relied upon his brother for style, his talent was in tracking the business end of their operation. Alan was becoming the public image of their young company; he was becoming the outside guy and the face of HS&C. Brian, on the other hand, was all about operations. He was the details guy on the inside. He had spreadsheets and lists for everything.

Soon they had a business going. They now had two sources of income: the store-credit business and the gray-market counterfeit sales. They took orders during the week and would have the merchandise in their backpacks on the following Monday—order by Friday, in your hands by Monday. That was their promise. Then they would arrange for a meetup, hand off the goods, and collect their money. They were like drug dealers, only they were supplying the most-wanted fashionable items.

During their weekly meetings in the Situation Room, they brainstormed new scams for making money.

"First thing on the agenda is figuring out other ways of bringing in cash," said Brian. He was standing in front of the whiteboard they used for outlining their strategies. The whiteboard hung over their flat-screen television and slid behind their bureau when not in use. Their bedroom was beginning to look more like an executive suite than a bedroom.

"Weed," said Alan. "We could become the suppliers of quality weed."

Brian shook his head. "Nah, these kids can get all the weed they want without us."

"True," replied Alan, "but we can sell individual joints. Only the rich kids can get quantity. The rest might be interested in buying single joints."

Brian scratched his head, thought about it for a few moments, and then asked, "How much do you think we could get for a single joint?"

Alan did a quick Google search. "A gram sells for two to three bucks wholesale. A single J contains less than a gram. We could probably get five bucks a stick."

Brian scratched his head again, paused for a moment, and then decided to write it on the board. "Okay, we'll consider it. It's time intensive. We gotta score the weed and then roll the joints. But it's doable. What else have we got?"

They went back and forth for a few minutes before Alan came up with another idea. "What about expanding our business to include special-order items?"

"What d'ya mean, special order?" asked Brian, staring at his brother with interest.

"Let's say a kid wants a bike, and we can find him one at way below retail. Word gets out that kids can place special orders, and we can get it for them," explained Alan.

"And just where are we gonna get a bike, steal it?" Brian chuckled, but he was clearly perplexed. His stomach began to churn. Stealing always caused an uptick in his anxiety. Despite his best efforts to be indifferent to illegalities and risk, he couldn't control his fears the way Alan could. It wasn't that he was morally against doing things illegally; it was more about getting caught that bothered him. He had no moral qualms if he thought he could get away with it. He could see where Alan was heading.

"Not us, but one of the wannabes," answered Alan. "You know, those guys we see around town looking like wannabe gangbangers or gangstas. They steal, we buy, we sell. We tell them what we want; they find it."

Brian smiled despite the bubbling in his stomach. "Whoa, that's a cool idea. We don't have to get involved. We just place the order. We could even sell through Craigslist or one of the apps. Or even eBay."

Alan began pacing their room. "This could be big, bro, really big."

"We don't do the stealing ourselves, and we don't have to keep an inventory," mused Brian out loud. "How cool is that? We just take and place orders."

"We could even find knockoffs from our downtown suppliers," added Alan. "We could take orders for Schwinns, Rolexes or any other name-brand item kids want. We become the middlemen. Some shit's stolen, some're just knockoffs."

"Large size items, like a bike," began Brian, "should be only by special order and with a down payment; we don't wanna get stuck with it, and we have no place to store it."

"Good point," replied Alan. "Maybe we should stick with small items and stay away from eBay. There's too much tracking, and we want to stay under the radar."

"I think we should be an all-cash business," added Brian, "and sell only person-to-person. We should go with Craigslist. We can arrange for a pickup location and spell out that it has to be cash only. That's typically how Craigslist works anyway. No one needs to know where we live."

The twins were about to enter the criminal world. They would be dealing in stolen goods. They became like the fences they saw in TV crime shows, the pawnbrokers of stolen goods. Even selling knockoffs was illegal, especially if they led the buyer to believe a knockoff item was genuine. Though Brian was worried about getting caught, he pushed aside his worries about the potential danger and focused on the money. If Alan could do it, so could he. But Brian had a nagging feeling that he and his brother were only identical on the outside—they looked alike, but did they feel alike?

They dabbled in selling weed and created a reputation for being able to find brand-name merchandise at low prices. Alan and Brian began hanging out with the school's outliers, the stoners, the streetwise, and those kids called thugs by both the students and the faculty. They were particularly looking for teen wannabe gangsters. They wanted kids who were trying to earn their stripes with gangs. West Los Angeles and Santa Monica, despite having some of the most expensive homes in LA, also had their share of street gangs. It was from this group that Alan and Brian wanted to recruit kids who would bring them what the twins called SOIs—Special Order Items.

When added to their weed, store-credit businesses, and knockoff businesses, they were making more money than they had ever expected. The metal box hidden in the wall of their closet was filling up fast, but most of their earnings went back into the business. They often had to make up-front payments for merchandise to develop trust with the gangs. And they had to be able to cover their losses. The gangsta-wannabes were not known for their integrity. The twins were often ripped off, especially in the beginning. Most of these kids, and the gangs to which they either belonged or wanted to belong, understood that Alan and Brian were a good source of ready cash. The twins had relationships with the students, the gangstas did not. As long as Alan and Brian paid as promised, they were safe from being hassled.

To keep up with their classes and homework assignments, Brian and Alan used their newfound affluence to pay others to do their homework and write term papers for them.

They even paid kids to feed them test answers.

They learned it was good for business that they were in different classes; they could reach out to more students. They told the school counselor that they found it better for their studies for them to be in separate classes. They told the counselor about their grammar-school experience, saying that the teachers would always separate them and that the separation kept them out of trouble.

The counselor was willing to oblige, believing that it was both insightful of them to realize being separated was a smart decision and one that would work better for the teachers because it would be easier to tell them apart. However, from the twins' point of view, once they were in separate classes, they could practice the art of deception by sitting in for one another in class. This way each one could get to know all the same classmates and the styles of more of the teachers. The more they knew, the better it was for their business and the better for a con when necessary.

In addition to developing their various businesses, Alan and Brian also cultivated a small crew of their own. They had befriended about a half-dozen kids who supported them and admired them and would do whatever they wanted them to do. These kids, often less popular, were like groupies; they liked associating with the infamous twins. Most of them were either nerdy, physically unattractive, or had unique, uncool interests in things to which the average teen couldn't relate, such as history, astronomy, or even snakes. But they were all smart, and Alan and Brian needed smart kids to help them. In turn, by associating with the twins, these kids were tolerated, if not completely accepted by the in-crowd. Alan and Brian began to feel the power of being the center of attention and having control over others. By the time they were ready to graduate from middle school, everyone knew them, and if they didn't know them personally, they knew who they were.

Despite their newfound popularity, the twins were very cautious about letting anyone too close. They had learned from their grifter movies never to reveal their secrets or trust anyone, not even their mother. When around her, they played the part of the good sons, lugging school books back and forth in overstuffed backpacks. When asked about school, they would make up a story about tests they were studying for or projects they had to complete. These stories were enough to keep her satisfied. She was preoccupied with her own life, so it didn't take much to satisfy her. As long as they stayed out of trouble, she left them alone.

No one knew exactly how they did what they did, nor did anyone know how much money they were making. Not wanting to raise the suspicions of bankers, they kept their money in the back of their closet as always, except they now put it in a strongbox with a combination lock—a portable, fireproof safe. They would periodically change the smaller denomination older bills into crisp, new hundred-dollar notes that would stack neatly in their new strongbox. The hundred-dollar bills would take up less room. Alan, the neater of the twins, liked just looking at them. When they finished middle school, they had over fifty thousand dollars stashed in the wall of their closet.

Their newly acquired popularity, affluence, and power had a dramatic effect on their self-esteem and self-confidence. By the time they were fifteen, Alan and Brian had learned to control their emotions to the point that very little could hurt their feelings. Even Brian's stomach felt calm, though he had to work harder at it than Alan.

For Alan it was easy. He was becoming more emotionally cutoff every day. He could even be in the presence of their explosive, critical father without feeling anxious. Brian was getting better at it. The more explosive Lucas became, the calmer the twins felt. They no longer felt intimidated by his volatility. Lucas took notice, not only of the fact that his boys were no longer afraid of him, but also of their overall increased self-confidence. He was also keenly aware of their newly acquired affluence.

One afternoon while the twins were in the middle of a strategy session, Lucas burst in.

"Where are you losers getting the money to buy all that stuff?" Lucas demanded.

Brian and Alan stared at him.

"That is none of your fuckin' business, asshole!" declared Alan. "And how the fuck did you get into this apartment?"

"Simple," replied Lucas with a smirk, dangling a key in front of Alan. "I used this. And who the fuck are you calling an asshole?" He jutted his chin as if ready to fight.

"You, asshole! Why don't you just take your sorry ass back out the way you came in?" snarled Alan.

Lucas was enraged. "Who in the hell do you think you're talkin' to, punk?" he growled. His faced reddened. He took a step toward Alan with clenched fists.

The twins glared. "We're talkin' to you!" exclaimed Brian. "You want a piece of us? Do you think you can take us both on?" Alan picked up the baseball bat they kept next to the closet in their room in case of an emergency.

Lucas taunted, "What? You gonna hit your father with a bat, huh?"

"What don't you test me, asshole? Just get the fuck out of here before we forget you're our father," exclaimed Alan, holding the bat at the ready.

Lucas glared at his sons. Sensing they meant business, he backed out of their room. The twins followed him as Lucas walked out of the apartment, cussing under his breath.

Alan and Brian looked at one another with a satisfied grin, feeling good about having finally stood up to their abusive father.

"That prick has a key to the apartment. Mom must have given him one in case of an emergency. Stupid idea! We have to get her to change the locks on the front door. And we have to get a security system and a real lock for our Situation Room door," said Brian. "I don't trust anyone, and we've got a lot of cash in there."

"Agreed," replied Alan. "I think we should get a security camera for inside the Situation Room as well. We should know if anyone snoops around."

"Once we tell Mom that Dad just walked in, she won't have a problem with it," said Brian. "I'll get on it."

\*\*\*

Along with their increased self-confidence came an increase in arrogance. The twins became cocky. And their cockiness created jealousy. They developed a few enemies who wanted to take them down.

Success bred the envy of others, and as their stature in the school grew, so did the envy. While most students looked up to them, others wanted to see them fall. Their crew not only helped the twins, but they also reported back to them whenever they heard someone talking trash about them.

Two weeks before graduating from middle school, Vice-principal Gordon Kahn, a tall, balding gentleman, met them at the school entrance and escorted them into his office where two police officers stood waiting.

The twins remained calm.

Normally a kindly, smiling man, Vice-principal Kahn glared at them, stern-faced. "You boys have been accused of possession of and selling marijuana on school grounds," he said. "That's a serious crime."

The police officers approached the boys without a word and took their backpacks. The twins knew it was pointless to resist. Fear gripped Brian; his stomach flipped. Alan was calm.

"We have reason to believe that you are in possession of marijuana with the intent to distribute," said the older of the two officers.

The other officer began emptying the backpacks. Inside, they found a copy of *GQ* magazine, the books *Catch Me If You Can* and *Think and Grow Rich*, and some textbooks. There were also a couple of watches. From one of the side pockets, the officer removed twenty joints. In the other backpack, he found ten.

"We're going to have to take you boys in," said the older officer, placing a firm hand on Alan's shoulder. Alan's eyes welled up.

Similarly, the younger officer had his hand on Brian's shoulder. Brian remained externally stoic despite his internal apprehension; he felt the sweat rolling down his armpits, and his hands were practically dripping.

He looked over at Alan and did a double take, staring in disbelief as he saw tears rolling down his brother's cheeks. He couldn't believe that after all the practicing, Alan would let these people see him cry. Alan looked at Brian and gave him a slight two-finger salute.

Brian suddenly realized what Alan was doing. He gave his brother a raised eyebrow and let the tears he had been holding back fall. Within moments, both boys had tears rolling down their cheeks. They were almost sobbing.

"We're sorry," began Alan, pleading. "We were just trying to make a little money."

Brian began to sob out loud. "We don't want to go to jail!"

Vice-principal Kahn looked at the boys and then at the police officers. "Officers, is there anything we can do short of taking these boys to police headquarters? They've never been in trouble before."

"Possession with intent to sell is pretty serious, sir," replied the older officer. "What did you have in mind?"

Realizing it was now or never, the twins began to beg. "We'll do anything," they pleaded in unison as they put on their most innocent and contrite faces.

"My understanding of the law in California is that juveniles who are caught for possession of marijuana with the intent to distribute can be fined up to two hundred fifty dollars or be placed in juvenile hall for up to ten days, correct?" asked Vice-principal Kahn.

The younger officer nodded. "Yes, that's true for a first offense."

"So, how about this," began the vice-principal, rubbing his chin. "The boys agree to contribute two hundred fifty dollars each to the school library fund and spend two hours a day reading to elderly people at in the local Senior Citizens Center?"

The boys held their breath and hung their heads in shame, waiting for a response.

The police officers conferred with one another for a few moments. The older officer turned to the vice-principal.

"If you're willing to take responsibility for insuring that these two show up to the Senior Citizens Center every day for the next six weeks and pay the fine to the school, we'll let them go with a warning. But there will be no second chances. The next time we get called in, it's off to juvenile detention to await standing trial."

The vice-principal nodded. "I understand." He turned to the twins. "Do you understand the terms described by the officer?"

"Yes, sir," they said, nodding vigorously.

"I'll make a call to the director of the Senior Citizens Center and tell her what we have decided here," said the vice-principal. "I know she will cooperate and be willing to sign an acknowledgement indicating they showed up each day. Thank you, officers."

"Thank you, officer," said Brian, still looking contrite.

"Thank you," said Alan in barely audible tone.

The two police officers nodded, turned, and left.

"Today you were lucky, boys," said Vice-principle Kahn. "Now I have to call your parents. They have to agree to your going to the Senior Citizens Center for the next six weeks."

The twins tried to talk the vice-principal out of it, but without success. He wouldn't budge. He placed the call and asked Martina Suarez to come to the school as soon as possible. Within the hour, Martina rushed into the administrative offices. She saw her sons sitting on a bench outside the vice-principal's office. As she approached them, Vice-principal Kahn stepped out of his office to greet her and invited her to join him. Once inside his office, he explained what had happened and what was decided. A tearful Martina agreed with the plan. Vice-principal Kahn brought the boys into his office where Martina glared at them, mascara-filled tears leaving streaks on her cheeks.

"I can't tell you how disappointed I am in you," she said. "I hope you have learned a valuable lesson."

"We're sorry, Mom," said Brian looking remorseful.

"We're sorry, Mom," echoed Alan, biting his lip.

"At least, now I know how you paid for those new clothes I've seen you wearing," said Martina. "Don't think I didn't notice."

Seeing their mother in pain gave them a pang. Neither of them could tolerate hurting her. Despite not being demonstrably affectionate with her, they felt great sympathy toward her. Brian's stomach ached as he saw his mother's anguish; he could feel his eyes well up. Alan was much more stoic; he just stared ahead. Though he felt bad, he showed no visible signs of discomfort. Their mother was their only other human attachment and the only person whom they cared about. However, despite not wanting to hurt her, they were more driven toward their own ambitions. Her disappointment would not deter them from their mission of being rich and powerful.

"I told your mother about the Senior Citizens Center," said Vice-principal Kahn, "and she has agreed to the plan. I also called the Senior Citizens Center and spoke with the director. She will be expecting you to begin on the first Monday of summer vacation. You will sign in for at least two hours every day and do whatever the director tells you to do. The director will set up your schedule. Do you understand?"

The boys nodded.

Martina drove them home from school. Tears rolled down her cheeks as she drove. Brian and Alan didn't know what to say.

Martina was thinking, *They were selling dope right under my nose, in my home. How could I be so stupid to believe everything was going so well? Now I know how other mothers must feel when their kids get in trouble. They blame themselves for not being better moms. I must pay more attention.*

"It's my fault," she finally said out loud, sniffling. "I'm a terrible mother. I should spend more time with you."

Alan and Brian looked at other, shaking their heads. That was the last thing they wanted, a snoopy mother.

"No, Mom," began Alan. "It's not your fault. You're a great mom." He elbowed Brian.

"Yeah, Mom, he's right; you're a great mom—the best," Brian exclaimed. "We're sorry. We just got mixed up with the wrong people. We've learned our lesson. We promise."

Martina looked at her sons and smiled.

***

During their next strategy session, the twins talked about what had happened.

"We were lucky," said Brian. "Man, I sure didn't want to end up in a juvie." He was quiet for a moment. Then he asked, "Where did you learn how to turn on the tears?"

Alan smiled. "Practice, brother, practice. It's all part of the con."

Brian chuckled. "It sure came in handy."

"I wonder who ratted us out," mused Alan. "That's what happens when you become successful. Someone always wants to bring you down."

"Yeah," acknowledged Brian. "Ya know, I think we should get out of the pot biz. It's too risky and it's messy." He was hoping that his brother would agree. Alan always had more temerity and could deal with the consequences. Brian often could adopt a bravado, but not nearly as well as his brother. With Alan, there were no cracks in the façade.

"You're probably right, bro," replied Alan. "And besides, we're heading into high school, and high-school kids have more money than middle-school kids. They also have wheels and can score their own dope. And besides, there's a lot more competition."

Brian let out a sigh of relief. His stomach relaxed. "And we've got to be more careful now that Mom knows we've been selling dope," said Brian. "The last thing we need is for her to snoop around, ask questions, and want to know more about what we're doing."

"It's enough that we have to deal our asshole father," replied Alan. "Maybe we should spend a little more time with Mom. You know, have dinner with her or something."

"You mean taking a preemptive strike," replied Brian. "We take charge and set the time and agenda rather than have her spring something on us."

They high-fived, nodding.

They put having a weekly dinner with their mother on their calendar.

***

The twins were becoming much more sophisticated as entrepreneurs. They realized that if they were going to be doing business that was illegal or shady, they would have to be even more cautious. They wanted to keep up their business of taking special orders to provide discounted merchandise. They told their suppliers they didn't want to know where anything came from. Even if someone fingered them, no one could prove that they knew it was stolen. For all they knew, some stuff they bought might have fallen off the back of a truck. They wanted plausible deniability. Since they weren't warehousing the merchandise and didn't know how it was procured, they believed it was a pretty clean business.

Within short order, the twins gave up both the pot business and the store-credit business, leaving themselves with the direct sales of both gray-market and knockoff items and their special-order operation.

# CHAPTER FOUR

# Summer of 1997

Alan and Brian weren't looking forward to serving their time at the Senior Citizens Center; it wasn't how they had hoped to spend their summer vacation before starting high school. They viewed it as a chore to be endured and couldn't wait for the six weeks to pass.

When they arrived at the center, they were greeted by the director, Natalie Jefferson, a middle-aged African American woman with a jovial countenance. She gave them a tour of the facility and an introduction to what was done there.

"People arrive early to have their morning coffee and donuts," began Natalie. "It's like a social hour before they go about their activities. This is a community center where people who come here are looking for companionship. Making friends when you get old is difficult. There is no workplace, which is where people often meet others. And unlike young parents, for whom raising children gives them something to bond over, the elderly often have nothing but their advancing age in common with one another. So, they come here where they can play card games, board games, or watch television. Every so often, they go on an outing to a museum or other local event. Through these activities, they get to know each other and find other things they might have in common. That's how they build friendships."

Alan and Brian listened as they walked through the Center.

"Do you have any questions?" she asked.

The boys were silent, so she continued.

"The main purpose of the Center is to provide a social experience for the members. It gives them a chance to be with others rather than to be stuck at home. Social contact is vital to the health and emotional well-being of all people, but the elderly tend to withdraw from social contact. That's why the Senior Citizens Center is so important. The members have come from different walks of life, held a variety of jobs, and had a lot of experiences. I hope you boys will get to know a few of the members and find working here interesting. Remember, old people were once young, too, and each has a story to tell. You might be surprised to see what you can learn from them."

Brian and Alan saw some people in wheelchairs, some watching television, and a few playing dominos, chess, and other board games.

Alan whispered to Brian, "These six weeks are gonna feel like forever; it can't be over soon enough."

Brian gave him a nod and then excused himself to go to the restroom. Ms. Jefferson assigned Alan the task of taking one of the wheelchair-bound seniors on a walk. She introduced him to Mrs. Rose Schwartz, an eighty-two-year-old former television soap opera actress.

Rose weighed under a hundred pounds and was always in full makeup in an attempt to cover her many wrinkles. She wore bright-red lipstick and was a consummate flirt. She held a cigarette holder between her thumb and forefinger, more for effect than for smoking, and often used it to emphasize a point she was making while talking.

Alan and Rose left the center to go on their first walk. As Alan pushed Rose around the neighborhood, she flirted with him—it didn't matter that he had just turned fourteen. She also flirted with every other man she saw at the Senior Citizens Center and all along the street as they walked.

Rose loved to talk about her television career. "It was the same for television as it was in the movies. You had to be pretty, especially in the early days," she said. "Talent was important, but being pretty is what really mattered. If you weren't pretty, you wouldn't even be considered. And I was a cutie." She looked up at Alan, giving him her most coquettish smile.

Alan couldn't help but smile. Rose knew how to play her audience.

"All the big stars loved me," Rose continued. "James Arness from *Gunsmoke*, Carroll O'Connor before he was on *All in the Family*. And even some of the stars from the big screen, like Gregory Peck." Rose smiled wistfully as she told her stories of the years gone by.

Alan didn't know most of the actors she mentioned; they were before his time. Much to his surprise, he found himself captivated by the way she told her stories. She did it with such a dramatic flair that Alan looked forward to hearing them. Whether her stories were true or not didn't matter.

Rose wanted to go to the nearby park, so that's where Alan took her. This would become their daily routine.

When Brian returned from the restroom, Ms. Jefferson introduced him to his charge—a gravel-voiced eighty-four-year-old gentleman named Nick Pomeranz. Slim and debonair looking with wavy white hair and goatee, Nick was originally from Brooklyn and had never lost his accent despite not having lived there for over forty years. Alan later learned that Nick worked hard at keeping it. He would say, "Ya can take da boy outta Brooklyn, but ya can't take Brooklyn outta da boy." Nick sat straight in his wheelchair and wore a black cotton turtleneck under a black blazer with a red pocket square neatly displayed. He would change his pocket square daily; he seemed to have dozens of them. Brian thought that Nick could have played a part in *The Sopranos* hanging out at the Bada Bing Bar and Grill.

"Why're you doin' this, kid?" asked Nick when he met Brian. Nick talked out of the side of his mouth when he spoke, giving him a wise-guy look like the mobsters Brian had seen in movies.

"Why am I doing what?" replied Brian.

With squinted eyes, Nick stared at Brian. "Why're you here? Why're ya spendin' your summa vacation volunteering to push a bunch of decrepit old farts around da neighborhood? Ya should be goin' ta da beach, hittin' on chicks, and gettin' laid."

Brian laughed at the old man's candor. He hesitated, not knowing how to answer the question. "I'm trying to earn a merit badge in the Boy Scouts," he lied.

Nick just continued to stare. "Don't bullshit a bullshitter," he exclaimed. "You're no more a friggin' Boy Scout than I'm a twenty-year-old! Keep pushin' and start talkin'." Nick nodded toward the door to the street.

Brian did what he was told. They began walking; he began talking. "Truth is, I am here as a punishment. I got busted for carrying weed on the school grounds."

"Possession or distribution?" asked Nick.

"Both," replied Brian.

"How'd it happen? How'd you get caught?" asked Nick without judgment.

"Someone had squealed on me," said Brian. "The cops and vice-principal were waiting when we got to school."

"We?"

"Yeah, me and my brother. We were in business together," replied Brian.

"That sucks," said Nick. "Why and how were ya doing it?"

"Money. We sold joints to kids who couldn't afford a bag," said Brian.

"If you guys wanted money, why didn't ya just get a job?" asked Nick.

Brian gave him a raised eyebrow. "Two reasons. We're kids. People don't hire kids. And second, there's not enough money in working. Minimum wage at best. That sucks."

"You guys like to hustle?" asked Nick as they continued walking. "Ways to make a fast buck?"

Brian looked at the back of Nick's head as he wondered where this was going. He wasn't sure how much he should say. After all, they had just met.

"Well, yeah," he replied.

"Brian, do ya know the difference between a hustler, a grifter or conman, and a gangster?" asked Nick.

Brian thought about the movies and television shows he and Alan had watched. "They're pretty much the same," he replied. "Both work out scams for making money outside of the law."

Nick shook his head. "Nah, that's not it. A hustler is anyone who moves quickly to take advantage of opportunities or situations. Their activities may be legal or illegal. For example, a pool hustler tries to fool people into thinking that he doesn't know how to play pool. He gets into a game with them, and when the stakes get high enough, he shows his stuff and cleans them out. It's not illegal. What grifters or conmen do is always illegal or at least borderline illegal. They come up with a scam to convince people they're legit, and then they take advantage of them. They're different than gangsters; they're much subtler and have more style.

"A gangster can be anyone from a burglar to a drug dealer and anyone else who breaks the law. And gangsters physically hurt people or are, at the very least, ready to do so. A grifter figures out a plan that outwits the cops and the mark. And before they figure out they've been taken, the grifter's gone. Even a pool hustler could be called a grifter, I suppose; they lie about their ability to play the game until they find a sucker. Not exactly against the law, but the grifter scams other players by making them think he doesn't know how to play the game. Then he takes them down. Hustlers are usually very skilled at what they do. They're not fighters; they're thinkers."

"So, a grifter is a scammer who figures out how to make a fast buck and doesn't really care about the law," replied Brian, "but he uses his brains and has a plan to minimize the risk. Is that it?"

Nick twisted in his wheelchair so that he could see Brian's face. He smiled, nodding his head. "Ya learn fast, kid. I think it's time to get back to the Senior Citizens Center. We'll continue chattin' tomorrow. You *will* be back tomorrow, right?"

Brian nodded. "For sure, I'll be back."

The twins met outside the Senior Citizens Center and headed home. They shared their experiences of hanging out with Rose and Nick. Brian told Alan about how Nick distinguished been a gangster and grifter.

"I always thought of them as being the same, but they're not. Grifters use their brains to make money. They are very skillful."

"But gangsters are more powerful," replied Alan. "People are afraid of them."

"Ya know, I think this may be less of a punishment than we thought," said Brian. "Ms. Jefferson was right. Everybody has a story."

They both looked forward to seeing their charges the following day, thinking that perhaps they could learn something from the old geezers, just as Ms. Jefferson had suggested.

When they arrived at the Senior Citizens Center the next day, Brian made a pit stop while Alan went into the communal room. Rose was seated in her wheelchair in front of the television laughing at an *I Love Lucy* rerun. When she saw Alan, she smiled. Without waiting, Alan took off with Rose to the park.

A few minutes later, Brian came out of the restroom looking for Nick. He spotted him playing a game of dominos with another old guy. He slipped up behind him, grabbed the wheelchair, and spun Nick around.

"Where to, Nick?" he said cheerfully.

"Where else? Down the boulevard," Nick said, pointing in the appropriate direction. Today, Nick was sporting a blue pocket square with red polka dots.

"Lookin' good, Nick," said Brian, and off they went.

Brian and Nick continued their conversation about grifters and gangsters. The more they talked, the more Brian found himself identifying with the grifters rather than the gangsters. Grifters seemed cooler and tended to work smarter. Gangsters didn't seem to have much class; they were primarily muscle and threats rather than brains.

Brian also liked the idea that grifters weren't into physical violence. Being a grifter required more brains than brawn and hence was less dangerous. This fit more with Brian's self-image; he was not a fan of physical violence, mostly because he didn't like to get hurt. The thought of being clever and outwitting others made him smile.

"I've been a grifter my entire life," said Nick. "Started as a kid in Brooklyn, working a hustle on the stoop of the apartment where I lived. Hustling was just a part of life back there. Nobody had nothin'. No money. No stuff. If ya wanted to eat, ya hadda hustle."

Brian was very interested. Here was a guy with experience in doing the things that he and Alan were trying to learn how to do.

*Maybe he can help us with our business*, he thought, *teach us a few things.*

"All da years I spent hustling, conning people, I never been busted by the cops," Nick told Brian. "I don't even have a rap sheet. No matter what state I lived in, you can't find nothin' about me in a station house. I'm as clean as a whistle."

"How'd you manage that?" asked Brian, fascinated by the old guy.

"Hey, kid, I'm not sayin' that I didn't have some close calls. But I got the gift of gab, you might say, so I could talk my way out of it. But one of the things I learned is like the song says, 'Ya gotta know when to hold 'em, know when to fold 'em, and know when to walk away.' When I saw that I was slowing down, I folded. I retired and walked away. So, here I am." Nick spread his arms as though greeting an audience.

Brian listened carefully, taking it all in.

While Brian was learning about some of the nuances of the con, Alan was engaged in conversations with Rose about acting. She told him how important it was to be able to tap into one's own experiences when playing a role to make the character more believable.

"All actors are cons," mused Rose, as they sat in park watching the children at play. "Actors have to be able to make people believe they are someone they are not. If you're going be any good at it, you must know people. You have to study them. If you're going to play 'em, you've got to know 'em."

Alan smiled. He liked Rose. And Rose liked him.

During their strategy sessions, Alan and Brian talked about what they were learning from Rose and Nick. They realized that given their size and age, they'd be better off identifying more with hustlers and grifters than with gangsters. They would take advantage of every opportunity to make a buck, and they didn't care whether it was legal or not. They also realized they were going to have to become better actors. Rose could help them. And, of course, Nick could certainly teach them a few things about the art of the con.

Much to their surprise, Brian and Alan had developed a friendship with these two elderly people. They no longer found it a chore to visit with them. In fact, they looked forward to spending their time at the Senior Citizens Center and decided to continue it through the summer rather than quit after they had served their six-week duty.

They found themselves giving up their stereotypes of old people as feeble-minded, complaining, and just waiting to die. The more they learned about the members of the Senior Citizens Center, the more they realized that Ms. Jefferson was right: they all had a story to tell. Given the direction that Brian and Alan were going with their lives, Rose and Nick were becoming their mentors.

*** 

Alan and Brian also realized that it would be very helpful for them to become physically fit. Even pushing the wheelchairs was sometimes challenging for them, especially when they went uphill or for longer walks.

Having been born preemies, they had always been thin, small, and not very athletic. They gasped for air when running one lap around the school track, and they wheezed when climbing the hills in their neighborhood, having to stop halfway up the slightest grade. Even lifting light weights was a struggle. When they talked about their television heroes, they realized that most of their role models were athletic and expert in a variety of activities. Angus MacGyver and James Bond were extraordinary. Tony Soprano was just big.

As grifters, Alan and Brian agreed that they should at least be able to defend themselves. Alan hadn't given up admiring gangsters, but he realized that to be a gangster he had to be physically strong. Brian wanted to do whatever he could to avoid a fight, but he didn't want to be afraid either.

The twins decided that they would spend the summer and their high-school years jogging, weight training, and learning some form of martial art. They also recognized that girls liked guys who were not only sharp dressers, but who were also buff. Instead of feeling sorry for themselves because of their physical stature, Brian told Alan that Nick had told him that the key to success was to utilize all assets available and capitalize on their abilities.

Brian remembered something Nick had told him, "Make use of the gifts God gave you; ya never heard of a giraffe wishing it was a kangaroo."

The twins were slim and relatively short in stature; therefore, being flexible and wiry could be an advantage in both yoga and the martial arts. After all, Bruce Lee was only five feet seven, but in the movie *Game of Death*, he beat Kareem Abdul-Jabbar, who was seven feet two.

The twins joined a gym that had karate and yoga classes and the latest and best equipment. They also took advantage of the physical trainers provided by the gym, hiring one to develop a workout plan for the two of them. They were lucky to be brothers; they could challenge one another, push one another, and have a built-in training partner. Another asset.

That summer turned out to be pivotal in their life.

Alan and Brian decided that since Rose and Nick were becoming their mentors, it was time to have the two of them meet so that they all got to know each other better.

Rose knew Nick and had flirted with him, just as she had done with every other man at the Center. Nick, in turn, flirted back, but they had never spent time together other than occasionally watching a television program along with several other seniors. One morning, after making his customary pit stop, instead of taking their usual walk, Brian decided to take Nick to the park where Alan and Rose usually went. As Brian approached Rose and Alan, both Rose and Nick did a double take upon seeing the identical twins.

"Whoa," exclaimed Nick looking up at Brian. "Ya never said anything 'bout ya brudder bein' a twin!"

Brian smiled. "Yeah, well—I thought it would be a surprise."

"Surprise, hell," said Nick, "it's a potential game-changer. Just think of all the possibilities ..." His mind drifted off just contemplating this new bit of information.

"Amazing!" exclaimed Rose. "What stories you kids could tell. Imagine: identical twins! Why, just think of an actor who could substitute his brother on stage and no one was the wiser, especially if they were equally good."

"And the fun of literally being able to be in two places at da same time!" interjected Nick with a chuckle. "The only real challenge would be insuring that others, especially in a con, didn't know there were two of you."

Rose laughed out loud.

Alan's and Brian's heads jerked up as they stared at one another. It often happened that they would simultaneously have a similar thought.

"Hey, Rose, tell Nick what you told me about actors," said Alan. "I think he would appreciate it."

"I told the boy that I thought all actors were cons," replied Rose with a twinkle in her eye. "And maybe all women are actors." She looked over at Nick with a slight flutter of her eyelashes.

Nick chuckled. "And men are the mark?"

Rose smile demurely. "Or the Nick," she replied giving him a playful wink. A flicker of a smile swept across Nick's face.

"Hey, dese kids could con us, Rose," said Nick. "How are we gonna tell 'em apart."

"Why would I care?" said Rose with a glint of mischief in her eye. "They're both cute."

Nick chuckled.

And so it went throughout the rest of the summer. Alan and Brian spent their mornings with Rose and Nick, sometimes staying at the Center through lunch, chatting it up with other folks as well as Rose and Nick. Then they headed over to the gym where they worked out with a trainer several times a week, enrolled in the karate class, and jogged every day.

By the time school started, they were in much better physical condition. They continued this program even after school started. They were determined to become physically fit and capable of defending themselves in any altercation.

They also continued to meet with Rose and Nick on Saturday mornings. They had many conversations about the direction they were heading. They discussed whether they were they going to be grifters or gangsters. They took in what Nick had to say about the distinctions between gangsters and conmen—brawn versus brain.

Nick had said conmen were the ultimate hustlers. Alan could feel himself wanting to be both, but he felt pulled toward becoming intimidating. The impact of his father's intimidating style pushed him toward wanting retribution.

Brian continued to lean toward being a grifter; he felt an affinity for the grifters who were fearless, could play multiple roles, and could dupe their marks with impunity. He liked that they had nerves of steel. He actually loved outwitting his father.

While Alan and Brian continued to model themselves after both styles, they each had their preferences.

"Ya know, if I had my way, I'd be a grifter," said Brian. "I'm not crazy about being a tough guy. I'd rather use my brain."

"Yeah, I know," replied Alan. "But after years of being afraid of our father, bullied in school, and always being afraid of the big kids, I want people to be afraid of me. For me, it's payback."

"I hear you," said Brian. "I don't want to be afraid either. I just get more excited about being able to outthink others, talk my way out. Like Nick. He said he had the gift of gab. And he never got busted."

Alan paused for a moment. "Maybe we could be both," he said. "Maybe it's more about emphasis. I mean, like you could emphasize the con, the brain, and I could just kick ass along with a con—you can be a brain who can take care of himself!"

They laughed and gave each other a bump.

The one thing they were sure of was that they wanted to be hip, slick, and cool. They preferred to use their brains to come up with scams. Part of the fun was planning and then executing the plan. However, they were not opposed to doing things that were outside the law.

They also liked power. They liked the idea of getting others to do their bidding. Grifters tended to be loners. No one got close to a grifter. While Alan and Brian didn't get close to others, they did like having a crew and people to work for them, like the kids in middle school who did their book reports and term papers.

They discussed all of this with Nick and hoped that he might help them come up with what they referred to as a "business plan" that would combine the best of both the grifter and the gangster.

They also enjoyed their long conversations with Rose about learning how to develop a character. She taught them how to use their own experiences and emotions to make a character real. "You have to become the character," Rose told them. "You can't appear to be acting if you want to be believed."

This presented some difficulty. For most of their young lives, they had worked to suppress emotion, to avoid feeling. Now Rose was telling them they had to be able to access their feelings in order to be effective as actors. Brian remembered how Alan was able to turn on tears when they were busted for selling weed.

*Was he accessing real emotions or was he able to simply fake it?* wondered Brian.

Rose told them that good actors had to make themselves vulnerable in order to access their true feelings. This presented a real problem for them. They had spent their lives trying to avoid being vulnerable; after all, Harry Callahan never revealed emotion. Now Rose was telling them this was required if they were going to be believed.

The twins would have to work on this. They would have to find a way to be believed while maintaining their emotional shield.

They also asked Rose to teach them about using makeup and other ways of changing appearances for different roles. Rose was more than happy to teach them. And Alan and Brian wanted to learn. They even did their own online research on the subject. They learned about costumes, masks, gaining and losing weight, mannerisms, and loads more.

Rose suggested that they watch people. "If you're going to play a character, you've got to study the character you're playing," she had said.

Nick told them that good poker players learn how to pick up a tell—an unconscious behavior that gives up information about their opponent's hand.

"You know, like when you scratch the back of your head when you're thinking," said Nick, looking at Brian.

Brian's eyes popped open. "I do what? Nah, I don't—"

Alan laughed. "Yeah, you do, bro," he said.

Brian's hand immediately went to the back of his head. Catching himself, he too laughed.

Alan and Brian began watching people, observing body language. Some people tapped their foot when they were nervous; others bit their lip. They watched poker players on television, and practiced behaving like people they met, trying to imitate them. They practiced reading little behaviorisms to see if they could *tell* when a player was bluffing.

\*\*\*

In addition to conning, hustles, and making money, like most fourteen-year-old boys, Brian and Alan were into girls. They thought about how Rose had said that all acting was a con. Coming on to girls was a con. They wanted to learn how to hustle girls into going out with them.

Simply asking a girl out like their friends did was no fun and wouldn't fit with being hip, slick, and cool. They had to do better. In addition, getting rejected would hurt. If they were acting, they would feel more comfortable. This was where they thought that Rose could be most helpful. Hustling for money was one thing; hustling for girls was an entirely different ballgame.

The twins wanted to learn how to move on girls in a hip, slick, and cool way, not like most of their peers. Even at this age and in this arena, the twins were into maintaining their unique brand. Rose gave them a lot of insights into how girls thought and what was important to them.

"Contrary to what is portrayed in some movies, especially pornography, girls are not interested in being mistreated," said Rose during one of their outings. "Girls like gentleness. They like affection."

"But what about all of these badass dudes I see on television?" asked Alan. "The chicks seem to love them."

"Yeah, well, that's Hollywood for you," replied Rose. "Remember, most of the directors are men, most of the writers are men, so they write what they think women want. And keep in mind, that while some girls will like the bad-boy style in the beginning, it has a short shelf-life. It gets tiresome pretty quickly. It's not good for the long-term relationship."

"I'm a kid, Rose," said Alan. "I think my brother and I are not in it for the long game. We'll take the short run and have some fun being badasses." He smiled.

Rose nodded and gave a chuckle. "I understand. But be nice badasses."

***

By the time they were ready for high school, the brothers had put on some weight, all of it muscle. They could run five miles in under forty-five minutes and had advanced toward becoming black belts in karate. They even engaged in local competitions between karate clubs much like what they had seen in the *Karate Kid* movies. And, more often than not, they won. During practice sessions outside of the dojo, they sparred with each other. Sometimes one would be an attacker and the other would defend himself.

They particularly wanted to become adept in defending against scenarios that might come up on the street. They wanted the martial arts to be practical, not just for tournaments. Given that they lived together, they could practice more frequently than most other martial artists. They practiced in parks and at the beach as well as in the dojo. Hence, they made rapid progress. This was their way. Once they got into something, they would persevere until they became fully competent.

They had renegotiated their agreements with the independent street hustlers to supply them with merchandise as needed. They reaffirmed their relationship with the kids who wrote their papers and reports, and even found a kid who was a whiz at computer hacking and was willing to hack into the school's system to change a grade if necessary. For a buck, they could find people to do most anything they wanted. Money was power. The piece that was missing was the new idea for the business.

# CHAPTER FIVE

# High School

## *1997-2000*

Just as middle school had been a training ground for high school, Alan and Brian used high school as a training ground for college.

They focused on practicing the art of deception. They recognized the truth in what Nick and Rose had said about capitalizing on their identical appearance and the importance of an actor learning how to develop a character.

They bought a theatrical makeup kit and several forms of disguise and spent hours online watching YouTube videos, learning how to apply them. They had mustaches, beards, wigs, change-of-eye-color contacts, and a palette of theatrical cosmetics that could change their facial appearance, including materials for aging and for adding wrinkles and scars to their faces.

They practiced putting makeup on themselves and on each other. They even went so far as to sign up for theater arts classes where they could practice acting under the guidance of their teachers. They figured that if they were going to be good grifters, it would be wise for them to learn the craft of mastering disguises and playing different characters. The Situation Room became not only their strategy headquarters, but their dressing room as well.

"You know," began Brian one Saturday morning, "we could ask Mom for some help with this."

"Huh? Mom? What—" exclaimed a surprised Alan.

"Look, remember we said we wanted to be proactive with Mom to prevent her from prying into what we've been up to," explained Brian. "Well, she's a cosmetologist. And she's a girl. Why not have her help us with makeup?"

Alan thought about it for a moment. Tapping his finger to his head and then pointing at Brian, he said, "Good thinking, bro, good thinking. Why not call her in now?"

Brian left their bedroom in search of Martina. Alan followed him. Finding her in the kitchen, he said, "Hey, Mom. We could use some help with a school project. Gotta few minutes?"

Martina froze, almost dropping the knife she was using to prepare some vegetables. This was the first time her sons had asked her for help. Pulling herself together, she replied, "Sure. How can I help?"

"Alan and I have signed up for a theater class at school, and we have to learn how to put on makeup," explained Brian. "We thought that maybe being a girl and a professional in cosmetology, you could help us."

Obviously pleased, Martina smiled. And then she laughed. "Oh, my God, I'd be delighted to help! I never thought I'd be asked to help my *boys* put on makeup!"

Brian and Alan blushed and then laughed along with their mother.

The three of them spent hours over the course of the next few weeks learning some of the tricks of the trade. Once the twins got the basics down, they would periodically consult with their mother, which made her very happy. Now when they had their weekly dinner together, they had something more to talk about. For the first time, they had something in common: makeup. Martina knew from first-hand experience of her sons' ability to close people out of their lives. She didn't want to say or do anything to mess up this fragile relationship. As much as she relished her time with her boys, she also felt apprehensive when she was with them.

Alan and Brian watched people walk and listened to how they talked, paying specific attention to various accents. They practiced playing different roles in their acting classes, as well as when they went out shopping. Rose was helpful in tutoring them and giving them exercises and assignments that challenged them to fool different people.

They went to ethnocentric areas of LA—Little Italy, Olvera Street, Little Persia, Little Armenia, Greektown— trying to pass as natives. They shopped in the local markets and strip malls. Their complexion allowed them to pass as Latino, Italian, Greek, and most other cultures where being olive-skinned was common.

They kept their hair short so that it would be easy to wear a wig when needed. They figured if they were going to be effective at conning people, it would be good to be able to change places with one another without people knowing that they were identical twins. They used brown contact lenses to cover their green eyes, wearing them when they went on their various excursions. They would also exchange places at will and be in the same place at the same time while looking different from one another.

They would be identical or different, as the con required. They were in control.

One of Rose's homework assignments was for Alan and Brian to change their appearance enough to fool their own mother. She figured that if they could fool their mother, they could fool anyone. It felt like a final exam.

"I have an idea," said Alan. "How about trying to introduce Mom to a friend from school? One of us could be the friend."

They sat in their room working out a plan for introducing one of them to their mother. They flipped a coin to see which of them would be the friend. Brian won the toss.

"I'd love to find out how Mom always is able to tell us apart," said Brian. "We still don't know how she does it."

"Maybe it's smell," replied Alan. "You know, like the way dogs smell their puppies. Maybe we give off a smell that only mothers can detect."

"Yeah, she gives us the sniff test," said Brian.

They laughed at the thought.

"Okay, that sounds great," said Brian. "First, we have to get busy creating a disguise. I think we should do a Mexican accent and long hair. I'm pretty good with a Mexican accent."

"You need to use the brown eye contacts and some putty to fatten your face, along with a darker skin-tone makeup," added Alan.

"And we can use some of that body padding to make me look a little heavier," said Brian.

"Let's try the wig," said Alan.

Brian put on the long-haired wig and stared into the mirror. "What do you think, keep it loose or put it in a ponytail?"

Alan stood next to Brian, looking in the theatrical three-sided mirror they had bought to configure the dressing room. He reached out and pulled the wig back into a ponytail to get a look.

"What d'ya think?" asked Brian.

Alan looked closely into the mirror and then looked back at Brian. "Hey, what's this on your ear, bro? I never noticed this before."

"What? What do you see?" asked Brian, leaning closer to the mirror.

"This mark, like a freckle or a beauty mark," replied Alan. "I don't have one."

"I never paid any attention to it sitting there on my earlobe," said Brian.

"That's how she does it!" exclaimed Alan.

"How who does what?" asked a puzzled Brian.

"Mom," replied Alan with a wry smile and a nod. "That's how she tells us apart. You know she notices everything!"

"Well, I'll be damned!" exclaimed Brian smiling. "Well, that decides it. The hair stays down, covering my ears."

"And now we know how we can fool even Mom," said Alan pointing to the birthmark. "We just have to create one of those for me."

Brian smirked. "And now we have the upper hand."

They both laughed. "And we learned something very important," said Brian. "It's all in the details. We can never be too careful—we must examine things with a fine-tooth comb. Look at everything under a magnifying glass!"

They nodded in agreement. "The devil is in the details. Now we know what that really means."

While their mother was at work, they spent the next few hours in their room applying the makeover. By the time they were done, Brian no longer looked anything like his identical twin brother. He looked at himself and found the transformation amazing. He hardly recognized himself.

"We need a larger shirt," said Alan, "to cover the padding and give a loose fit."

They spent the next several days developing a strategy, including a plan for telling their mother that Brian was staying at school for a project while Alan and his friend Pedro were studying in his room. They practiced the dialogue and even created some lines to work on Brian's accent, especially for Spanish words that all people with Mexican heritage pronounced correctly but Anglos often didn't.

They went to the mall as Alan and Pedro to see whether anyone from school would recognize them. They bumped into several friends who just accepted Pedro as Alan's friend.

When at home, Alan pretended to have phone conversations with Pedro within earshot of his mother, including a conversation where they mentioned the possibility of getting together to study within the next few days. This exercise helped them with the details of developing a successful con. When they felt ready, they set the day for the big test.

Alan and Brian went to school as they usually did. At the end of the day, they found an empty bathroom and used a stall for Brian to change costumes. Alan and Pedro left the school and walked home to their apartment. It was a Friday afternoon. Martina always came home early on Fridays. It was showtime.

Alan and Pedro walked into the kitchen where Martina was preparing dinner. Pedro was a dark-complexioned, jowly Latino with shoulder-length brown hair and brown eyes. He wore a plaid, flannel shirt over a black tee shirt and cargo pants. He looked about twenty pounds heavier than Brian, and his work boots made him taller.

"Hi, Mom," said Alan with a cheerful smile. "This is my friend, Pedro, from school. We're going to do some work on a school project together."

"*Mucho gusto*—uh—pleased to meet you, Mrs. Suarez," said Pedro speaking softly with a slight accent.

Martina looked up from the sink and smiled. She stared at Pedro for a moment. "*Encantada conocerte*, Pedro," Martina replied. It wasn't often that she spoke her native tongue around the house, but it came automatically when she was addressed in Spanish.

Martina turned and looked at Alan. "Where's your brother?"

Alan smiled. "He's still at school. He had some stuff to do."

Martina turned toward Pedro. "Would you like to join us for dinner, Pedro?" she asked.

Pedro hesitated. He turned toward Alan and then back to Martina. "Uh, well, uh, thank you, Mrs. Suarez, but I, uh, I only can stay for a little while. I work after school and must be there by five o'clock. But, uh, *gracias*, uh, thank you."

"You're welcome," replied Martina. "Perhaps another time."

"Come on, Pedro, we'd better get busy," said Alan. "We don't have much time."

The two of them left for the Situation Room. Martina stared after them for a few moments before returning to her cooking.

Once inside Alan's bedroom, they closed the door and let out a sigh of relief. They gave each other a high five. They hung out for a couple of hours discussing their next steps before Alan escorted Pedro to the door. Pedro said goodbye to Martina and left.

Twenty minutes later, Brian walked in.

"Hey, Mom, what's for dinner?" asked Brian as he strolled past the kitchen with his stuffed black backpack slung over his shoulder.

"I made a meatloaf," replied Martina to the back of Brian's head as she watched him walk by.

*Something strange is going on*, she thought. *I can't put my finger on it. Probably because this is the first time either of the twins has brought someone home to study. Hmmm. Maybe this acting class is good for them.*

"Great. I'm starving," said Brian. "I just passed Pedro on the street. He said he was here. Why didn't he stay for dinner?"

"He said he had to go to work," replied Martina, smiling. She was feeling good about the new bond she felt with her sons.

Brian nodded and smiled. Then he closed the Situation Room door. The twins pumped the air and gave one another a thumbs-up.

Once they had passed the test of fooling their mother, they felt completely confident in being able to either present themselves as two different people, as twins, or as one person, depending on the circumstances.

They began a series of adventures to test out their newly acquired skill. Using their ability to be in two places at the same time, they signed up for races where they would figure a way of substituting for one another at the halfway mark. They competed in 10K races, as well as half-marathons. They even substituted for one another in karate competitions.

They even loved dating the same girl, swapping places with one another—and the girl wouldn't know who she was with at any given moment. They could even substitute for one another in bed. They enjoyed this activity the most and did not feel either the jealousy or competition that other brothers might have felt. They were more invested in the scam than the relationship. For the twins, it was simply a game.

During one of their Saturday visits with Nick and Rose, Nick asked if Alan and Brian had ever gone to bed with the same girl. The twins looked at each other and chuckled out loud.

"Yeah," said Alan. "We love doing that."

"Remember the time we went over to that girl's house when her parents were away for the weekend?" asked Brian looking at his brother. "What was her name?"

"For sure, I remember doing it, but I don't remember her name," replied Alan. "I took her to the movies, and then when I took her home, you had already snuck into the house through the bathroom window."

"Yeah, I was just sitting there waiting until you guys got back," said Brian smiling as he recalled the incident.

"The girl and I started making out on the couch; she was all prepared," chucked Alan. "Had the condoms hidden under the sofa pillows. She was ready. After I did the deed, I went to the bathroom to flush the condom and take a leak."

"Right," said Brian. "And you told me where she kept the condoms. Beverly, that was her name. I just remembered. Then I went back into the living room while you split through the bathroom window. Beverly was happy that I was ready to go again so quickly."

The twins laughed at the memory.

"When Beverly and I were done," continued Brian, "I kissed her good night and left by the front door. I remember promising to call her."

Nick, Alan, and Brian shared a laugh. Even Rose had to smile despite her not liking how the twins had treated the young girl. Although she had learned how to use her femininity to get what she wanted in a male-dominated world, at heart Rose had become a feminist.

The twins only thought about sex for their own pleasure. For them, it was simply a sport. It was all about the numbers; they kept a running tab on how many girls they took to bed. They even created a spreadsheet so that they could keep track of what they said and to whom. The devil was in the details.

It didn't take long before word got around at the high school that the twins were players. The boys thought they were cool. Except for a few of the more promiscuous girls who liked the idea of bedding twins and even wanted to do them both at the same time, most of the other girls stayed away from them. The twins developed a reputation for being interested in only themselves and couldn't be trusted. It was a reputation they deserved.

Alan simply shrugged it off. It didn't bother him at all, but Brian, always the more sensitive, struggled with it. The comments and being thought of as a jerk hurt him. It bothered him even more that it bothered him at all. He didn't like the fact that he felt anything; it didn't fit his ideal of being impervious to what others thought of him. But he couldn't help it. Brian knew he had to continue to work on perfecting his game.

Alan and Brian continued to meet with Nick and Rose at least once a month throughout high school. Instead of meeting at the Senior Citizens Center, they met in Rose's apartment. Nick and Rose were now living together. Their combined Social Security checks made them more financially secure and increased their quality of life; they were also able to look after one another.

"What's going on with you boys?" asked Rose as she prepared a pot of tea. The four of them sat around the kitchen table and chatted.

Alan and Brian filled them in on what they've been doing and reported on the reputation they'd been developing and their desire to find a bigger market for HS&C.

When the twins finished their update, Rose said, "Well, boys, it looks like you'll have to move on to greener pastures."

"One thing I learned a long time ago, fellas," said Nick smiling wistfully and taking a sip of his tea, "don't shit where you eat."

Alan raised his eyebrows. "What does that mean?"

Nick became serious. "It means that you've outgrown your high school. Everyone knows you, and you can't keep scamming the same people or foolin' around with the same girls all the time. Not only is it bad for business—people talk—but it can be dangerous as well. As Rose says, it's time for ya to move on to fresh territory. You've practiced in your backyard, where ya eat; now it's time to go beyond."

Alan and Brian sat quietly staring down at the table for a few moments and reflecting on what Nick said.

Finally, Brian looked up. "We have one year left before going off to college. We should be thinking beyond our senior year in high school."

"We should be thinking about other high schools, not just our own," added Alan.

"And you should be thinking about getting into the best and biggest college you can get into," said Rose. "The bigger the school, the easier it is to get lost and the more marks there are."

"Think big, boys," said Nick. "Think outside of the box. Be creative. There's a big world out there."

Alan and Brian looked at each other for a long moment and then became quiet. They finished their tea, chatted about what else was going on in their respective lives, and after an hour, they left. Their conversation with Nick and Rose had given them lots to think about and became the major topic at their next strategy session.

"Remember what Nick said about thinking big?" began Brian. "I think he's right. We've been thinking only about our 'hood and high school. We gotta go outside the box, like he said."

Alan nodded in agreement. "Yeah. Think big." He paused. "Hey, what about the internet? That big enough? It's global."

Brian stopped scratching his head. "Right! Wow, you're right. Instead of just buying shit online and selling to our high school, we could sell stuff online all over the country. Kids are kids wherever they live. We could do our entire business online. We could do the same business through eBay. We could go global!" exclaimed Brian.

"There's a whole network of gray-market merchandise being produced in Asia," said Alan. "They even make knockoffs of every major brand out there. It's just a matter of connecting with the suppliers and working out an arrangement."

Brian scratched and nodded. "Yeah, right. Most kids in our market don't give a shit where or how the stuff is made as long as they have the style and, of course, the label," replied Brian. "We could create an eBay store that pulls together merchandise from all over the internet into one site—a virtual one-stop shop for brand names that kids love. All for cheap. They go to one place, order what they want, and we ship it."

They spent the next several days hammering out a plan for finding gray-market suppliers, knockoff vendors, and making lists of the type of merchandise they would best be able to sell to low- and middle-income kids around the world. They also made plans to contact internet-savvy friends about making sure their internet address could not be traced back to them and to discuss the ins and outs of online banking.

They set up a virtual private network because it gave them more security over the internet, hiding their actual location. They knew everything bought online was done through e-commerce, so they would have to set up a PayPal account, merchant account, or some such online billing mechanism. They made a detailed list of everything they would have to learn for this new venture and divided the tasks between them. Their plan for building their business was underway. They intended to launch it the summer before they entered college.

\*\*\*

"One of the other things that Rose said," began Alan, "is that we should give more thought to going to college. All the kids at school are talking about college. We never gave it any thought. But now it might be a good idea."

"Having a college education would give us more credibility, especially as we get older and have to deal with the adult world," replied Brian. "And it should be a big school, like a UCLA or Berkeley. Remember what Rose said: the bigger the school, the easier it is to hide. We want to fly under the radar. And UCLA is just a few miles from here."

"And it will give us a larger population," added Alan. "UCLA has around forty thousand undergraduate students. College students have money. Who knows what kind of cons we could pull?" He grinned. "The big question is, how the fuck are we gonna get into UCLA? Our grades are okay, but not great, ya know. And we both have to get in. UCLA is not exactly second-rate."

"Yeah, I know," replied Brian. "But, hey, don't forget who we are. We can figure a way to hustle our way in, right? And we're California residents. We get priority."

Alan smiled knowingly. "True dat, bro," he said. "But we're entering our senior year in high school. That means we should finish off this year with a bang—we gotta ace our senior year. And we're gonna have to get a high enough score on the SATs. It looks like we might have to spend some time studying, or at least paying attention in class, huh?"

They chuckled.

With a couple hundred dollars, they bought some help from a friend who hacked the school computer system. The twins got a few of their grades changed to put them in the running for admission to UCLA. It wasn't that they were stupid. Quite the opposite; they were often told that they were not living up to their full potential. Being naturally gifted, they were able to coast by and still get above-average grades, especially with a little test-taking assistance from their crew. They were just not interested in academics. They only needed a little help from the hacker to bring a few of their grades up to the top nine percent of their class. They knew that once teachers submitted their grade sheets to the administrative office, they never paid further attention to a student's GPA, especially not in a large public high school like theirs. The more difficult part was obtaining a good-enough SAT score. Being California residents with a Hispanic surname helped. But they still needed at least a midrange score.

They did it the old-fashioned way. They decided to study. They hired a tutor and took an online SAT preparatory course. Much to their surprise and that of their high-school counselors, they scored in the upper twentieth percentile. At first, they were put on a wait list for admission to some of the University of California campuses, pending the outcome of their senior year.

They did well enough that year to get them admitted to UCLA. Martina Suarez was ecstatic. She never expected that her boys would get into UCLA. Martina needed her boys to be successful; she harbored a lot of guilt for divorcing their father and for not being a strong-enough parent. If her sons were successful, in some way she felt vindicated.

Once Alan and Brian had graduated high school, were admitted to college, and had turned eighteen, they again revisited the idea of opening an eBay store. They could apply for credit cards and bank accounts on their own. They no longer had to worry that their mother might discover they were using her Social Security number to get credit cards. This made growing their business a lot more convenient. Now they could buy and sell merchandise all over the world.

Alan and Brian had set up an eBay store selling brand-name merchandise at drastically discounted prices. They found that almost every high-end brand of clothing for men and women, as well as handbags and watches, were available in the gray market. They had already made connections in the LA garment district with odd-lot jobbers—vendors who bought mixed sizes and styles from manufacturers and large retailers who could not sell their entire inventory. They also connected with small boutique retail stores that needed to clear out space for new merchandise.

They decided to rent a storage unit in a self-storage place near the downtown area where rents were cheaper than on the Westside of Los Angeles. It was also closer to their suppliers. They would have to spend time at their new space, and since they would also have to keep Martina from inquiring about what they were up to, they told her they were able to land after-school jobs that would require their coming home around dinner time most days. Between after-school acting classes and their new *job*, they were able to account for their time.

The storage unit was about the size of a one-car garage. They used it as a warehouse for the goods they purchased and began to sell the merchandise on eBay.

They set it up as a mini-warehouse, complete with clothing racks, a desk, and a computer. They spent their after-school time inventorying, packing, and shipping merchandise. Keeping records was an important aspect of their business. They needed to know what they bought, sold, and didn't sell, and what goods people liked in different parts of the country. They were learning the skills necessary for being successful entrepreneurs.

As Nick always said about a good con, *the devil was in the details.*

When they first started the business, they only bought older styles and odd lots of authenticated merchandise from legitimate vendors. They learned that kids in the Midwest didn't mind being one season behind the latest fashions.

Rather than selling at high markups, the twins decided to make their money by selling in quantity with low profit margins. Alan and Brian took full advantage of eBay and Craigslist and all other online opportunities for selling merchandise. They knew their market: young people who wanted to stay current in style and fashion but did not have access to their parent's credit cards. There were a lot more kids who had limited funds out there than there were wealthy kids. Alan and Brian served them.

Instead of just operating locally, Alan and Brian went national. Kids were the same throughout the country. HS&C—Hip, Slick, and Cool—brought the most popular stuff under one umbrella, saving kids the time of having to do their own internet search for deals. Brian and Alan knew kids and knew what they wanted. They even took some special orders.

The twins had become what eBay referred to as "power sellers." They were raking in twenty to thirty thousand dollars each month with minimal overhead. This status brought them into contact with other wholesalers from around the world who wanted to do business with them. Most of their vendors in the garment center were willing to warehouse the merchandise for them for weeks or longer, given they were such good customers. They stored the merchandise purchased overseas in their storage warehouse.

The topic of how much counterfeit merchandise they should buy became a focus for one of their Situation Room chats.

"Hey," began Brian, "we got a decision to make. We have been getting quite a few requests from overseas companies to handle their goods. But their stuff is definitely counterfeit."

"Yeah, so?" replied Alan. "Do we give a shit? As long as the stuff looks legit, that's all that matters. Our buyers only care about the label."

"I know, but selling knockoffs is against the law," said Brian, his brow raised. "Big time. Passing off imitations as the real deal is like passing counterfeit money. A federal offence. And now we'd be doing business on a large scale—and we're no longer juvies. We're talkin' potential felony convictions if we are busted. At least gray-market stuff is not illegal to sell as long as we don't advertise that they're the real deal."

"No risk, no reward," replied Alan smiling. "Did Tony Soprano give a shit if he was on the other side of the law? The bigger question is, where do we store the stuff? Our little storage unit is not big enough to store large quantities, and these overseas dudes are not gonna hold the stuff for us."

"Maybe we can make some connections downtown," replied Brian. "I bet our suppliers know some gray-market vendors as well as knockoff vendors. For all we know, they've been slipping some knockoffs in our orders on the sly."

Brian was about to scratch his head but stopped. He had been working on stopping the tell ever since Nick had made him aware of it. At times he was more successful than at others.

"Now you're talkin'!" replied Alan.

Brian and Alan talked to their vendors downtown, and through them, they were put in touch with some suppliers who had connections in China as well as other countries. Some of these countries were known for being able to imitate anything from jeans to watches to handbags. Even the labels looked authentic, and that was most important.

This began their forays into the world of knockoff merchandise, items that were imitations of name brands made to look exactly like the genuine articles. The twins knew that selling counterfeit merchandise was against the law, but they were not deterred. It was all about the money. Brian's stomach issues and sweats picked up, but he didn't care. He only saw dollar signs.

They didn't care about the authenticity of the items; they only cared about the profit margin. The customers who bought from them were less concerned about whether the articles were genuine than they were about the label, the look, and the price. They were more interested in keeping up with the latest fashions and style than they were in quality. Hip, Slick, and Cool catered to that demographic.

The twins connected with dozens of distributors from all parts of the world to supply them all the major, trendy brands. Some of the items were knockoffs, some were gray-market, some were factory seconds, and others were odd lots of discontinued styles. They sold it all.

Their business grew a lot faster than they had expected, and money continued to roll in. They were using PayPal to collect their fees and then transferring the cash to their bank account. This raised some serious concerns for Brian. He did some legal research on the internet. It was time for a major sit-down in the Situation Room.

"Look," began Brian. "We're making too much money for it not to be noticed. We gotta do something to make ourselves look legitimate. We gotta pay taxes. While PayPal doesn't report our income to Uncle Sam, it's gonna happen soon. Same thing for eBay. And banks are required to report deposits of 10K or more, and even multiple large deposits require reporting. And now that we're using our own tax ID number and accounts, we're exposed to a potential audit. We're not flying under the radar."

Alan stared at his brother. He squinted his eyes and furrowed his brow, deep in thought. "Fuck! You're right, bro! You are fuckin' right. Shit! So, what are we gonna do?"

"Well, I'm thinking that we need both a lawyer and an accountant," replied Brian. "I did some research and heard about offshore accounts, credit cards in other countries, and shit like that."

Alan was quiet for a few moments. "Nah, I think we should set it up like a legitimate business. Including paying taxes. I don't want to fuck around with the IRS. It's one thing to pocket the cash when we were small-time operators. But we're not so small anymore. And as you said in our last meeting, we're not kids."

Brian nodded. He was pleased that his brother was being careful. He didn't like being the only one voicing caution. "Okay, then. We should search around for a lawyer, and maybe he can refer us to an accountant.

"We should also consider getting our own website rather than just being an eBay store. Hip, Slick, and Cool Enterprises International. We can cut out eBay and do our own advertising. And we should get our own credit-card-processing account so that we can accept credit-card payments directly."

"We could keep the eBay store for selling individual items," said Alan, "and refer people from eBay to our website where we can offer a larger variety. eBay would be like a portal to our website. We should sell only gray-market stuff through eBay. That would give us a little less exposure."

"Cool," said Brian. "You're right. Our website will be our portal for all sorts of merchandise including special orders. We would be brokers finding special items on request. Customers could contact us directly through email with no eBay trace. But one thing we need to do is to be careful about the people we buy from and how we advertise. We don't want someone to rat us out. We should never say anything about things being *authentic* or *genuine* brands. Just show pictures of the merchandise with a brief description. Let our low prices speak for themselves."

"We can use the eBay store for selling gray-market items and our website for selling everything else, including knockoffs," said Alan.

Brian felt nervous. He knew that selling counterfeit goods was just as much against the law as selling stolen merchandise. He also knew that doing it through the mail was a federal crime; it was mail fraud. But Alan was enthusiastic. He just didn't care about the legalities. He was focused on the money.

They hired a lawyer who walked them through all the steps for setting up a business. The attorney was a no-nonsense guy whose style was direct and to the point. He did not sugarcoat anything.

"The first thing you need to know is that whatever you tell me is covered by what is known as attorney–client privilege," explained the lawyer. "In other words, whatever you tell me remains with me. I am not permitted to tell anyone whether what you are doing is legal or illegal. My job is to tell you what the law is and what the consequences of your actions might be. Do you understand?"

Brian and Alan looked at each other and then back at the attorney. They nodded. They took turns outlining all of their business plans. They told him about the gray-market and counterfeit items, the special-order items, and the odd-lot business.

"Okay, then," continued the lawyer. "First of all, what you are intending to do—selling stolen merchandise—constitutes a felony. If you are caught and found guilty, you go to prison, and you will have a permanent record. Secondly, selling counterfeit goods is also a felony. And since the merchandise you are selling comes from overseas, it is a federal crime. So now, we're talking about a federal prison. Get it?"

Brian's stomach flipped. Alan was stoic. They both listened carefully as the attorney went on.

"I suggest that you boys stick to selling odd lots, seconds, and even gray-market items. Gray-market items are different from counterfeit items. Gray-market items are legal in the country in which they are manufactured and cannot be sold in the United States. They are essentially the same as the U.S. version, but are not guaranteed by the manufacturer in the U.S. They are frequently made of different and/or cheaper materials. What is illegal, however, is selling gray-market items as if they were authentic U.S. goods. For example, selling a pair of gray-market jeans as if they were the genuine article is a crime. Get it?"

The twins nodded. They had understood this from their internet research. But hearing it from an attorney made it real.

"Selling counterfeit items or knockoffs," continued the lawyer, "is a crime. These items are made to look like the real McCoy but are fake. Selling them constitutes fraud and trademark infringement. This would be a felony. A federal offence. Not a good idea to mess with the feds. Are you with me?"

"What if we don't know where the stuff comes from?" asked Brian. "I mean, sometimes we buy stuff from people, and we don't know where they got it or whether it is gray or counterfeit."

"What do you mean you don't know where it comes from?" asked the lawyer. "Exactly whom do you do business with?"

"We do business with a lot of different people," replied Alan. "Some of them are not necessarily businessmen." Alan was trying to be circumspect, not wanting to reveal the fact that they often dealt with thieves.

The lawyer was a street-smart, savvy guy. He could sense that the twins were hustlers and not above doing things outside the law.

"Look, if you guys bought your merchandise legally and sold it as used, there's no problem," explained the lawyer. "But if you either passed it off as new, obtained it illegally, or were party to obtaining stolen merchandise, you are committing a crime. My advice is to stay clear of knockoffs and stolen merchandise. Don't buy stuff from guys who tell you that the crate of jeans fell off the back of a truck. Get it?"

The twins nodded in unison. "We get it," replied Brian.

The lawyer introduced them to a CPA who set up their books and found them a bookkeeper who managed their accounts. HS&C became an official business.

Their visits with the attorney and the accountant gave them a lot to think about. The more they thought about it, the more Brian was convinced that they should stop dealing in stolen merchandise. He believed they should continue selling gray merchandise in addition to the factory seconds, odd lots, and overstocked inventories. He remained uncertain about selling knockoffs.

"Knowingly selling knockoffs is against the law, right?" began Brian. "We can become vendors of gray-market items exclusively. That way, we're legit. We can capture the fashion market in our demographic."

"The truth is that most people know the merchandise is gray," said Alan. "But they don't care. They just want the stuff. Even if we sold knockoffs, they wouldn't report us because they would have to admit to buying illegal merchandise. It's just like when people buy Rolexes from the dude on a street corner showing a display of name-brand watches. People know they're counterfeit, but they don't care. They just want the look."

"But those guys sell them on a street corner," said Brian. "They pack up and split when a cop comes by. No one even knows their name. We're a business; we have a website; we pay taxes. And we're looking at being in the business for a while."

As much as he hated giving up on knockoffs, Alan finally conceded. "Okay, it's agreed," he said. "We're going to do just gray."

Brian felt relieved. "What are we going to do about the special-order items?"

Alan hesitated, looking Brian directly in the eyes. Brian knew that look. His stomach jumped.

"What about keeping the Craigslist operation for the SOIs?" asked Alan.

"I thought we were giving that up when we decided to go legit," said Brian. "It's a fencing scam."

"I have a hard time leaving money on the table," replied Alan. "I see a huge opportunity."

"And besides, it takes a lot of time meeting people to give them their product," pressed Brian.

"Nah," replied Alan. "If the profit is right, we can use a delivery service or hire some people to make the drops and collect the money. Always in cash, just like we've been doing."

"We're still selling stolen merchandise," said Brian. "Entirely illegal!"

"What's your problem, bro?" asked Alan, becoming irritated with his brother's pushback. "It was your idea to begin with. You were the guy who said we could do it online using email for taking special orders. Now you want to back out? Wassup with that?"

Brian could feel his stomach grumbling. "That was before we spoke to the lawyer. And before we decided to go legit. We're talking federal crimes here. I don't like leaving money on the table either, but ..."

"Look, we don't know where the stuff comes from, bro, and we don't ask," argued Alan. "As long as it is genuine, looks good, and functions, we're good. I'm telling you, people don't give a shit about pedigree." Alan smiled. "People who buy on Craigslist never question where their stuff comes from, and they know they're taking a chance on the stuff working. *Caveat emptor. Let the buyer beware.*"

"What about the exposure?" said Brian with less intensity. He knew his brother would win the argument. "These street vendors can't be trusted. Any one of them could demand more money or threaten to rat us out."

"We just have to make sure that doesn't happen," replied Alan. "We've got to make sure they know not to fuck with us."

Brian's heart began to pound. He could feel his breath catching in his throat. Fortunately, the feeling quickly passed. While the idea of being fences dealing in stolen merchandise and making a ton of money appealed to him, the thought of get caught made his stomach turn, his hands sweat, and his heart pound.

Alan could see the look in his brother's eyes. "Hey, bro, stop worrying. It's all cool. We can have the gray-market business both on eBay and our web store, and the Craigslist resale, special-order business. We've diversified." Alan chuckled.

Brian tried to control his breathing. *Shit*, he thought, *for Alan everything is a game. Nothing bothers him. Fuck! I wish I could be more like him. We look the same, can even act the same, but we sure don't feel the same.*

Alan rarely worried about anything. He was all about action. End results mattered. While he sometimes wondered about his brother and how Brian always seemed to be so cautious about things, he rarely gave it much thought.

# CHAPTER SIX

# College Years

Alan and Brian spent the summer months before entering UCLA taking care of the details of their new business plan. They streamlined their business, reorganized their storage facility, and developed an inviting HS&C website, complete with pictures and a shopping cart. They spruced up their eBay store, had the bookkeeper set up detailed accounts for tracking all sales and expenses, and created spreadsheets for keeping track of all of their vendors, both abroad and local.

They had turned eighteen and were now legally adults. They had lined up their people: mentors Nick and Rose, a lawyer, an accountant, a bookkeeper, street vendors, apparel district vendors, overseas vendors, a computer technician and hacker, and their crew to whom they turned to for writing papers and doing other odd jobs as needed.

It was quite an operation. The summer had been profitable on all fronts. They made money and worked out many of the kinks inherent in running a business. Now they were ready to focus on school, girls, and growing their business.

Three months later, Alan and Brian entered UCLA. It excited them to be able to buy whatever they wanted, whenever they wanted, and not have to even think about it. Instead of wearing knockoff watches or even gray-market clothes, they could buy the genuine article. Even their sunglasses were top of the line. They no longer had to shop for bargains, at least not for themselves. Less than a third of their gross went for merchandise and other expenses, leaving them around one hundred fifty thousand to support their lifestyle. And the business was growing—and it was legit, at least the internet part was.

Connecting with people, other than how they could serve their own aspirations, became less and less important to the twins. The only people with whom they felt emotionally connected, other than one another, were their mother, Nick, and Rose. To the rest of the world, they were detached, remote, and calculating.

During one of their acting classes, the teacher had described the twins as robots, saying that they had to get more in touch with their feelings if they wanted to be effective. While other students would have felt criticized, the twins smiled when they heard her describe them that way. They had achieved their goal of becoming like James Bond.

Brian recalled an evening that he and Alan had spent with their mother. Martina, who was now feeling more secure in her relationship with the twins, had said, "Sometimes I worry about you boys. You seem so, I don't know, uh, unemotional. You seem like, what's that guy's name from Star Trek?"

"Mr. Spock?" said Brian.

"Yes, that's him, Spock," said Martina. "All brain and no feelings."

Both boys smiled.

"Why does that worry you, Mom?" asked Alan.

"Well, if you are ever going to be in a relationship with a girl, she's going to want to see some show of feelings. You know, some emotions. Some sign that you care."

Brian recalled that both he and Alan had smiled at the description.

From time to time, Brian was concerned about taking advantage of someone, but for the most part, he had it under control.

*As long as I don't physically hurt someone, I'm cool with it*, he rationalized.

Despite their mother living only a few miles from the UCLA campus, Alan and Brian decided to rent their own apartment adjacent to the university.

"You know we're going to have to talk to Mom," said Brian. "If we're going to move out, she's gonna want to know where we got the money. She's gonna ask questions."

"You're right, bro," replied Alan. "I guess, we're going to have a convo with her ASAP."

Later that week, they had dinner with their mother. While discussing their beginning college, Martina told the boys how proud she was for their having gotten admitted to UCLA and for wanting to go to college. She asked them how they felt about it.

"We're excited about it, Mom," said Brian. "And we want to do well there. People keep telling us that having a college degree is important for our careers no matter what we do."

"Yes," replied Martina, "that's true. What are you going to do? I mean, what are you going to major in?"

"We're thinking business," answered Alan. "We like making money and are thinking about having our own business." Alan smiled thinking about all the money they were already making.

"As a matter of fact, Mom," added Brian, "we started our own business a little while ago buying and reselling CDs and other electronics. We do some of our own mixing on request, making CDs for people. You probably heard the loud music coming from our room. Well, our business is doing well enough already, so we are thinking about getting our own apartment near campus."

Alan was blown away by his brother's ability to think on his feet. And the story was close enough to the truth that it didn't sound like a lie. He remembered Nick having said that the best cons are based on having enough truth that they are believable. He couldn't help but smile.

"Your own apartment near UCLA?" exclaimed Martina. "You boys must have some business. I thought you were only working part-time while going to school. But to be able to rent an apartment, wow, that must be some business! My sons are entrepreneurs."

Entrepreneurs. The twins liked the way that sounded.

"Yeah, well, it's growing," said Alan trying to be as circumspect as possible. "It looks like it could really take off. And if we're careful with our money, we should be able to swing the apartment. And living near the campus, we would be able to spend more time in the library studying."

"It would also give us more time to get involved with college life," added Brian quickly.

"Well, I know how hard it is to start a business," said Martina. "I hope you are not working so much that you won't be able to do your school work. Getting into college is one thing, but graduating is a whole different thing. It's not like high school, I can tell you that much!" She recalled her years in college and had occasionally thought about finishing her own degree.

Martina could hardly believe what she was hearing. She had often wondered what the twins were doing behind the closed door of their bedroom and had had concerns about their future. She also realized that she had been so wrapped up in her own life after divorcing their father that she hadn't been as involved in their lives as she should have been.

She had worried whether she was a good-enough mother. Their apparent success left her feeling better about herself. She felt in some ways exonerated for her failures as a mom. She had been more concerned with avoiding contact with Lucas, her explosive ex-husband, who always seemed to show up in her life unexpectedly—at her work or school or even in the supermarket, each time making a scene.

When she had decided to go into business for herself, her parents had loaned her the money to open a hair-and-nail salon. She had spent most of her waking hours developing the business, and now that her boys were in college and on their own, she could even think about opening a second salon. She spent seven days a week, working sixteen-hour days in developing the business. It became her life. She did not want to be financially dependent on her parents, nor did she ever want to be dependent on a man ever again.

"Will you be able to pay for tuition, books, and an apartment?" she asked with some hesitation. "I could help with a little. I have saved some money and would be happy to pay something. You boys haven't asked for much of anything since your father and I got divorced. I would like to help."

"That won't be—" Alan began, oblivious to their mother's desire to participate in their lives.

Brian interrupted, sensing their mother's desire to be more of a mom. "While not necessary, Mom, that would be very nice of you. How about paying for our books? College books can be very expensive."

Martina beamed. "Yes! I can do that. You tell me how much, and I will write a check." She was ecstatic. Her boys were finally allowing her to be a small part of their lives. She felt hopeful.

Once back in their room, Alan asked, "What was that all about, bro?"

"Look, Mom just wants to be helpful," replied Brian. "She's tried her best to get her life together. I know, she hasn't been much of a mom to us, and that was fine with us. But since she began helping us learn about makeup and we began having dinner with her, it has made her happy and kept her out of our business. She's pretty much given us space to do our thing. What's the harm in letting her pay for the books if it makes her happy?"

Alan just looked at his brother, thinking, *Who is this guy? It never would have occurred to me to let her give us money.*

He just shook his head and said, "Okay, bro. No problem."

"One more thing," continued Brian. "I think it would nice for us to continue having dinner with Mom at least once a week like we've been doing. She's off early on Fridays so that would work, okay?"

Alan remained quiet, thinking about Brian and his sudden desire to stay in touch with their mother. It was not something he would have thought of on his own.

After a moment, he replied. "Sure, bro, sure. Good idea."

***

They spent the next couple of days packing up their stuff and moving to their apartment. Gradually, their Situation Room was transformed back into a normal bedroom. They made sure to seal up the hole in the wall where they had stored their cash.

The twins furnished their apartment to resemble the pictures that they had seen in the upscale magazines showing the coolest bachelor pads, Hollywood style. The apartment itself was a two-bedroom affair, each with its own bathroom, separated by the living room and kitchen.

For the first time in their lives, they had separate bedrooms. The apartment was totally hi-tech and ultramodern. A section of the living room was set up like an office. They had identical desks facing each other placed in front of the windows at one end of the long room. They each had a big-screen computer. That setup made it easy for them to talk to one another.

"Now that our business is running smoothly, we have our apartment, and we're starting college," began Brian, "we ought to be thinking about how we're going to get through school with the least amount of effort. We have to continue to focus on growing the business. College life will definitely make that more difficult unless we come up with a strategy."

Alan nodded. "You are absolutely right, bro," he replied. "You got a plan in mind?"

"As a matter of fact, I do," said Brian. "Three things. Number one, I don't think we should be twins at college; we should just be brothers. We should keep our being idents hidden so that we can switch places when needed. Number two, I think we should make some connections like we did in high school, finding kids we can buy off to take exams for us when necessary. And lastly, we should find a good computer hacker who can fix grades. I think we've outgrown the guys we've been using. Time for a change."

"Whoa, bro, I'm impressed," replied Alan. "You've been doing some serious thinking about this."

"That's what I do best—think," acknowledged Brian with a sly smile. "For better or worse, my brain is always buzzing."

"I hear ya," replied Alan. "That's what makes us such a good team. You're the thinker, and I'm the doer. You've got the ideas, and I develop the plan of action. I'm the point person, and you're operations."

They high-fived.

"The first step is for us to come up with a disguise to differentiate ourselves from one another," continued Brian. "It's got to be something quick and easy that both of us can use. Like it's easy for us to use the color contact lenses. One of us can be brown-eyed. We could use a wig, so one us would have long hair, the other short. Things like that."

"How about glasses?" added Alan. "We could get some really cool specs. One brother wears glasses with brown eyes and long hair, the other natural."

"That would be enough," said Brian. "Remember Rose said a good actor keeps it simple and uses his own personality to carry the part. It's the subtle details that matter. So, given our personalities, you being the more outgoing one and me being the more serious one, I could have long hair, brown eyes, glasses, and be more reserved. You've always been the out-there guy, so it's a natural."

Alan nodded and smiled. "Let's give it a try."

Within a few minutes, Brian had inserted the brown contacts, put on the glasses, and donned the wig they had used to fool their mother. When they stood side by side, the transformation was clear. They looked like brothers, but not identical twins.

They used their cell phone to take a photo. Then they switched identities; Alan put on the wig, the contacts, and the glasses. Again, they looked in the mirror and took a picture. They studied the photo and concluded that no one could tell them apart. They each could become the other in less than five minutes.

"Okay, from now on, you have to wear the disguise whenever we are out and about near the university, and especially when on campus, right?" confirmed Alan. "And we have to keep our hair short to make it easy to put on the wig."

"And one thing we have to watch out for," said Brian. "We have to stay away from anyone who might know us from before. They could bust our cover."

Alan nodded. "That could be a problem, bro. There are a lot of people from our high school who know us, and many of them might be attending UCLA. Also, we lived on the Westside all of our lives."

"What's most important is that new people not know that we are twins," replied Brian. "As long as we keep each other informed about who we meet and what was said, we can just play each other's part as needed. It'd be just like when we'd hustle chicks; they never even knew we were idents. And if we're together when I'm wearing a disguise, no one will know who I am. Remember, we fooled Mom. If we could fool her, we can fool anyone. We just don't want anyone we know to see us together as they knew us; we don't want them introducing us to their friends. It might become necessary for one of us to always be in disguise just to be safe."

Alan was impressed with his brother's attention to detail.

With the first step of their three-part strategy in place, they set out to find a hacker. Finding students to take exams for them would take a bit longer. Hackers hung out in the computer labs. They were a special breed of students known to most of the ordinary students in the lab. The twins just had to ask around to find the right candidate for their purpose.

When school started, Alan and Brian hung out with the campus outliers—the stoners, the nerds, the punks—anyone who was marginalized. Contrary to what most people believed, despite their attitude and appearance, these kids were often much brighter than the average student. Alan and Brian knew this was where they would most likely find people who would buck the system, especially if the price was right.

The twins spent a lot time in the Student Union checking out the various clubs that met there: chess club, literary club, math club, and any other club that might serve their purpose. They even interviewed tutors, figuring that some tutors could be bought if they offered the right amount of money. Gradually, they put together a group of people who were willing to work for them as needed; they were freelancers.

Alan and Brian themselves attended classes, enrolling in different sections of the same class, swapping places with each other, and always making sure to enroll in the largest classes they could find where the likelihood of being singled out was small. They didn't care what the subject was as long it was required for graduation or was a major that had a large enrollment.

The larger lecture classes were usually taught by teaching assistants rather than professors. Teaching assistants were themselves graduate students and didn't really care whether a student attended a class or not. And in the large lecture halls, teachers rarely took attendance. When they first thought about going to UCLA, Alan and Brian had found out the two departments that had the largest enrollment were psychology and economics, so they figured this would be their major: economics with a minor in psych.

They settled into their routine and were ready to focus entirely on their budding business. The business took off, and they were making more money than they ever thought possible. It turned out they didn't have to resort to counterfeit merchandise; there was enough profit in gray-market clothing and the odd lots. In fact, they were developing a reputation for being the go-to source for retailers to dispose of their inventory.

They had targeted the right demographic—kids in the areas of the country who didn't have access to the latest high-end fashions and who didn't much care about guarantees or quality. They just wanted style, the correct label, and a low price. If the merchandise looked good, that was enough. And

Hip, Slick, and Cool Enterprises was just that—all about the look. It was the same approach they took to life; it was all about the look, the appearance, the pretense—never about the value or the quality. They were nothing if not shallow.

Just as they figured out that regular contact with their mother would keep her from prying, they also figured out that the best way to keep their father from suddenly showing up out of nowhere was to hire him to work for them. By hiring him to run errands and to ship goods at the warehouse, they could keep an eye on him. They had learned from their mother that he had blown his inheritance through drinking, acting like a big shot with his friends, buying them drinks, and living the life of the high-roller—until he went broke. His parents gave him a monthly allowance, but he usually spent it before the end of the month.

Lucas had to stay on the twins' good side if he didn't want to lose the job. Alan and Brian weren't crazy about the idea of having Lucas involved in their business at all but kept him anyway, thinking it would be better to keep him close to better to control him. And they did like giving him orders and sometimes would send him on meaningless errands just to humiliate him. They treated him like a gofer, sending him on various errands and tossing him a few extra bucks for doing so. Having him on the payroll kept him from showing up at their apartment or from bothering their mother at odd hours looking for a handout.

Brian and Alan decided it would be better to set a regular meeting schedule once each week where they would spend an hour or so with Lucas in the storage unit and give him a list of things to do for them. This way they had more control over him, and control was very important.

They made the deals with the vendors and had Lucas pick up the merchandise, take it to the storage unit, inventory it all, and ship it to the buyers. They hired another person, Rafael, to do the shipping and help with the sorting. This freed up Alan and Brian to negotiate deals and network with people who could advance their agenda. It also freed them to focus on their college work and, most importantly (next to making money), women.

"Now that we've got some serious coin comin' in," began Alan as they started one of their Sunday business meetings, "I think it's time for us to make our name in the club scene."

"You're not interested in finding a girlfriend are you, my brother?" chided Brian.

"You're kidding, right?" replied Alan. "I am interested in getting laid, nothing more. And how can we be hip, slick, and cool without having a chick on our arm? It's all about the image, bro."

Brian smiled. "I think you're right," he replied. "It's time for HS&C to go Hollywood."

"The first thing we should do is hire a stylist," said Alan. "I'm good at putting shit together, but it's time for us to go pro—someone who could put together a wardrobe for us. We've got our brand to think about; we're all about the look. No sense relying upon chance."

"Yeah, we gotta be *perfecto!*" exclaimed Brian.

"The second thing we have to do is locate all of the Hollywood clubs that admit kids under twenty-one," added Alan. "Once we're inside, we can negotiate our way to the VIP area where drinks are sold. Money talks."

They both smiled and nodded at the thought.

"Ya know, maybe we should make a couple of visits to check these places out," said Brian. "You know, kinda do a reconnaissance on the places. We can see whether we can grease some palms, check out who's in charge, you know what I'm sayin'?"

"Yeah, we wouldn't want to be embarrassed by trying to make a move to the VIP area and be turned away," replied

Alan. "That wouldn't be too cool, especially if we had some chicks on our arm." He shivered at the thought.

"What we want is to establish a couple of relationships at these places so that when we show up, they treat us like VIPs," said Brian.

Alan nodded in agreement.

"Okay, so let's make a list of all the clubs that seem cool," said Brian, turning toward his computer. "I'll do a Google search; you write the stuff down. We can set up a calendar, and one by one, we can pay the clubs a visit. Ready?"

Alan opened his computer and set up a spread sheet, ready to write down information. He included columns for the club names, addresses, cover charges, names of bouncers and managers, and a space for comments. The twins were very methodical in their approach to everything that had to do with business. And this was business. Once Alan had the spreadsheet set up, Brian began rattling off names, addresses, phone numbers, costs, and dress-code information, and Alan filled in the columns.

The next step was for Alan and Brian to visit the clubs.

On their first night out doing their recon of the clubs, they dressed in their most hip, slick, and cool outfits appropriate for clubbing. They dressed in high-end men-in-black, matching outfits: tight black jeans, black silk shirts, and black leather jackets along with the latest pointed black boots. They topped it off with orange-tinted sunglasses and a faux-diamond ear stud. They were creating a brand.

Brian wore the disguise just in case they ran into someone they knew. No sense taking chances. He put in the brown contacts, pulled his long-haired wig into a ponytail low on his neck, and added a bit of tan to his already swarthy appearance just to further differentiate himself from Alan. They rented a black Mercedes for the occasion and hired one of their crew to chauffeur them around; this way they didn't have to waste time parking or waiting for a valet.

They planned on covering several clubs in one evening. At around nine thirty, after giving each other a high five, they left their apartment and climbed into the back seat of the waiting black Mercedes, looking every bit the hip, Hollywood duo.

The Mercedes pulled up in front of The Hollywood Vibe at about ten o'clock. There was a long line of young men and women waiting to get in. The valet opened the car door, and the twins got out. They were in character, playing a part they had rehearsed many times; they were the bad-assed boys-in-black.

They looked at the line of people, glanced at the doorman, and gave a quick nod to one another as they ignored the line and went directly to the front. Many of the folks standing in line jeered and called out to them for cutting. The twins didn't pay attention to the disgruntled masses.

Alan smiled up at the three-hundred-pound, six-foot-six doorman and extended his hand, acting as if they were old friends. The doorman was about to send them to the rear of the line until he spotted the hundred-dollar bill in the palm of Alan's hand, a little trick Alan had picked up from a James Bond movie. He shook Alan's hand, palmed the bill, pushed open the door, and ushered the twins into the club. They could hear the hoots and feel the glares from the guys they had bypassed in the line. They smiled over their shoulders and gave the guys their trademark two-finger salute. They received a one finger salute in return.

The music inside the club was deafening. The bass caused the floor to vibrate. The dance floor was already crowded and becoming more so by the minute as the partygoers kept filing in. The girls were dressed in spiked heels and very tight, short skirts, gyrating to the music. The guys wore the latest fashions and sported high-end watches. The twins took it all in, sizing up the clientele and taking in the vibe. They casually walked around the perimeter of the club as if they either owned the place or were casing it for a heist.

At the front end of the extravagant bar that stretched across the entire wall of the club, there was a booth where customers showed their ID, indicating that they were at least twenty-one years old, and in turn had their wrist stamped. All customers were required to show the stamp to the bartenders if they ordered alcoholic beverages. It was a simple and efficient system in a busy club that catered to those eighteen and older. The bartenders had little time to check actual IDs.

Alan and Brian stood in the line. When it was their turn, they produced their driver's licenses showing they were twenty-one—another benefit of being connected with their street contacts. They were assured the licenses could not be distinguished from the genuine article. There were only two ways for a good forgery to be detected: a special blue light used by the armed services or a scanner used at the airports. Dance clubs typically didn't go to such extremes. The twins received their stamps and sauntered over to the bar.

"So far, so good," said Brian with a slight, self-satisfied grin.

"The devil is in the details," replied Alan with a nod. "Everything is going according to plan."

"What'll you have, gents?" asked the bartender.

"Two glasses of champagne, Tony," replied Alan, reading the bartender's nametag. "I'm Alan. This here is my brother, Brian."

Tony nodded and gave them each a fist bump. "Coming right up," he said.

"Hey, Tony," said Alan, "where's the VIP lounge? We may want to bring a group in next time."

Tony pointed toward a staircase at the far end of bar. A red velvet rope blocked the entrance, and another big guy, like the one at the front door, stood on guard.

"That's Alejandro standing there," said Tony as he placed their drinks on the counter. "You gotta be willing to buy a table for a grand to be seated. And you gotta either be somebody or know somebody."

"No problem," replied Alan without batting an eye.

Tony just looked at him. "Well, okay, then. That'll be fifty for the drinks."

Alan dropped a hundred-dollar bill on the counter while Brian left to go to restroom. The bartender turned to ring up the sale.

Alan twisted his head to look for Brian, but instead of seeing his brother, he was facing a steroid-loaded linebacker with a menacing scowl. Standing next him was a somewhat smaller version of the linebacker.

"Hey, asshole," began the linebacker, jabbing his oversized finger into Alan's chest. "You're the dickwad who skipped to the front of the line while me and my friends stood waiting."

Alan smiled and looked up at the big guy. He stared into his eyes and calmly replied, "I suggest that you remove your finger from my chest, my friend."

"Or what—what are you gonna do, twerp," said the linebacker, towering over Alan as he stared down on him.

Alan took a short step backward and without any warning kicked the man squarely in the testicles with the toe of his boot. When the big man doubled over in pain, Alan grabbed the back of the guy's head and forcefully brought it down onto his rising knee, crushing the man's nose. He followed up with a driving elbow to the man's spine, sending him to the floor.

Alan had executed the three karate moves so quickly that it took the man's friend a moment to react. Just as he was about to charge Alan, Brian returned from the restroom. Seeing what was happening, he tapped the friend on the shoulder. When the guy turned, Brian jammed his palm into his nose, and blood began pour out.

As Brian was about to follow through with another blow, two bouncers charged over and separated the four customers. They were about to escort all four patrons out of the club, but the bartender stopped them.

"Hey, Jimmy," said Tony to one of the bouncers. "The big guys started it. They were pissed off about something that happened outside."

Jimmy was the doorman the twins had met when they arrived at the club. A smile of recognition came over his face when he saw that it was Brian and Alan. "Hey, my man, how ya doin'?"

The twins smiled in return.

Jimmy turned to the two other guys. "I think it's time for you gentlemen to leave. And you might want to have a doctor take a look at those noses." He turned toward his partner. "Would you escort these two out?"

The other bouncer nodded.

The two guys glared at the bouncers. They knew better than to argue. They looked menacingly over their shoulders at the twins as they turned to leave, holding handkerchiefs to their bloody noses.

"You guys handle yourselves pretty well for a couple of lightweights," said the oversized doorman with a grin. "I'm Jimmy. What are your names?"

Alan and Brian introduced themselves.

"Have fun, and you take care, Brian and Alan. Try to stay outta trouble." Jimmy nodded, turned, and left.

"I think we could use another drink," said Alan, looking at his brother.

They turned back to the bartender. "Thanks, Tony, we appreciate your standing up for us," said Alan.

"Anytime. We watch out for our VIPs," said Tony, grinning.

The twins ordered another couple of glasses of champagne.

"That's the first time we had to use our karate skills for real, bro," said Alan. "It worked, and it felt great. I didn't have time to think; I just reacted. What a fuckin' rush! All the practice paid off. Did you see how that big dude went down?"

"Yeah, I saw it," exclaimed Brian. "And yeah, it felt really great. For a moment, I felt, like, all powerful! As though I could take on anyone! I can still feel the adrenalin rush. But we were lucky this time. Those guys were big! They just didn't expect what we gave them. I hope it doesn't become a habit." Brian looked at his palm and remembered the sound of the man's nose breaking and the spurting blood. He felt a little nauseous.

"Agreed," replied Alan. "But right now, let's celebrate." He lifted his glass and tilted it towards his brother. "To the bad-assed boys-in-black."

Brian clinked glasses with his brother and took a gulp of the bubbly, hoping it would settle his stomach.

They finished their drinks, thanked Tony once again, and placed another hundred on the counter. Alan and Brian made sure they wouldn't be forgotten at this club.

Before leaving, they had one more stop to make—the VIP section where they introduced themselves to Alejandro. Alejandro smiled broadly, greeting them as though they were regular VIP customers. He had seen what happened at the bar and already had spoken with Jimmy.

"Hello, gentlemen. Welcome to the Hollywood Vibe VIP Lounge," said Alejandro, extending his large hand. Their hands felt tiny when they shook his. "I saw what you guys did over there. I was impressed."

Alan and Brian grinned. "Jimmy is impressive," said Alan. "He's gotta be a linebacker."

"Jimmy is not just a doorman and bouncer," said Alejandro. "He's also the club manager. He likes to work the door for a few hours each night to check out the crowd and get a sense of how the evening might unfold."

The twins nodded.

"Alejandro," said Alan, "we'd like to get a tour of the VIP lounge. We sometimes get together with clients for an evening of fun. How about giving us a peek?"

Alejandro escorted them up the stairs and explained how the club operated.

"For five thousand dollars per year, you can buy a membership in the club," said Alejandro as he escorted Alan and Brian up the carpeted staircase. "That would give you preferential reservations to the VIP lounge. Non-members only get seated as seats become available. Then they have to pay a thousand for the table."

"Do you have to spend a certain amount once you're a member?" asked Brian looking around at the tables that contained ice buckets with champagne bottles sticking out.

"The management expects club members to spend at least a hundred per person at a table with a minimum of six people," replied Alejandro. "And you are expected to use the lounge at least once a month."

"Cool," said Alan, nodding. "That means five large per year plus a minimum of six hundred a month, right? Makes sense. The boss gotta eat, too, right?" He chuckled.

Alejandro nodded and smiled.

Alan and Brian took it all in. The lounge was filled with couches and chairs placed around large coffee tables upon which the drinks were served. Along one wall, there were booths offering a little more privacy. The room was dimly lit and elegantly appointed, with walls covered in mirrors which made it easy to see the rest of the club even when facing away from the action below. There were dozens of servers, dressed in black and white, scurrying around making certain that no one had to wait for drinks or hors d'oeuvres.

Alan and Brian were impressed. They thanked Alejandro for the tour, slipped him fifty dollars, and assured him that they would be back.

Brian called for their car. As they walked by the bar heading for the exit, they saluted Tony, nodded to Jimmy who was still manning the front door, and left knowing The Hollywood Vibe was going to be their club. They had already invested three hundred fifty dollars and a couple of broken noses in establishing themselves.

While Alan left the club feeling excited and energized by the experience of making his mark in a Hollywood club, Brian felt uneasy.

Brian convinced himself that he did not care about legalities, but simply was afraid of getting caught when they functioned outside of the law. He could keep it under control when he was conning someone, but he had more difficulty when it came to dangerous situations. He was becoming increasingly aware that he had an aversion to physically hurting people. Sometimes he wondered whether he was simply less confident that Alan. He often thought of himself as a wuss and had to fake it to act confident in dangerous situations.

Before going to the club that night, Brian had downed a couple of tequila shooters just to take the edge off. And if it weren't for the two drinks they had had while in the club, he doubted that he would have been able to hit the guy who had been threatening Alan. Normally, he ruminated over decisions, driving himself and his brother crazy. This time he just reacted without thinking. Now he had to deal with the aftermath. It was one thing to hit the guy, but hearing the cracking of the guy's nose breaking—like the snap of a tree branch breaking—left him feeling queasy. How was he supposed to be a grifter and cool dude if he couldn't control his emotions?

When he tried to talk to Alan about it, his brother just scoffed or teased him.

"The guy was being a dick, bro," said Alan. "He deserved what he got. You did good!"

"Yeah, but why do I feel so shitty?" replied Brian, shaking his head. "I'm not you. You can do this shit and feel good about it. How do you do it?"

"Like Nick has said many times, it's just a part in the show," replied Alan. "I just get into character and do what the part requires. Nothing to it. When I am in character, I am Jason B."

Brian looked at him feeling envious. "I think I have to practice more. It's hard for me to stop thinking of what might happen. My brain won't shut off."

"You think too much," said Alan. "This is all just a game, bro. Play the game."

# CHAPTER SEVEN

# Panic Attack

His heart pounded—he couldn't catch his breath. The elevator car felt like it was spinning, and its walls seemed to be closing in on him.

*What the fuck is happening to me?*

Brian clawed at his collar, trying to get more air into his lungs. His knees buckled as he leaned against the wall for support. He thought he was going to die.

*Fuck! I'm having a heart attack! Oh, my God, I'm dying!* After several seconds had passed, he thought, *Calm down, Brian. Just breathe. Eighteen-year-olds don't have heart attacks.*

And then, just as suddenly as it had started, it stopped.

Brian looked around him at the puzzled faces of the other passengers in the elevator. People stared at him, not knowing what they had just witnessed. While Brian's shirt and hands were drenched in sweat, his heartbeat and breathing had returned to normal. He was alive.

*Thank God, I'm alive! What the fuck was that?* he wondered, still frightened by the experience.

Brian got off the elevator at the next stop and walked over to the stairwell, still feeling a bit wobbly from the experience.

He placed one hand on the wall for support, and as quickly as he could, he made his way down to the subterranean garage to his car. Immediately upon climbing into his Porsche, he called his physician to make an emergency appointment. The doctor made room for him in his calendar for that afternoon.

The doctor performed a complete examination, including an electrocardiogram and a stress test. Brian ran on a treadmill while the machines tracked his heart rate and blood pressure. After it was over, the doctor told Brian, "Congratulations, my boy, you're a perfectly healthy young man."

"Then what was it that I experienced in the elevator?" asked Brian putting on his shirt. "It sure felt like a heart attack."

"I think you had a panic attack," replied the doctor. "Panic attacks mimic heart attacks. But they are caused by anxiety."

"You mean, it's all in my head?" replied Brian.

"No, not exactly," said the doctor. "They are real for sure, but they have psychological rather than physical causes. Have you been under more stress than usual? Brian, I know you're going to school and working. That's stressful in itself, but is there something else that's been troubling you? Is there something that might just be pushing you over the edge?"

Brian hesitated a moment. "Nah, nothing unusual. My life is just one stressful thing after the other," he said grinning.

"I think it could be helpful for you to talk with a psychologist who specializes in treating anxiety and panic attacks," replied the doctor. "The sooner you deal with it, the better. Research suggests that after one panic attack, they might occur more frequently if you don't treat it right away."

"A shrink!" exclaimed Brian. "You want me to see a shrink?" Brian was incredulous. "Aren't they just for whack jobs?"

The doctor smiled. "No, Brian. Everyone could use a little psychological help every now again. It doesn't mean you're a whack job. Just a guy under a lot of stress who experienced a panic attack."

The doctor rummaged through his desk and found a business card. "Here's the card of a psychologist whom other patients have found to be quite helpful. Give him a call."

Brian took the card, thanked the doctor for squeezing him in on such a short notice, and left. He glanced at the card as he walked to the elevator—Dr. David Albertson, Clinical Psychologist.

He shoved the card into his pocket thinking, *Fuck, now I am just like Tony Soprano, having to see a shrink! Not exactly the part of Tony I had in mind when I looked up to him.*

He pressed the call button for the elevator, but when it arrived, he thought better of getting on; he was not ready to get back into an elevator just yet. Instead, he took the stairs down to the parking garage.

He shook his head in disbelief. He and his brother were alike in most every way.

*How is it that Alan can so completely detach himself from hurting people?* he thought. Despite their obvious similarities, he often thought about how different they were.

*How is it that I gotta be so sensitive? Fuck! I gotta work on this. Alan is right. The guy deserved it.* Brian threw his shoulders back, stretched his neck, and flexed his muscles. *I can beat this thing. I don't need a shrink! No way!*

By the time he got back to the apartment, he was feeling better. He had resolved to become more like Alan. After all, he was a badass twin. He parked the Porsche, tossed his shoulders back, stood tall, and grinned as he walked into the apartment, showing confidence.

"What the fuck are you grinning about, bro?" asked Alan, looking up from his computer.

"Nothin'," replied Brian. "Just feeling good."

He knew he was lying.

*Fake it until you make it!* he thought.

Somewhere he had heard that expression.

\*\*\*

The twins began strategizing for their next foray into the Hollywood scene. They knew that if they were going to be successful both in their business and their social life, they would have to become more visible among the movers and shakers who set the trends. They would have to become savvy about the latest fashions and fads. Not only did they have to read about the current trends, but also they had to see what people were actually buying. They had to stay ahead of the curve if they wanted to remain relevant to their demographic.

Hollywood set the trends for young people around the globe. Even New Yorkers kept their eyes on what was going on in Hollywood and Beverly Hills where all things hot were happening, especially when it came to fashion.

Teens and twenty-somethings accounted for a significant percentage of the buying public, especially in their demographic. Alan and Brian were committed to capturing that market, particularly the wannabes—all those kids who could not afford the three-hundred-dollar jeans and two-hundred-dollar running shoes were their customers. If HS&C was going to keep up with the trends, Alan and Brian were going to have to keep their fingers on the pulse of those who set the trends.

They began frequenting not only their home base, The Hollywood Vibe, but other clubs as well. They got themselves invited to parties, raves, and after-hours clubs. And they were introduced to drugs. If they were going to be part of the in-crowd and not merely observers, they had to participate.

Alan, always the more adventurous of the two, jumped right in. Brian, being fundamentally shy and fearful, simply followed his brother's lead. Brian fancied himself as the planner in their business and social dealings, allowing Alan to be the public face of HS&C. As they moved forward in the Hollywood arena, Alan's fearlessness served them well. He could hobnob with the best of them.

It didn't take long for drugs to become integral to the scene. Coke, Ecstasy, OxyContin, and, of course, marijuana were only some of the drugs readily available at every venue. The management looked the other way.

Customers in the VIP lounge would snort a line on the club table or from vials they carried in their pockets. Same was true for pills. People were generous, willing to share with those around them. Once again, Alan was ready to give it a try. Until this point, alcohol was the twins' only vice. But with the partying crowd, drugs supplemented booze.

Brian was hesitant at first, but much to his surprise, he enjoyed pot. He remembered that when he and Alan were selling individual joints, he hadn't liked smoking. Now, however, he found that the effects of dope reduced the anxiety that would often creep up on him. When he was high or buzzed, his hands didn't sweat. He didn't worry about things. It just mellowed him out.

Alan, on the other hand, enjoyed cocaine. When stoned, he was even more audacious than normal. He would become the life of the party, often dancing on tables at clubs and making himself the center of attention. Brian, stoned on marijuana, sat back and smiled, shaking his head as Alan carried on.

As they aged, more of their differences were revealed. Despite being identical twins, they were of different temperaments. Alan became even more extroverted, loved the limelight, and occupied center stage. Brian preferred to hang in the sidelines; he was the man behind the scenes. Fundamentally, he was shy, preferring to watch his television shows, alone. Alan loved partying.

The difference in their dispositions complemented one another. Alan looked at the world through a wide-angled lens, seeing the big picture. Brian, on the other hand, focused on the details. Alan was the dreamer and more action-oriented, sometimes verging on being impulsive; Brian was the details man, more practical. He could develop the strategy, leaning toward a conservative approach to most things.

People, especially the girls at the clubs, were naturally drawn to Alan. He was funny, outgoing, smooth, and charismatic. He had no problem moving in on a group of young women, chatting them up, and inviting them to join him at his table. Brian counted on Alan to make the first move toward girls and then to introduce them to him.

Alan always had more temerity than Brian. Even in middle school, it was Alan who made the overtures when it came to girls. It decreased Brian's anxiety to have the girls at his table rather than having to make the first move to introduce himself to a group of strangers. Sitting at the table and having them come to him made him feel like the *Godfather*. Once they had paid their respects, so to speak, Brian used his more serious look, his smile and dark-brown, contact-lensed eyes to seal the deal. He knew he wasn't as smooth as his brother, but it didn't bother him. Being in costume made him feel more comfortable. He knew he was playing a part. Being buzzed helped.

One young woman caught Brian's attention. She arrived with a group of five other young women, but rather than being animated and garrulous, she was subdued. She repeatedly glanced at Brian and then looked away. Brian found her appealing. Alan introduced her to Brian.

"Hey, bro, this is Linda," announced Alan. "Linda, this is my brother, Brian."

Linda smiled over the top of a glass of champagne. She stood about five feet five and had red hair and hazel eyes. Her smile could light up a room; her eyes sparkled. She wore the typical club attire—a tight-fitting, short skirt with a low-cut blouse revealing ample breasts.

Brian was immediately smitten. He extended his hand in a casual manner, offering her a seat next to him. Up close, she was even more beautiful. She smelled of rose petals.

"Do you come here often?" Brian asked with a smile.

"No, as a matter of fact, this is my first time in a club," replied Linda softly, her head shaking as she took in the room. "It's really not my thing."

Brian nodded. "Not your thing. What is your *thing*?" he asked with a sly grin.

Linda blushed. "You'll laugh at me if I tell you."

"No, I won't. I promise," he said, becoming serious.

"I dance. Ballet," said Linda. "This type of music is too loud for me. It hurts my ears."

Brian paused for a long moment. "Ballet? I've never met anyone who likes ballet. Have you been doing it long?"

Linda nodded. "Ever since I was five."

"Wow, that's a long time," said Brian. "You must be quite good by now."

Again, Linda blushed. "I suppose," she said, again averting his eyes.

"Maybe someday you can show me some steps," said Brian. "I've never seen someone dance ballet. But in the meantime, how about dancing with me to this, um, loud music?"

He put out his hand inviting her onto the dance floor. She shook her head.

Brian was disappointed. "Then why did you come here tonight?" he asked.

"My girlfriends," replied Linda, feeling awkward. "They like clubbing. And it's the blonde's birthday." She pointed in her friend's direction. "So, they coaxed me into coming to celebrate."

"Well, I'm glad they did," said Brian, giving her a broad smile.

"Even if I won't dance with you?" Linda smiled, tilting her head as she looked up at him with a twinkle in her eyes.

Brian chuckled. "And even if you don't like this loud music!" He grinned as he took a sip of his drink. He noticed that Linda just held her glass of champagne without drinking.

"Don't you like champagne?" he asked.

"I'm not old enough to drink," she replied modestly.

Linda and Brian continued talking while the others danced and drank. This was the first time Brian felt comfortable talking with a female. There was something about Linda that put him at ease. She was not brash like most of the club girls and seemed almost shy, similar to himself.

He learned that Linda was also going to be a student at UCLA and would be majoring in psychology and dance. She was a vegan and believed in animal rights. She wouldn't eat any animal, fish, or animal products. She ate only a plant-based diet. Brian had a hard time understanding why someone would give up eating meat; he loved a good steak. Linda was the opposite of Brian, yet they had an easy rapport. He couldn't help but wonder why she seemed to be interested in him.

Brian glanced in Alan's direction. As usual, he was the center of attention, joking and clowning around. People were drawn to him, especially when he was high. That wasn't the case for Brian. While he was more relaxed when using pot, he was never outgoing. He turned his head back to Linda.

"You and your brother seem quite different," said Linda as she glanced in Alan's direction.

"Yeah, I suppose so," replied Brian. "We were more alike when we were kids, but as we got older—"

In mid-sentence, Alan appeared between Brian and Linda. He bent over them and slid an arm around Brian's shoulder.

"How are you two getting along?" he asked, flashing his broad smile in Linda's direction.

"We're cool, bro," replied Brian.

Alan leaned close to Linda and whispered something in her ear. She stood up abruptly, knocking over her chair in the process. Then she looked at him open-mouthed, and without saying a word, she stormed out.

"What the—what the fuck did you say to her, Alan?" exclaimed Brian, jumping up from his chair.

Alan laughed out loud as he rubbed his nose with the back of his hand, obviously drunk and high. "I just asked her if she ever fucked brothers."

"Jesus Christ, Alan!" said Brian, giving his brother a look of disgust.

He tried to run after her, but Alan restrained him. "Let her go, bro, let her go. She's just another club whore. And remember, you're a bad-assed man-in-black!"

Brian just stared at his brother. He broke free and ran after Linda, shouting, "Linda, wait!"

He was too late. Linda had already disappeared into the parking lot. He heard the peeling of rubber on the asphalt and was in time to see Linda behind the wheel of a white Honda that was turning onto Hollywood Boulevard. He slowly walked back into the club feeling both disappointed and angry.

Back at the table, Alan was still in party mode. Linda's girlfriends barely seemed to have noticed that she had left.

"Hey, bro, come on. Have another drink. It's party time!"

Alan made some dance moves in time to the music, trying to liven his brother's spirits. Brian just stood there.

He was ambivalent. He knew he was not fitting the image of the hip, slick, and cool guys they were supposed to be. But he liked Linda. She was different from the other girls he had met at the clubs. His attraction to her surprised him. Usually he was attracted to girls who led with their sexuality; Linda didn't. She was different than her friends—they fit the image, but he wasn't drawn to them.

He stared at them. Now they were busy downing shooters. A couple of the girls came on to him, coaxing him to join them. The blonde birthday-girl stood so close to Brian that when he looked down at her the only thing he saw was cleavage. She began to gyrate to the music, grinding against him. Another girl gave him a shooter. He downed it. And then another. And another. Alan was way ahead of him.

***

Somehow, they made it home without getting pulled over by a cop and crashed. The next morning, while nursing hangovers, Brian and Alan had one of their strategy sessions. Brian told Alan that he wanted to pursue a relationship with Linda.

"Why do you want to tie yourself up with one girl when you could be having so much fun with so many?" asked Alan.

Brian sat on the edge of his chair staring at the floor. "I like her," he said quietly.

"I get that, bro, but getting involved is not part of our plan. It's the two of us building our business. Making big bucks. We gotta keep our focus, bro."

Brian remained quiet. He felt confused. "Why can't we go out on dates or even have girlfriends and still do our business?"

"It's simple," replied Alan with an air of confidence. "Chicks just get in the way. They divert time and energy from our path. We've got to finish college and grow the business. There simply isn't enough time for a girlfriend. You wanna get laid, go get laid. But getting involved, that's not in the cards. At least not now."

Brian knew his brother was right. And he knew that he needed to up his game if they were going to be successful. They had college to finish, and the business demanded their full attention. Going to clubs was supposed to be more about connecting with people who could help them with their business. It was not about developing romantic relationships.

"Okay," said Brian. "You're right. We gotta stay true to the plan. I won't go after Linda. But I can't keep drinking like this. I feel like shit."

Alan laughed. "You sure got into it after Linda left."

"It helped loosen me up," said Brian. "You're better at the club scene than me. You seem to love it. Even in disguise, I feel uncomfortable. Like I don't know what to say. Like an actor without his lines. You know how I like to plan every move."

"Remember what Nick and Rose taught us?" replied Alan. "You develop a character and then play the role. The world is a stage. We are actors. If you play the part long enough and well enough, you become the character."

"I think you're a better actor than me, Alan," said Brian, chuckling. "I still get stage fright." He recalled his panic attack.

Alan loved to party. He found clubbing, drugs, and sexy girls exactly what he craved. He was fulfilling a dream that he had been nurturing for years. He was no longer the skinny little kid he had been in grammar school. He was becoming a player. He loved being the center of attention, soaking up the adulation of the people around him. It didn't matter to him what others thought, so long as they catered to him. For years, he and Brian had shared the same dream of being rich, hip, admired, and fawned over. It all seemed so easy for Alan.

With the help of marijuana and a couple of shooters before they left for their customary weekend of clubbing, Brian became more comfortable with the role he and Alan had written for themselves. The inebriants helped Brian become more sociable, but he preferred to remain in the background. It was Alan who continued to occupy center stage.

# CHAPTER EIGHT

# Paternal Showdown

## *2002*

One afternoon, Alan and Brian went downtown to the garment district in search of some new fitness attire that was becoming very popular in Europe. They wanted to be sure to have ample stock on hand to meet the demand they expected. They needed to find several suppliers, so it took a while. They decided to stop by their storage warehouse to see how things looked since their father, Lucas, and the shipping clerk, Rafael, were managing the place.

As they drove up to the warehouse, they saw a skirmish taking place right outside their unit. In the middle of the crowd was Lucas. He was being shoved around by three angry men who yelled at him in Spanish. Rafael was trying to help him, but he was no match for the guys attacking Lucas. Everyone stopped when they saw Alan and Brian get out of their car. Alan was carrying a baseball bat.

"What the hell is going on?" shouted Brian.

"Who the fuck are you?" asked one of the men.

"We own this place," said Alan, staring back him.

"You know this asshole?" the man asked.

"Yeah, we know him. Why?" asked Brian.

"He sold my grandmother a TV that was supposed to be new and supposed to work. When she got it home, it didn't do shit. No picture, no sound, *nada!*"

"He sold you a TV!" exclaimed Alan. He turned and looked at Lucas. He raised the bat over his shoulder, ready to strike. "What the fuck have you been doing, Dad?" Alan was furious.

When the men saw that Alan was about to hit Lucas with the bat, they backed away, giving him room to swing. Lucas was terrified.

"What the hell have you been doing down here?" demanded Brian. "We trusted you to take care of our business."

"He's been selling all kinds of stuff to people in the 'hood," said the man. "He tells them that he gets it from a guy who handles overstocked merchandise and can get it really cheap. He comes around in his van with TVs, computers, and other electrical appliances and sets up shop on a corner. He cons these old people into buying this stuff and then splits. He knows that no one will turn him in to the cops because they're illegals themselves; they don't see cops as their friends. This time he just fucked with the wrong old lady."

Brian walked over to the man. "How much did your grandmother pay him for the TV?"

"A hundred bucks," replied the man.

"What if I give you two hundred? Would that be enough to make you and your grandmother happy?"

The man hesitated. "And what about him?" he asked, pointing at Lucas. "He just goin' to keep on scammin' these people?"

Brian shook his head. "No, he's not going to be doing business with anybody. We'll take care of him."

Alan was still holding the bat, looking like he was ready to smash Lucas. Lucas crouched, holding his hands in front of his face to protect it. As explosive as was, he knew better than to provoke his sons. Instead, he pleaded with Alan not to hurt him.

The man nodded and put out his hand for the money. "We'd better not see him around here again. Next time we won't be just talkin'."

Brian handed him the two hundred dollars. The guy and the other men sauntered off, muttering among themselves in Spanish.

Brian turned toward his father and Alan.

"Maybe we should have just let them take care of him," said Brian to his brother.

"Nah, I didn't want to give them the fun of messing him up!" replied Alan. "I wanted that pleasure all for myself."

And with that, he swung the bat and hit Lucas squarely in his ribs. Lucas fell to the ground screaming in pain. Brian was stunned. He couldn't believe that Alan had used the bat on their father. Alan was ready to swing again. Brian stepped in front of him.

"Enough!" he screamed. "Enough!"

Alan looked at him as though coming out of a trance. He gave a short nod of his head and lowered the bat.

"Let's bring him inside the warehouse," said Brian.

Brian and Rafael helped Lucas off the pavement. The four of them went inside.

"I need to go to the hospital, you crazy son of bitch!" yelled Lucas.

"Crazy like our father," said Brian. "How does it feel to be on the receiving end for a change, asshole?"

Lucas looked at Brian with squinted eyes and clenched jaw, but he said nothing.

"You're not going anywhere until you tell us what's been going on down here," said Alan, still holding the bat.

Lucas grimaced in pain. "Look, you guys are raking it in, making tons of money," he said, his jaw jutting out in defiance. "I was just tryin' to make a few bucks for myself."

"By using our warehouse to store your crap and then hustling it on the street?" asked Alan.

Lucas nodded.

"He's been pulling the Murphy game on people," said Brian. "Nick told me about it. It's where cons sell all kinds of shit to people, telling them it was stolen and therefore it can be sold for real cheap. Nobody can turn them in because they know the shit was stolen, and they would be considered accessories for buying stolen merchandise. It's a perfect con."

"I bet he's been skimming our merchandise, too," said Alan. "I bet he's been selling our stuff out there and keeping the money."

Alan and Brian glared at Lucas and then at Rafael, who was sweating profusely and cowering in the background. Rafael was mild-mannered guy trying to make a living. He stayed away from gang violence.

"I didn't do nothin'!" exclaimed Rafael. He stared at the menacing bat in Alan's hands, his eyes wide with fear. When he saw that Alan wasn't going to turn on him, he relaxed and walked over toward the long table where he sorted clothes. He tried to stay clear of the family argument.

Brian rummaged through the merchandise stacked on the shelves. He suddenly stopped and pulled one of the garments from a pile.

"What the fuck!" yelled Brian. "These are knockoffs! Selling knockoffs is a federal crime, you asshole! They're counterfeit! Have you been shipping these to our customers?"

"No! I didn't ship any!" exclaimed Lucas. "I just stored them here and sold them in the neighborhood."

"Lemme tell you something," said Brian. "Just having them in our possession or having them traced back to us is enough to bust us. Having you work for us makes us an accessory."

Alan stared at his brother. "Hey, bro, you sound like a lawyer. It wasn't long ago that we were considering selling knockoffs ourselves."

"Yeah, but we didn't," replied Brian. "We went gray and gray only, right?"

Alan didn't reply; he turned away, not able to look his brother in the eye.

"What?" said Brian, looking curiously at Alan. "Don't tell me that you've been doing some deals with knockoffs!" Brian knew his brother. He could practically read his mind. "Fuck, bro, why the fuck did you do that shit? We agreed!"

"I know, you're right," replied Alan with a touch of remorse. "I just couldn't let that money slip by. People don't give a shit about whether it's counterfeit. And we could make a bunch more cash."

"So, why are you gettin' so pissed off at me?" said Lucas with a sneer, trying to recover his machismo despite his obvious pain. Lucas wanted to punch Alan, but between his fear of being hit again and the pain he already felt, he thought better of it. "I'm just doin' the same thing you're doin'. I'm just hustlin' to make a buck. And I know you got a lot of other scams going on."

"Shut the fuck up!" exclaimed Brian. "You're selling counterfeit goods and doing it under our name. You brought people right to our front door. We've been flyin' under the radar with what we do. And besides, you're scamming us! You're using our operation for yourself without consulting us."

Alan was ready to hit Lucas with the bat again, more because of all the pent-up rage for the years of abuse than for the dealing in goods.

"Alan, no!" shouted Brian. "He's not worth it."

Alan stopped. He looked at Brian and then at Lucas. "You're right. He's not." Alan lowered the bat. "So, what do we do now? And what about Rafael?"

Brian thought for a moment and then turned toward Lucas. "Why don't you get the fuck outta here and take yourself to the ER," said Brian scowling. "And just stay clear of us, the business, and our apartment. We're done with you."

"What? Are you firing me?" asked a stunned Lucas. He looked from one face to another. He couldn't believe his sons would kick him out. "What the fuck!"

Alan and Brian looked at one another for a long moment as if trying to communicate telepathically.

Lucas looked at Brian and then at Alan, who still held the bat.

Alan pointed with his chin toward the door in support of Brian. "Just get the fuck outta here before I take another swing."

Lucas said nothing; he just grimaced as he slowly hobbled out of the storage room, clutching his ribs in pain. He was filled with rage.

*You'll get yours, pricks*, he thought.

Once Lucas was gone, Brian took Alan aside and said, "I think we should keep Lucas. It's better to have him around so that we can keep an eye on him. You never know what that irrational asshole might do if he doesn't have this job. He's crazy enough to burn the building down! Or take it out on Mom." Sensing his brother's skepticism, he continued, "Rafael could give us reports. He knows the business, and it wasn't his fault that Lucas scammed us." He paused. "And we gotta get rid of all the knockoffs and any other illegal merchandise."

Upon hearing his name, Rafael looked up from the table. He smiled to himself, happy that he still had a job.

Brian glared at Alan, challenging him to disagree. This was the first time ever that Alan had deceived him, and he felt a pang that he never felt before.

"I'm sorry, bro," said Alan. "I guess I just got greedy. There's gotta be a way to do this without it being illegal."

"So, what are we going to do with Lucas?" asked Brian. "Remember what Nick once told us: keep your friends close and your enemies closer."

Alan nodded. "Okay, but we gotta keep him on a short leash. And Rafael has gotta give us regular reports and check the inventory often, agreed?"

Brian gave him a nod.

Though furious with his brother for violating their agreement, Brian paused for a moment to think. Then, as if a light bulb went on in his head, he said, "What about Genuine Imitations?"

"Huh?" replied Alan. "What are you talking about?"

"Remember what our lawyer told us about the difference between gray-market items and knockoffs? What makes selling knockoffs illegal is trying to pass them off as the genuine article—that would be selling counterfeits," continued Brian. "But what if we told people up front that the items were imitations? What if we put together a line of clothes that looked like the real thing, but had some minor change and a lookalike label with a misspelling or modified logo? You know, replicas. We could call the line Genuine Imitations."

Alan smiled in appreciation of his brother's idea. "That's awesome, bro. Genuine Imitations—we could have a website that brings together cool stuff that is current and affordable."

"We could sell all sorts of merchandise as long as they were imitations containing subtle changes, but otherwise almost indistinguishable from the real deal," added Brian. "We could even get some things customized to our specs and put them online. As long as we're not deceiving anyone, we should be good to go."

What began as an argument between the brothers ended up giving birth to another HS&C business venture.

# CHAPTER NINE

# Different Paths

It was clear to Brian that he and his brother were beginning to move in different directions. Alan was far more comfortable taking chances and doing things that were borderline, if not downright illegal. Alan often had to persuade Brian to go along with him or threaten to do things on his own.

Brian's anxiety came and went, depending on what he and his brother were doing and how risky the scam was, but he discovered that deep breathing could help control it. In addition, Alan had made cocaine his drug of choice, while Brian went with alcohol and pot—and TV.

But when it came to making money, both men were entirely focused, often working well into the night making deals, setting up websites, staying abreast on the latest trends, and opening new markets. In addition to their online gray-market business, their fencing operation was working well. But Alan kept pressing Brian to be more adventuresome and go for more expensive items. He wanted it to become a full-fledged fencing operation. Their suppliers were willing to bring them whatever they wanted.

This led to many arguments between the brothers.

"It's not worth the risk," argued Brian, striking the table with his hand. "Remember our business plan. HS&C is all about selling the latest and greatest fashion items at way below market value."

"But think of all the money we could make," replied Alan. "People bring their junk to us. We give them pennies on the dollar, no questions asked, and sell it for way above what we paid. No more having to go out and hustle with boys in the 'hood. They come to us."

"You don't get it, Alan!" exclaimed Brian. "We'd be no different than pawn brokers and fences. And fences are connected to the mob. We don't want to fuck with the mafia. Under the radar, that's where we are and that's where we should stay. If we get too big, we might attract attention. The more expensive the items, the more attention we attract. And the more attention we attract, the more—"

"Yeah, I know," interrupted Alan, "the more likely we are to get caught. But the more risk, the more gain!"

"Under the radar," repeated Brian. "Under the radar."

He constantly used the refrain, "stay under the radar." Though he liked the money, he was not thrilled taking unnecessary chances. He repeatedly cautioned that the more they used their suppliers, the more they were putting themselves at risk of some unhappy gang member ratting them out to the police. He felt a lot more comfortable with just doing the gray-market business.

In contrast, Alan enjoyed the association with the underworld. The danger excited him. He never felt a tinge of guilt or fear. Just as Nick had predicted, the more he practiced the role of being detached, remote, and unfazed, the easier it had become. Except for his brother and his mother, and to a lesser extent Rose and Nick, he felt attached to no one. And he liked it that way.

During one of their strategy sessions, Alan brought up a new business venture that he was excited about. "What d'ya think about going into the money-lending business, bro?" he asked. "We have extra cash, and the banks don't pay much interest. There are lots of kids who spend more than the allowances their parents give them. We're always being asked by our friends to loan them a few bucks until payday. They're all good for it. We'll get the money back, ya know."

"Money lenders? You mean loan-sharking?" replied Brian, dismayed by the idea of yet another illegal activity.

Alan nodded. "Well, yeah, loan-sharking. Just small amounts. Nothing that would compete with the big boys. We'd still be under the radar. Nothing more than a couple hundred bucks to any one customer, a thousand tops. We could get twenty percent return—per week, bro. Just think. We loan some dude a hundred, and a week later, we get one-twenty back. Now that's a good return on investment."

"Twenty percent per week!" exclaimed Brian. "Geez, that's like, what, over a thousand percent annualized?" He shook his head in disbelief. Once again, the allure of money caught Brian's attention.

His heart thumped in his chest. *Breathe*, he thought.

Alan chuckled, becoming more animated as he thought about the numbers. "Even if we were to loan out only a total of a couple thou per week, we could be bringing in some serious coin, bro."

"But what about bad loans; you know, people who don't pay up?" asked Brian. "How are we going to enforce repayment?"

"I've thought of that," replied Alan. "Our street vendors … there's some heavy-duty muscle out there who would be willing to make sure that we get paid, you know what I'm sayin'? Collectors. Enforcers." He gave his brother a sinister grin.

*Who is this guy that Alan is becoming?* thought Brian. *He is far more bad-assed than me. Sometime I envy him. Other times I fear for where he is heading and where it might take us. And I don't want to go there.*

Brian was excited by the idea of making money, but the thought of getting more involved with gangs and engaging in illegal activities scared him. He felt an anxiety attack coming on. That, too, scared him.

*Breathe.*

"What do you think, bro?" asked Alan. "Are you game?"

Using a technique he had read about for treating anxiety, Brian focused on a spot on the floor and took several slow, deep breaths, forcing himself to calm down, but he could still feel his heart pounding in his chest. While he tried to act cool, inside he was a wreck.

"I dunno," he finally managed to reply. "I mean, I can see that there's good money to be made, but if we do it, we will have crossed a line. We'd not be grifters; we'd be gangsters."

"And so?" asked Alan, not really caring one way or the other. He was just interested in the money.

"And we would be going to bed with the street gangs even more than we already are," reasoned Brian. "I mean, it's one thing not to really know where the merchandise we're selling on Craigslist is coming from, whether it's stolen or it fell from the back of a truck. But it's another thing to do loan-sharking and then depend on gangsters to break the legs of deadbeats."

"What the fuck are you so afraid of, bro?" asked Alan exasperated by his brother's hesitation. "What happened to the bad-assed boys-in-black? What happened to Michael Corleone? WTF?"

Brian dropped his head. He'd been asking himself the same questions. "You're right, you're right," he replied shaking his head. "Something is going on with me that I can't figure out. I see how easy all of this is for you, but it ain't so easy for me. I wanna be that guy ... the guy that doesn't give a shit. But I'm not him. It's not that it bothers me to break the law. It's the thought of getting caught ... and physically hurting somebody." He remembered how he had felt when he had smashed the guy's nose in the club.

"You'd better get your shit together, bro, 'cause if you're not interested in doing this, I'm gonna do it on my own," declared Alan, giving his brother a defiant look.

Brian just stared back at him, not knowing what to say. Alan's comment shocked him. The idea that Alan would do something on his own without him took him by complete surprise. He was totally without words.

Though Alan and Brian were close, just as any brothers, they fought, argued, and cussed each other out. But this felt different. More like a crack in the foundation of their relationship. Never before had the threat of separating from one another felt more possible.

Brian wasn't sure which direction to go. On the one hand, he didn't want to lose out on the money that could be made, nor did he want his brother to view him as some kind of a wuss. On the other hand, he didn't want to have to deal with the anxiety that being involved in flagrantly illegal activities brought him. If he followed his brother's path, he feared not only potential physical harm from the people with whom they would become associated, but from the legal system.

He felt fear *for* his brother, but not fear *of* his brother.

Brian didn't know how to respond to Alan. He could feel his heart pounding and was having difficulty breathing. His throat tightened. He felt the sweat building under his arms. His mouth went dry, and his nostrils flared. If he didn't do something quickly, he would be gasping for air.

Not wanting Alan to suspect what he was going through, without saying a word, Brian stood up, went into the bathroom, and closed the door behind him. He loosened his shirt collar and splashed water on his face trying to abort the panic attack that was beginning to overcome him. At least, he had a name for it; he knew he wasn't going to die.

*Where did I put that shrink's card?* he thought. *Maybe it's time I made that call.*

# CHAPTER TEN

# Looking Inward

D
r. David Albertson's office was located in a 1930s Craftsman-style home that had been converted into individual offices. One had to walk through a white picket gate and past an English garden outside the building to reach the front door to the building. It seemed like an oasis amidst a bustling commercial street. Brian had expected the typical modern high-rise building common for most medical practitioners. This building was anything but typical.

Dr. Albertson opened the door to the waiting room and greeted Brian with a smile.

"Hello, Brian," he said speaking in a soft, welcoming tone. "I'm David Albertson. Please come in."

Dr. Albertson stepped back into the office, allowing Brian to enter. Brian scanned the room, which looked more like a living room than an office, complete with a leather couch and matching large leather-upholstered chairs. Books and artwork adorned the walls. A Persian carpet lay over the dark wood floors.

It was a comfortable, dimly lit space that Brian found immediately inviting. Dr. Albertson fit right into the space. He was a middle-aged man of average height with gray beard and hair, and an athletic build. Dressed in Levi's, penny loafers, and a black Henley shirt, David Albertson was the opposite of hip, slick, and cool.

Brian took a seat on the couch across from Dr. Albertson, who sat in one of the leather chairs.

"So, Brian, tell me what brings you in today?" he said, sitting back in his chair with his fingertips touching just under his chin.

Brian searched the room as if looking for an answer. "Uh, panic attacks," he replied, reciting what the physician had told him.

"Panic attacks. Hmm, scary, aren't they? Feels like you're going to die," said Dr. Albertson.

Brian looked directly at Albertson and nodded. "Definitely," he said. "The first time I had one, I was so scared I called my doctor and asked for an emergency visit. I thought I was having a heart attack."

Albertson gave him a sympathetic smile. "Yeah, panic attacks mimic heart attacks—shortness of breath, pounding in the chest, dizziness ... the whole nine yards. But no one dies from a panic attack. These attacks usually pass in about twenty minutes."

"You got it, Doc," said Brian with a sigh of relief. "What do I do during those twenty minutes? And how can I get rid of them?"

"There are some techniques you can learn to control and ride out an attack," replied Albertson, "but getting rid of them, that's another story. First, we have to figure out what's causing them and what triggers them. And that takes time."

"How much time?" asked Brian.

Albertson smiled. "That all depends on how much time you are willing to invest in examining your life and how comfortable you will be in talking to me about the things that trouble you. I usually see people once or twice a week for fifty minutes each visit."

"Wow, that makes it expensive," said Brian. "How long will I have to be in treatment? A few weeks? A month?"

"It could be longer," replied Albertson. "Therapy is a significant commitment of time and money. And panic attacks usually take a while before they make their first appearance. Things build up unconsciously and eventually make their appearance when you least expect them. The thing is, once they do make an appearance, it takes less and less internal pressure to bring on another one. So, we may have to go back in time and find out a lot about you, how you were raised, what happened along the way to get you where you are today.

"Teaching you techniques for learning how to control them won't take very long, but you will have to practice them before they become effective. And not just when the attacks occur, but before they come. It's like with swimming. When you're drowning is not the best time to learn how to swim; you've got to learn how to swim in the shallow end of the pool before you find yourself in a dangerous situation. Make sense?"

Brian nodded. He felt comfortable with Dr. Albertson and liked his straightforward approach. While he wasn't sure that he wanted to make a long-term commitment to treatment, he decided that he would schedule a few appointments. What he actually wanted was something more immediate, like a pill, a quick fix. He left the office with his head buzzing.

Brian did not tell Alan that he had begun therapy. He was afraid Alan would think that he was either weird or, worse yet, weak. Alan's opinion of him always mattered a great deal. The two of them were part and parcel of one another. They were bonded at the hip. They would joke that not only were they roommates, but they also were womb mates, and together they made one whole person.

Their bond was greater than the bond between most twins. The combination of being identical twins and being abused without a strong mother to rely upon forced them to rely upon each other just to survive. But something between them had changed; Brian could sense it. Alan and Brian seemed to be separating, doing things differently from one another, leaving Brian feeling uncomfortable. Until recently, he hadn't recognized how heavily he relied upon Alan.

His work with Dr. Albertson progressed slowly. It wasn't easy for Brian to share his innermost thoughts and even more of a challenge for him to disclose his feelings. He wasn't particularly psychologically minded, making engaging in intimate dialogue awkward at best. In addition, the years of practicing being detached from his feelings, trying to emulate his fictional, emotionally detached role models, made the work of psychotherapy even more challenging.

In the beginning of the treatment, Brian mostly talked about day-to-day matters. He would talk about how the business was going and the daily struggle of dealing with vendors. He asked Dr. Albertson for advice and suggestions.

He was reluctant to share his life history except in the most superficial way. When he spoke of his father's temper and his tight bond with his brother, he didn't go deep into his feelings. He didn't trust Dr. Albertson, not because of anything the doctor had done, but just because it was difficult for him to trust anyone. The adult world represented a threat. The twins didn't trust anyone except each other. This was the first time Brian was looking to someone other than Alan to help him.

Gradually, he began sharing bits and pieces of what it was like to grow up as an identical twin and some of the pranks they pulled on their parents, like how they would undermine their parents'attempts to tell them apart through clothes and body markings. He spoke about the differences between their mother's reaction of frustration and amusement and their father's reaction of anger.

It was more difficult for Brian to talk about life with his alcoholic, abusive father. And it was virtually impossible to talk about his mother except in the most glowing terms. When Dr. Albertson tried to address Brian's relationship with his parents, Brian would be evasive, speaking in generalities rather than delving into his feelings toward them.

"My mother is a very loving and sensitive person," said Brian. "I am much closer to her than to my father. He's just a prick."

"How was he such a *prick?*" asked Dr. Albertson.

"He was always yelling about something, everything, no matter what," explained Brian. "And we never knew when or how he was going to explode. That was the worst part, the not knowing. He would sneak up on us and give us a smack on the head."

"What was that like for you?" asked the doctor.

"Me and my brother just stayed away from him," replied Brian. "We were glad when they finally divorced."

"How did you mother react to him?" asked Dr. Albertson.

"She was afraid of him," replied Brian.

"How did she react when your father yelled at you and your brother or hit you?"

"What could she do? She was afraid for herself," replied Brian in a monotone.

"And how did you feel when your father yelled at your mother?"

"We hated him," replied Brian.

It was clear to Dr. Albertson from Brian's flat, emotionless tone in response to the questions that Brian was not yet ready to fully explore the depth of his emotional reaction to the family drama that enveloped him.

Brian saw his mother as a victim of Lucas's violence and fearful for her own life. It never occurred to him that she should have put herself between her abusive husband and her children. Dr. Albertson knew that it was not uncommon for abused children to be protective of their mothers. He knew it would take a while before Brian could entertain the idea that it was his mother's job to protect him, not the other way around. He anticipated that he would learn that Brian would have difficulty connecting with women as a result.

As Brian began to trust to Dr. Albertson, he shared his obsession with becoming like his heroes—Jason Bourne, Harry Callahan, Soprano, and Bond—and how he and Alan would practice copying their unemotional style.

"My brother and I always admired the television and movie characters Angus MacGyver, Harry Callahan, and James Bond. They showed no fear, no matter how dangerous the situation. They trusted no one, kept their emotions totally under control, and were, I dunno, not needing anything or anyone."

"They were self-contained," said Dr. Albertson, "is that it?"

"Yeah, exactly, self-contained," replied Brian, grinning. "We also liked Tony Soprano. He was a man who could keep his business life totally separated from his family life. He dealt with his business associates through fear, using raw power to keep them in line. I wish I could be like him."

"Exactly what parts of Tony Soprano did you want to be like?"

"Power and respect," replied Brian. "And he got it through intimidation. People feared him."

Dr. Albertson had other male patients who had been similarly abused and bullied as children and who also admired Jason Bourne, Tony Soprano, Harry Callahan, and James Bond, and for the very same reasons. These fictional characters became an alter ego, someone they could attempt to internalize, so they could function in what they experienced as a dangerous world. But none of Albertson's other patients had worked so hard at actually trying to become these fictional characters. They idealized them and tried to act like them in some instances, but these patients didn't work at becoming them complete with their persona. It was very upsetting to Brian that he was not able to be as good as becoming like them as his brother. It frustrated and angered him that he felt anxious and couldn't do some of the things that had the potential for making money.

Dr. Albertson was familiar with *The Sopranos* television series and was able to use it to help Brian understand the roots of his anxiety.

"Brian, do you remember why Tony Soprano went to see a therapist?"

"Do you watch the show, Doc?" Brian asked with a smile.

Albertson returned the smile nodding. "So, do you remember?"

"Yeah, he was having panic attacks and fainting spells," replied Brian. "Just like me."

"Right, and why was he having panic attacks," asked Albertson, probing Brian to reflect.

"I dunno. I never really understood that," answered Brian. "And I never got why he suddenly ended up vomiting after hitting his bodyguard—it's like he felt bad or something."

"Why do you think he would have felt badly?" asked Dr. Albertson.

Brian hesitated for a moment. "Well, he was picking a fight with his bodyguard for no reason. He beat him up just to show his posse that he was still the boss."

Dr. Albertson nodded. "So, he felt guilty. A pretty human feeling, don't you think?"

"I guess," replied Brian.

"How'd Tony feel about his family?" asked Albertson, continuing to probe.

"He loved his family," replied Brian thoughtfully, "especially his wife, Carmela."

"So, how was Tony different from Harry Callahan and Bond?" asked Albertson.

"Never saw Bond have feelings for any woman or anyone else," replied Brian. "And Harry cut off all feelings, even for pain."

"Who do you think you're more like, Tony or Jason?" asked Albertson.

Brian thought for a moment. "Probably Tony," he replied. "I want to have a girlfriend and even get married someday. I think I would like to fall in love. Not like Harry or Bond. I think Alan wants to be more like them."

"Maybe the price for wanting a relationship with others is that you can't get rid of all feelings, Brian. What do you think?"

Brian remained quiet.

"Think about it, Brian. We'll talk about it more next week." This was Dr. Albertson's customary way of indicating that the session was over.

Brian left the session deep in thought. It troubled him that he and Alan were becoming different people.

# CHAPTER ELEVEN

# A First Real Date

## *2003*

One afternoon in his junior year, Brian was leaving a class when a young woman crashed into him as she rushed from the classroom. His glasses clattered to the floor.

"Oh, my God!" the woman exclaimed, "I am so sorry."

She and Brian bent to retrieve the glasses at the same time, and their heads collided.

"Ow!" they both exclaimed, followed by laughter as they rubbed their foreheads.

Brian picked up his glasses and placed them back on his nose. When he saw who the woman was, he froze. It was Linda, the woman he had met at the Hollywood Vibe the summer before he started UCLA. She was the one who got away.

Linda was clearly embarrassed and blushed. She did not recognize Brian since he was wearing the wig, brown contacts, and glasses. "I'm so sorry. Please forgive me," she said. "I should have watched where I was going. I'm so very sorry."

"No problem," said Brian. "No harm, no foul. I'll survive and so will my glasses."

Seeing Linda embarrassed and flustered gave Brian a feeling of comfort. She was more uncomfortable than he was.

He introduced himself. "Hey, my name is *Brad*. I'll let you make it up to me by having lunch with me." He gave her his practiced HS&C smile.

She gave him an awkward smile, nodded, and said, "OK, uh, my name is Linda."

"Hi, Linda," replied *Brad*. "Let's go down to the Student Union."

They walked down the path toward the Student Union, chatting about the class they had both attended, and in addition, learning more about one another. Brian learned that Linda was a junior like himself, she came from Missouri, and was the oldest of three children. She was majoring in psychology with a minor in dance and lived in one of the dormitories on campus. Brian remembered that she had studied ballet, but he could not reveal this to her without giving up his true identity. It was as though he was getting a second chance to make a first impression.

Linda was not typical of the young women Brian dated at the clubs. Though pretty, she did not wear much makeup and was not as fashionably dressed as many of the campus coeds. It was quite a contrast to the way she was dressed when he first met her at the dance club where she had worn typical club attire. Minus the high heels, she stood about five feet three inches, with a lithe, athletic build. Her red hair was pulled back into a pony tail, with bangs framing her face, and she had hazel, almond-shaped eyes that gave her a catlike appearance.

Brian found himself attracted to her just like he had been when he first met her—but not in a lustful way. He just enjoyed her company.

"It's getting late," said Linda after they were together for a couple of hours. "And I have homework and a bunch of other stuff to do."

"Yeah, me too," replied *Brad*. "It's been great chatting with you, Linda. I'm sure glad we bumped into each other." He rubbed his forehead and chuckled.

Linda laughed as well, remembering how they had met. She picked up her books and was about to leave.

"Hey, Linda," said *Brad* holding his breath, "I'd like to see you again. Maybe we could have lunch tomorrow?"

Linda smiled. "Sure, that would be great. See ya tomorrow."

Brian let out his breath and nodded grinning.

They met once or twice a week on campus, sometimes having lunch on the grass around the quad and sometimes in one of the campus eateries that were clustered in the Student Union. They chatted a bit about Linda's life in the Midwest and how different it was than life in Los Angeles. But mostly they talked about *Brad*.

When she asked him about his life in LA, Brian found it difficult to answer at first. He knew it was a simple question, but given that he and Alan had kept everything about themselves and their lives a secret, he wasn't sure how to respond. Hence, he made up a story about having been born in Argentina and moving to California when he was a youngster.

He made himself an only child and described his home life as coming from a wealthy family living in Beverly Hills. He found it fun to create a totally bogus life and started playing the part that fit the life he described. He described the Hollywood scene, name-dropped, talked about the stuff he owned, and how he would wear the latest fashions when attending class. He was a clear representative of the HS&C brand, and he wanted to impress Linda.

Linda was curious about *Brad*. Coming from the Midwest, she had never been exposed to anyone like him. She was fascinated by his stories and his depictions of life in his world.

Brian found it easy to talk with her, but rarely would he ask her anything about herself or her life. He simply wasn't very interested in too much detail. He knew she was from Missouri, loved ballet, majored in psychology and dance, and didn't like loud music. That was good enough for him. In addition to enjoying her company, he mostly liked being with her because she gave him an opportunity to talk about his fictional world and because she appeared interested in him.

"You're so different from any of the boys I have ever met," said Linda as she took a bite of her sandwich during one of their afternoon lunches.

*Brad* smiled. "How am I different?"

Linda thought for a moment. "You seem so sure of yourself," she said. "Most of the boys I know seem to be uncomfortable, you know, awkward. You're not."

Brian was pleased with how she saw him. He was working on giving that impression.

"Maybe it's because I was born into a family where I was always being introduced to strangers," he explained. "My parents were always having people over for dinner or cocktails—mostly diplomats and business people—and I was constantly being introduced to them. After a while, meeting people became easy."

In truth, Brian felt awkward any time he had to meet people. That was one of the benefits of the lessons he had been learning from Rose and his acting classes. When playing another character, he felt more like the character he was playing than himself. He was pleased with himself. His grifter persona was working. He was acting like so many of the fictional grifters he watched in movies, totally comfortable with being someone they were not.

Brian and Linda continued to meet for lunch at least once a week. Brian told Alan about her, reminding him that they had previously met her at the Hollywood Vibe when they were just starting UCLA. He told him about how well he was doing being a grifter and gave him all the details he could remember about their conversations.

One afternoon, Alan decided he wanted to meet Linda. Brian was wearing the wig, brown contact lenses, and glasses, so there was no danger that Linda would be able to detect that they were the twins she had met at the Hollywood Vibe. As far as she was concerned, Alan would be just a fellow student and coincidently a friend of *Brad's*. He knew where they would be having lunch and decided to walk by.

Seeing them sitting at one of the benches near the Student Union, he meandered up to them. "Hey, *Brad*, how're you doin'?" he asked in a casual way, giving Linda his most charming smile.

On seeing Alan, *Brad* briefly lost his composure, but quickly recovered. He smiled.

"Hey, Alan, wassup?" said *Brad*. He turned to Linda and said, "Linda, this is my friend, Alan. Alan, this my friend—"

Alan looked at Linda. "I know you; we've met before."

Linda smiled. "Yes," she replied. "I remember, you. You have a twin brother, right? I forget his name." The smile left her face as she recalled the events of that night.

"Yeah, that's right. I do have a twin brother." He hesitated. "Hey, Linda, look I'm sorry about what happened back at the Vibe. I had had too much to drink."

Linda blushed, remembering that night. "No problem. It was a long time ago," she replied.

"What are you majoring in, Linda?" asked Alan.

"I'm thinking about psychology," she replied. "I find studying people interesting, ya know?"

"Yeah, I know what you mean," he said. "No two people are alike. Not even twins."

"Exactly," replied Linda. "And what are you majoring in, Alan?"

"Whatever is not going to interfere with my social life." He laughed out loud.

Linda smiled.

"Alan is just a party animal," added *Brad*. "He majors in having a good time."

While Alan continued to flirt with Linda in his relaxed, laid-back style, Brian smiled. He knew that his brother was toying with her, wanting Brian to finally make a move and ask Linda out on a real date rather than just having lunch on campus.

The brothers were always competing with one another, but always in a playful way, more to goad each other on than to win. It was an integral part of their relationship. But watching Alan engaging Linda, Brian began to look at her in a different light. She was cute, had a milky complexion, a great figure, and an incredible smile. And unlike the first time they had met, she seemed to be into him. That was a big plus.

Once Alan left, Brian pushed himself back into character and said, "Hey, Linda, how about we go out on a real date sometime?"

Linda looked up at him, at first a little puzzled by the shift. Then she replied, "I think I'd like that."

"How about Saturday night?" said *Brad*. "We can have dinner at one of my favorite restaurants."

"Sure," replied Linda with a girl-next-door smile.

On Saturday night, Brian picked up Linda at her dorm. He was driving a rented Ferrari convertible. He wanted to give Linda a taste of the high life, and making a big impression was important to him. Following the advice of his stylist, he wore all the latest fashions representing the HS&C brand, including a Rolex.

When Linda walked out from the dorm, Brian was leaning up against the hood of the Ferrari, arms folded on his chest and a broad smile on his face. Linda wore a floral dress that clung to her, showing off her shapely figure. Her hair was loose and hanging shoulder-length.

Brian flashed back to how Linda had looked at the club two years ago, remembering that she could look hot. On seeing him, Linda's jaw dropped.

"Oh, my God," she said. "A Ferrari? Is that yours?"

*Brad* nodded as he stepped forward smiling. "You look great, Linda," he said. "This is the first time I've seen you with your hair not in a ponytail."

He stepped around to the passenger side to open the door for her. Once she was comfortably seated, he moved around to the driver's side, slid in, and started the engine. He gave it a little extra gas to make sure that everyone around would hear the roar of the oversized engine. Then he turned up the music and hit the gas, leaving a bit of rubber on the asphalt.

"Uh, could you slow down a little ... uh, please," said Linda with a note of fear in her voice.

"Oh, sure," said *Brad*, "I just thought you'd like to feel the wind in your hair. Have you ever been in a Ferrari?"

Linda shook her head. "No. There are no Ferraris back where I come from. Most every guy I know drives a pickup truck. I guess, you would describe my friends as just a bunch of hicks compared to the life you live here in LA."

*Brad* smiled. "Hey, I just want you to have a good time and to show you how the other half lives. Money can buy a lot of cool things that they probably don't have back in Missouri."

Linda frowned. "It's not that there aren't a lot of rich people back in Missouri. There are tons. But they don't drive Ferraris. People in Missouri live a different lifestyle than here, even the rich ones. They're pretty low key. It's a lot simpler life, with a lot less attention to bling."

*Brad* nodded. "So, you don't like upscale stuff? Jewelry? Trendy clothes?"

"It's not that I don't like it," began Linda, "it's just not that important. I'm just not a *thing* person."

Brian felt confused. He'd never met a woman who wasn't into fashion, jewelry, cars, and other outward displays of affluence. "What do you mean by *thing person*?"

"Well, it's just that people back home are not into buying stuff just for the sake of buying," said Linda struggling to explain herself. "They're more into functional things, things that serve a real purpose, like farm equipment or tools or even kitchen appliances. Am I making any sense?"

*Brad* thought for a moment. "Yeah, I think so. But what about the girls, the women? They're into farm equipment? Functional stuff? Nothing just to look pretty?"

Linda laughed. "No. The girls back home like to look pretty. They like their jewelry and nice clothes. But it isn't a way of life. And they don't look for that in the boys they go out with or the men they marry. At least not in the small town where I come from. I imagine in big cities, like St. Louis, there are those who like their stuff, but not in the smaller towns. And I'm just a small-town girl."

Linda's comments sobered Brian. He felt a bit deflated given what he had planned for the evening.

They arrived at the restaurant, a very well-known Hollywood eatery where people went to be seen and to rub elbows with the rich and famous. One parking attendant opened the door for Linda, while another opened Brian's door. Brian gave him a twenty-dollar bill. The attendant nodded. He understood that Brian was asking him to park the car in front.

Once inside, the maître d' showed them to their table. The place was bustling with activity. Wait-servers and busboys moved quickly throughout the restaurant, carrying drinks and platters of artistically arranged food. Conversation and laughter created an atmosphere of high energy with the feel of success.

When the server approached their table and asked whether they wanted a cocktail, Brian ordered a bottle of champagne with two glasses. He produced his counterfeit driver's license, showing he was twenty-one. He also slipped the waiter a twenty, giving a knowing nod toward Linda to avoid having her carded. The server returned the nod, recited the specials of the day, handed them the menus, and departed.

Once the server left, Linda leaned across the table and whispered. "What did you show him? You're not twenty-one."

*Brad* gave her a sly smile. "It's all about knowing how to play the game and knowing the right people."

Linda stared at him, shaking her head. "Well, I don't play games, and I don't drink." She began to look through the menu. "And these prices are outrageous. Thirty-five dollars for a hamburger!"

"Don't worry about the cost; just order whatever you would like," *Brad* assured her. "The food is amazing. And it looks pretty on the plate."

"Do you come here often?" asked Linda.

"I go to a lot of different places," he replied. "I always like going to the best places and the latest finds. It's fun going to the new restaurants."

"How can you afford these kinds of places and a Ferrari? And wear a Rolex? And go to school?" asked Linda.

"I have a business that does pretty well," replied *Brad*. "My partner and I share the responsibilities, so it gives me time to go to school. I'm an entrepreneur. I like money, and I like nice things. My hope is to be a millionaire by the time I'm twenty-five." He gave her a self-satisfied grin.

"You are ambitious," replied Linda. "I suppose that's a good thing. But don't you care about society? Look at all the people who are hungry and have nothing. Don't you care about them?"

*Brad* was at a loss for words. He had never thought about anyone except himself and making money. He did not know how to respond to Linda. "What do you mean? People should take care of themselves. Why is it my responsibility to be concerned about people who don't work?"

"I think if we are able to help others who are less fortunate than us, we have a responsibility to help them," said Linda. "Not everyone comes from a wealthy family or has the means to go to college. "Don't you feel empathy toward other less fortunate people?"

"Empathy? What does that even mean?" asked *Brad*, genuinely perplexed.

Linda raised her eyebrows. "You don't know what empathy is? Like when you feel for another person's situation as if you were walking in their shoes. To feel what another person might be feeling."

"Nah, I don't think much about that. What's the point?" replied *Brad*.

"It's how we connect with others," said Linda.

"I feel sorry for some of those people—old people, sick people, disabled people—but not all," added *Brad*. "If people want to get ahead in this world, they have to work for it. I don't believe in handouts."

The more time Brian spent with Linda, the more confused he became. It was clear that she was not impressed with his attempt to show her how the other half lived. She was not interested in material things, expensive lifestyles, making a lot of money, and fancy restaurants. All the other women he had met at the Hollywood clubs were impressed with his ability to show them a good time. Linda was not. He felt off his game. Sweat formed on his hands.

*Brad* was disappearing, leaving him with just being himself, Brian.

Fortunately, the server came just at that moment to show Brian the bottle of champagne he had ordered. Brian looked at the bottle and asked the waiter to take it back and bring them a bottle of Perrier instead. Linda smiled appreciatively.

"I think we should order our food," said *Brad*, changing the subject and trying to get back into *Brad* mode.

"I'll have the grilled vegetable salad," said Linda as she closed her menu.

"That's it? A salad?" said a surprised *Brad*. He had forgotten Linda had told him she was a vegan. "I thought you Midwesterners were big meat eaters."

"We are, but not me," replied Linda. "I'm a vegan."

"A vegan? You mean, you eat only vegetables?" asked *Brad*.

"Yep. Only a plant-based diet, no animals or animal products," replied Linda. "It's better for my body and better for the environment."

Brian stared at her for a moment. He was incredulous. He shook his head in disbelief before ordering a rack of lamb with a baked potato. Not having a drink was one thing, but not having his meat was a different ballgame altogether.

They spent the next hour talking about movies and television shows that they each liked. Linda was drawn to those that were character driven with lots of human drama, while Brian favored action shows with violence, money, and power.

The differences between them were quite evident. Brian could not understand why anyone would be interested in watching relationship-based shows. He couldn't relate to the feelings of the characters and lacked insight into their motivations. Linda, on the other hand, could not relate to the violence and deplored people who made money at the expense of others.

"You mean, you actually like television shows like *The Sopranos* and movies like *Die Hard*?" asked an incredulous Linda. "Those guys are despicable!"

"They're cool," replied *Brad*. "Nobody messes with them. Tony Soprano and John McClane are real men." He felt defensive. "And they take care of their families as well."

Linda shook her head in disbelief. "The next thing you'll be telling me is that Jason Bourne is your role model. A guy with no compassion, no feelings, no humanity."

By the time they finished their dinner, they were barely talking with one another. The date didn't go as Brian had imagined. Rather than becoming a romantic evening with Linda being impressed with his ability to show her a good time, Linda seemed to be withdrawing. Even their friendship seemed in jeopardy.

On their way back to the UCLA campus, Linda said, "Look, Brad, I have enjoyed our friendship. All the lunches on campus were fun. But tonight, I found out that we are very different from one another. You are all about money, excitement, buying stuff, impressing people, being cool, and living life in the fast lane. I'm not. I am more about people, wanting to make a difference in their lives, helping others. I enjoy the simple things—a good movie, sharing a pizza, and meaningful conversation. I am not into Hollywood. I'm a girl from Missouri, a place where people have potluck dinners and barbeques, where people help each other out. We are very different from one another, Brad."

*Brad* didn't say anything. He knew she was right. They were very different.

When they arrived at Linda's dorm, she got out of the Ferrari and said, "Thanks for dinner, Brad. See you on campus."

*Strike two*, thought Brian. *That's the second time I've struck out with this girl. Shit!*

# CHAPTER TWELVE

# Party Central

Whesn they graduated from college, Alan and Brian continued to live together. They decided they no longer needed to hide that they were identical twins since their businesses didn't require the scam. With the continued help of their stylist, they differentiated themselves in their clothing and accessories, using their bodies to advertise their merchandise.

Alan wore the most avant-garde of their merchandise, always on the cutting edge, while Brian tended to be more mainstream—fashionable, but not eye-catching. They wore trending watches, sunglasses, shirts, suits, and pants that were coveted by their peers, most of whom were either still in college or just beginning their careers. The twins, having started early, were way ahead of them in making money.

Their apartment had become party-central. They gave parties that elevated their social standing and even went so far as to hire a publicist to create buzz. Once a month, they held a lavish party at their apartment, complete with the best alcohol and wines, and cocaine and pot available for the taking.

The food was catered. Servers carried trays of champagne and hors d'oeuvres. They envisioned themselves as the heavy-duty players of West LA catering to the millennials. They had developed a reputation for being the go-to people for partying and buying anything that was trending. And, of course, the source for borrowing money to tide one over until the next paycheck.

At one of their parties, Brian spotted a familiar face. A young woman wearing tight-fitting jeans, spiked heels, and a pullover top hanging off one shoulder and knotted over her right hip. It was Linda.

Brian wondered whether she would recognize him. As far as she was concerned, they hadn't seen each other since their junior year and the fiasco of a date he had had with her when he was disguised as Brad. She wouldn't know him as Brad, the guy with the Ferrari, but as Brian whom she had met years ago at the Hollywood Vibe when they were just entering UCLA—the guy with the twin brother.

Brian sauntered over to her, carrying a flute of champagne and flashing a big, toothy smile. "Hey, Linda," he said in a self-assured manner. He had never forgotten that she was the one that got away—twice. "How've you been?"

"Hi," she said, returning his smile. "I've been good. Which one are you, Alan or Brian?"

"I'm Brian. You remember us?" replied Brian. "It's been more than four years since you ran out of the club." He recalled that she had told Alan when they met on campus that she had forgotten his brother's name. It made him smile.

"Yeah, well, that was a long time ago," replied Linda. "And you're unforgettable. You and your twin brother."

"Hey, I'm sorry about that night," said Brian. "I ran out into the parking lot after you, but you were already burning rubber."

Linda laughed as she recalled that night. "I was pretty pissed off that night. But it's water under the bridge. What are you up to these days?"

Brian looked around the room and made a sweeping motion with his right arm. "This," he replied.

"This? You mean this is yours?" asked Linda in wide-eyed awe.

Brian tipped his glass toward her. "Yep. Mine and my brother's."

"Wow, you've done well for yourself," she said. "Did you graduate from UCLA?"

Brian nodded. "I did, and you?"

"I did. And now I am finishing up my master's in social work at USC."

"Impressive," replied Brian. "We should get together to catch up."

"I don't think so, Brian," said Linda making direct eye contact. "You have a very different lifestyle than me. Frankly, I don't think we have much in common."

Brian maintained his cool, detached demeanor as well as his smile. "And you don't like people with different lifestyles?"

Linda flushed. She liked to think of herself as tolerant and accepting. Brian's comment bothered her. "Uh, it's just that I can see we live in two different worlds. It's obvious that you are into money and glamour. My world is one where I want to help others, and yours is, well, one where you want to buy things."

Brian looked Linda up and down, noticing her designer jeans and shoes. "Seems like you like to buy things, too. We have that in common." He gave her a smile.

Before Linda could respond, Alan joined them.

"Hey, Linda, how's it going?" Alan gave her a once-over with his eyes. "Lookin' good." Then, without waiting for a reply, Alan turned to Brian. "Bro, I need to talk with you."

He motioned with his head for Brian to follow him as he walked toward the kitchen.

Brian looked at Linda. "To be continued," he said, and then he followed Alan out of the room. Linda watched him leave.

"What's up?" asked Brian.

Alan replied, "There are a couple of guys here from New York who say they have serious connections in Hong Kong and can connect us directly with factories that can copy anything we want from clothing to jewelry. They want to meet with us to discuss some kind of joint venture. What do you think?"

"We've never had partners before," replied Brian. "Why should we start now? We're doing fine on our own."

"It could be a way to really grow our business," said Alan. "I think we should at least meet with them."

"I'm not so sure," said Brian. "My guess is that we would be moving back into selling knockoffs as the real deal, not just for our Genuine Imitations division, and that would leave us wide open to criminal charges. And when we bring others into the business, we are even more exposed. I don't think it is a good idea."

Alan glared at his brother and shook his head. He didn't like his ideas being dismissed so quickly.

"Man, what's with you?" he exclaimed. "Where are your balls? The older you get, the more of a pussy you become!"

Alan stormed off, leaving Brian staring at his back.

Brian felt the sting of Alan's rebuke as he watched his brother walk away. Gradually, he pulled himself together and walked back into the living room where everyone seemed to be enjoying themselves. He had the bartender pour him a vodka on the rocks and drank half the glass in one gulp, glancing around the room as he did. He was happy to see that Linda was still there. She saw him looking at her and walked toward him.

"So, where were we?" asked Brian.

"You were saying that we were alike," she replied. "I thought about what you said. Maybe you're right, at least in part. I do like nice clothes. But I don't identify with the clothes. If I can afford them, I buy them. If not, I don't. They do not define who I am. I think that for you, they define you. Your clothes, your car, your jewelry, and even this apartment. They define who you are. And that's how we're different. Things don't define me. They are just things."

She had made similar comments about him when she thought he was Brad. He just stared at her, feeling deflated as though someone had sucker-punched him. Finally, he pasted an artificial smile on his face, more of smirk, and managed to utter a few words.

"Whoa, where did that come from? You barely know me."

"Yeah, but I know your type," said Linda. "You and your brother are so full of yourselves. You just use people to get what you want—especially women. Women exist only for your pleasure and conquest. You guys haven't changed since I first met you six years ago."

A part of Brian's brain knew she was right. He and Alan had designed their life according to the principle: *look out for number one.* Ordinarily, being dissed by a woman wouldn't bother Brian. He had worked on becoming impervious to insults or any other criticism. But ever since he had begun therapy, he had become more sensitized to other people's feelings, including his own.

"If you are so sure that you 'know the type,'" began Brian, using finger quotes to make his point, "then why are you here? When we first met years ago, I seem to remember that you were at the club because of a friend's birthday. What's your excuse this time?"

"You want the truth?" Linda asked, looking at Brian with a slight tilt of her head as though taunting him.

Just as he was about to answer, he heard his name being shouted.

"Brian, come quickly," yelled a panic-stricken female. "Something's happened to Alan!"

Brian turned and ran toward the voice that had come from the direction of Alan's bedroom. As he entered, a woman clad in only bikini underwear was pointing into the bathroom. Brian went in and found Alan on the floor, half dressed, with his eyes rolled back in his head. His body was shaking in random jerks, spittle dripping from his mouth.

"Call 9-1-1!" shouted Brian to the crowd that had gathered in the bedroom.

As he bent down to pick his brother up, he noticed the line of cocaine on the vanity countertop. He half-carried, half-dragged Alan into the bedroom and managed to get him up onto the bed. He tried to get him to stop shaking, using his own body to help calm him down.

Within a few minutes, he heard sirens outside the apartment house, followed by pounding on the front door. Unlike many poorer areas, West LA had a very responsive emergency dispatch center. The paramedics quickly took control of the situation, put an oxygen mask over Alan's nose and mouth, and placed him on a stretcher to take him to the UCLA emergency room.

"Okay, everybody," Brian shouted over the din, "party's over. Sorry, but we have an emergency, and we need to clear out. We'll be in touch."

With the aid of some of the hired help, Brian quickly ushered everybody out of the door. He was in take-charge, command mode.

Once everyone was out, Brian jumped into his car and sped over to UCLA to be with his brother. Brian knew that Alan had been using cocaine and had experimented with other drugs, but he did not realize how often and how much his brother had been using. Seeing Alan on the bathroom floor had scared him.

*Fuck*, Brian thought, *maybe Linda is right. We think too much of making money and buying shit, and not much about anything else, even each other. Once you recover, bro, we are going to have some serious conversations.*

Brian arrived at the UCLA ER and found out that Alan was in the OR having his stomach pumped.

"Mr. Suarez," began the doctor, "we found not only cocaine, but also oxycodone in his system. This, plus alcohol, well, he could have died. Good thing you found him when you did."

*Fuck. I didn't know. How fucked up is that? I thought I knew him. Maybe I don't really know anyone, even my brother ... or myself.*

CHAPTER THIRTEEN

# Showdown

The doctors kept Alan overnight in the hospital for observation. The next afternoon, Brian took him home. He looked a bit drained but none the worse for the wear. They didn't talk much on the ten-minute drive from UCLA Hospital to their apartment.

"We need to have a strategy session, bro," said Brian.

"Wassup?" replied Alan.

"Wassup? You almost fucking died, that's wassup," replied Brian. "That stunt scared the shit out of me, man. Just seeing you on the bathroom floor, shaking and all, spit drooling down from the corner of your mouth…" He paused, stared as his brother, and almost in a whisper, said, "You fuckin' almost died."

"But I didn't. I'm still here," replied Alan, grinning.

"How much shit have you been using, Alan?" asked Brian. "What's happening to you?"

"Look, bro," replied Alan. "I just like to party. Things got a little out of hand. No big deal. Let it go." Alan tried to make light of the situation, but his glare at his brother warned him to back off.

Brian shook his head. "Nah, bro, I ain't backin' off," he said. "We've gotta talk. I mean seriously talk. This shit's not workin' for me." For one of the few times that Brian could remember, he wasn't feeling overawed by his brother. It felt good.

Alan raised his eyebrows, giving Brian a look of surprise. "What d'ya mean, it's not working for you."

Brian stared right back at him. "I mean you and your drugs. And us," began Brian. "I've been thinking about how blind I've been to the symptoms. I went online and read about drug addiction."

Alan interrupted. "Addiction? What the fuck are you talkin' about. I'm not an addict. I just enjoy a little blow and maybe some oxy now and then. Like I told you, I like to party."

Brian continued, "You've been jumpy, irritable, unable to focus, willing to take increased risks, and in general, being a prick. It's the drugs, man. I just never paid attention. We haven't had a real strategy session in months. I have no idea where we're heading. You just keep coming up with these crazy ideas for making a quick buck that don't make any sense. We're not kids any more. Unless you clean up your act, I'm gone."

Now it was Alan's turn to be surprised. And if Brian was going to be honest with himself, he surprised himself as well. He hadn't prepared to tell Alan that he thought about moving out on his own.

"Gone?" asked Alan, bewildered. "What d'ya mean gone, bro?"

"I can't live with you, my brother, if you're gonna continue to use," said Brian. "I don't want to go through what I went through last night ever again. I don't want to be called by someone or come home and find you laid out from another OD. So, you gotta stop, or I'm gonna find my own place."

Neither Alan nor Brian had ever envisioned a time when they wouldn't be together. It was always the two of them, the twins, the bad-assed boys-in-black. They were a team, inseparable. But now Alan's back was up against the wall.

Without thinking, he blurted out, "You can't go. You can't manage without me. You wouldn't survive on your own. Without me, you're nothing!" His eyes were ablaze. He sounded contemptuous.

Brian was too stunned to move. His eyes welled up.

When Alan saw the look in Brian's eyes, he immediately realized that he was out of control. "I'm sorry, bro. I didn't mean that. Maybe you're right. Maybe I have been doing a little more shit than I realized," he said in a softer tone. "I know you're only trying to help me, bro. Maybe it's time for a major strategy session."

Brian nodded in agreement. He felt his body relax.

*** 

Over the course of the next several weeks, Brian and Alan had multiple lengthy strategy sessions discussing every aspect of their lives from business to personal to the future. Brian managed to tell Alan that he was in therapy. Instead of ridiculing him, as Brian had expected, Alan told Brian that since his overdose, he had been thinking of getting some counseling himself. He realized that he had been partying too hard. This disclosure surprised Brian.

"Wow, bro, good for you," said Brian, giving Alan a pat on the shoulder. "Seeing you on the bathroom floor scared the shit out of me. I can only imagine what you felt."

Alan smiled appreciatively. "Maybe it's time for us to reassess our goals and where we are heading."

Brian nodded. "Yeah, I've noticed that we haven't been as tight with each other as usual," he began. "You know, like we've been going in different directions. It's been weird since we have always been in synch, but lately not so much."

Alan stared at his brother for a long moment. "Maybe you're right. We have been on different pages."

"I miss you, bro. It's been like I've been losing my best friend," said Brian.

"What d'ya mean?" asked Alan. "I'm right here."

"Yeah, but you know, you've been wanting to do more illegal shit, getting involved in more hardcore activity. And you seem to get pissed off at me when I say I don't want to go down that road," explained Brian, surprised by his own directness.

"I hear you," replied Alan. "And I'm sorry for some of the things I've said to you about being a pussy and all."

Brian smiled. This was the first time he could recall his brother apologizing.

"I appreciate that, Alan," replied Brian. "So, are we gonna be in business together, or are we going our separate ways?"

"I want to still make a bundle of money," said Alan. "And I want to party. I like being a player. I like fucking different chicks. Call me shallow, but that's what I like. And I like to buy stuff."

Brian laughed. He wished he could have been as candid with Linda as Alan was being with him. But he also knew that he wasn't like his brother. There was something in what Linda had said to him that was true. He had been using people, and it was beginning to bother him. It didn't bother Alan.

"All our lives together, we've been of like mind," Brian said solemnly. "It was almost as though we were one person. But maybe we are learning to *individuate*, as my therapist says, meaning that we are beginning to become separate people rather than just 'the twins.' We tried to become like the guys we loved to watch on TV. We wanted to be tough, cool, and without feelings. But it is not as easy for me as it is for you, never has been. You've been able to become Harry Callahan, detached and not give a shit about what others say. I've become more like Tony Soprano, complete with panic attacks, though not as tough. I don't like hurting people, and I want to be in a relationship. Here I am, twenty-five years old, and I've never even had a girlfriend. Do you even think about wanting to be in a relationship?"

Alan sat silently reflecting on what Brian said.

"It's true," Alan began. "I am not as sensitive to others as you are. In fact, Mom has called me a robot more than once. She says I don't show any human emotions. The only things I care about are money, respect, power ... and you. It's not a whole lot different today than it was when we first started Hip, Slick, and Cool. And about women, I am not really interested in anything long-term. Women serve a purpose—to please men. That's it."

"And what about the law?" asked Brian. "How do you feel about being a criminal? About jail?"

"Hey, bro," replied Alan with a smirk, "if that's what it takes to get to the top, it's worth the risk. But if we could figure out a way to make the big bucks without breaking the law, I'm all in."

Now it was Brian's turn to reflect. He knew that Alan would risk jail time to make money.

"I have an idea," began Brian. "How about we take a short time-out, ya know, a break. It would give us a chance to think about which direction we want to go. Maybe come up with some new ideas. What d'ya think?"

Alan remained quiet for a moment. He let the idea of taking some alone time sink in. They rarely took time away from one another.

"What did you have in mind, bro?" asked Alan.

"How about my going to Vegas for a couple of weeks? Or maybe Palm Springs?" replied Brian. "You could stay here and take care of business, and I could go chill for a couple of weeks."

Alan said, "Okay, I'll take care of the fort and you can go."

Brian smiled, happy that there was no argument from his brother.

# CHAPTER FOURTEEN

# The Necklace

Brian drove to Palm Springs. He was looking forward to his two-week vacation soaking up the rays, doing a bit of gambling, and getting drunk on margaritas. He put the top down on his Porsche, turned up the music, and took a leisurely drive on the freeway, making it from LA to Palm Springs in less than two hours.

He checked into the hotel, tipped the bellhop, and proceeded to unpack his suitcase. Then he called room service for the first margarita of his vacation.

He spent his days lounging by the pool just as he had planned. He did some reading and thinking about his future business plans and what it might be like to live apart from Alan. He found it strange that he didn't miss being with Alan as much as he had imagined. Nor did he miss the parties.

*So, this is what R & R feels like*, he thought. *Kinda nice.*

In the evening, he visited the casino where he played mostly blackjack and chatted it up with the dealer and other players.

About ten days into the trip, he was lounging around the pool and nursing a frothy margarita on the rocks when he received an urgent call from Alan.

"Hey, bro, I need you to come home, pronto!"

Brian sensed an excitement in Alan's voice that he never heard before. His stomach dropped. *Is this good news or bad?* he wondered. Aloud, he said, "Wassup, bro?"

"I can't talk about it on the phone," replied Alan. "Just get back ASAP!"

Before Brian could say anything, the line went dead. He hesitated for a moment before gulping down his drink and jogging back to his room. He quickly packed his things and checked out. He was on the road in thirty minutes and made the ninety-mile trip back to Los Angeles in well under two hours.

Within minutes of entering their apartment, Brian learned that Alan had been accused of stealing a three-million-dollar necklace from a client.

Brian was stunned. "Three mil ... What the fuck!"

Alan stared at his brother, emotionless. "This is a first-class con, bro. Primo! Sit back, relax, and let me tell you a story you won't believe." Alan gave his brother a self-satisfied smile.

Brian pulled himself together and focused. "Okay, bro, tell me everything. Give me a play-by-play. Leave nothing out." Brian sat back, hands behind his head, assuming the same posture he took when watching TV. He was ready to listen.

"A while back, I met a guy named Joseph Faraday who came to me for a short-term loan of twenty thousand dollars," Alan began. "Joe is a high roller who lives large. Everything he does is over the top: from the house where he lives to the cars he drives. Joe's wife comes from money. She inherited millions from her aunt, who was also her godmother. While Joe earns a bundle on his own, he spends more than he earns. He thinks he has to keep his wife happy by buying her stuff like she's been used to. He makes a lot of money as an investment banker, and it keeps rolling in, but he spends it just as fast. I became his go-to source for quick, short-term loans—ten thousand, twenty-five thousand, and even fifty. He repaid the loans quickly and became a regular client. Even though his wife's super-rich, Joe told me that she was not particularly generous. Joe had to earn his own money.

"Faraday's always bragging about the price of the things he owns and how much money he and his wife have; he loves showing off the stuff. His cell phone is filled with selfies showing him standing next to Ferraris, Lambos, celebrities, and wearing expensive jewelry and clothes. He especially loves his diamond-faced, purple-dialed thirty-thousand-dollar Rolex and the two-hundred-fifty-thousand-dollar Aston Martin he drives. He wears five-thousand-dollar suits and custom-made shirts and shoes. I am a suspicious guy, so I challenged Faraday to prove the stuff was real, not just knockoffs. After all the time we've spent in the knockoff world, I wanted to be sure the stuff was legit. I played into Faraday's egotistical nature, challenging him to prove he was financially successful and not just a bullshitter. Faraday took on the challenge and invited me to visit his home up in the hills of Pacific Palisades. I knew it would flatter Faraday, so I used my cell phone to take a video of the place and included Faraday in the video. He strutted around showing me his stuff, all puffed up. You know the type. Couldn't stop talking."

Alan showed Brian the pictures. The video was like watching someone taking a tour of a museum. The home was one of those McMansions built to maximize the square footage and fill every buildable square inch of the lot and show off the magnificent view of the Pacific Ocean.

The house was furnished to the hilt, everything high-end—appliances and features shown in *Architectural Digest*. Included in the tour of the house was Faraday showing Alan his wife's closet. The closet was larger than most people's bedroom, with a safe located on one wall of the closet. Alan had filmed Faraday punching in the security code to the safe and pulling open the door. Inside the safe, everything was on display in glass cases. It looked more like a jewelry store than a safe in someone's closet.

Brian nodded. He had calmed down considerably, completely absorbed by the story that Alan was telling. When combined with the video, it was like watching a reality TV show.

Alan continued, "Faraday is the kind of guy who puts a price tag on everything; whether it's the rugs on the floors, the paintings on the walls, or the jewelry in the safe, everything has a price tag. It was during this visit that Faraday showed me the diamond necklace which he tagged at approximately three million dollars. And it was at that moment that I hatched a plan for scoring big. I began devising a plan to steal this necklace.

"After giving it a great deal of thought and spending many hours going over the plan with Nick, our mentor, we came up with an idea that would require that you be out of town when the con went down so that you would be able to cover for me if I got caught. It was Nick who told me to keep his plan secret from you so that you could not be convicted of collusion. If I had told you about the plan beforehand, you would have been considered an accomplice, and we both could be convicted. All I had to do was figure a way to get you to go on vacation. But you solved that problem when you suggested we take some time apart. It was perfect timing. As always with us, you must have picked up on my wavelength."

"No wonder, you gave so little pushback when I suggested taking time apart!" replied Brian. "You were setting me up."

"Protecting you, bro," said Alan. "Protecting you. And making us a bundle."

Alan resumed his tale. "Once you were on the road, I was ready to execute my plan to steal the necklace. I had already figured out how I was going to gain entry to the Faraday house when Joe and his wife were going to be out of town. Joe Faraday loved to talk about their home in Cabo San Lucas and how they were planning to be there for the weekend. With you on vacation and the Faraday house empty, I was ready."

After he watched the video, Brian figured out that Alan must have used the security codes he had filmed to gain access to the house while the Faradays were away for the weekend. Alan told him that because they were identical twins, he knew that there was no way anyone could prove that it was he rather than Brian who had taken the necklace. Faraday had never met Brian and did not know that Alan was one of identical twins.

"And that's exactly how it went down. I heisted the diamond necklace, left behind a counterfeit one which would delay the reporting of the crime, and through Nick's connections, I lined up a fence who was ready to take the necklace off my hands for a third of its value. And I received cash for over a million dollars, which I parked in a safe-deposit box."

He dangled the key for Brian to see.

Brian shook his head in disbelief. "That's one hell of a con, bro! What a story! What's going to happen now?"

"Our lawyer will be meeting with us and will run through the steps. He'll question you, and then the police will want to question you. No doubt, there will be an insurance investigator involved as well. I'm sure the jewels are insured."

And this was exactly what happened.

When Faraday's wife found out that her precious necklace was stolen, she had called both the police and the insurance company. They both questioned Joe Faraday, who in turn told them that he had shown the necklace to Alan. The police brought Alan in for questioning. And Alan brought his lawyer with him. The detectives told them that the forensic team that had examined the crime site went over every inch of the closet and the safe and found a hair that didn't belong to either Joe Faraday or his wife. They asked Alan to submit to a DNA test.

At first, the lawyer objected, but Alan had no problem giving them a DNA sample. He knew that as an identical twin, both he and Brian shared the same DNA. When the results of the DNA test came back, the police once again brought Alan in for questioning. This time, in addition to his lawyer, Alan brought Brian with him. Brian had given the lawyer the all-cash receipts from his trip to Palm Springs proving his whereabouts at the time of the burglary.

When the lawyer summarized the facts of the case against Alan, the police and the assistant district attorney assigned to the case realized they had no grounds for filing an indictment against Alan. They could not prove the case against him despite believing that in fact at least one of the twins had been involved in the robbery. Neither the police nor Faraday could prove which twin had been actually in the closet.

The burden of proof lay with the police and the DA, and they had not met the requirement. They realized that proving a case against one of a pair of identical twins would be difficult, if not impossible. Even if they took the case to court, the jury would find it difficult to find one guilty. There simply wasn't enough evidence to prove a case against anyone. Proving collusion was even more difficult; there was no evidence that Brian had foreknowledge of Alan's plan to steal the necklace. They could neither prove which twin had committed the crime nor that they had colluded. And with insurance cases, the LAPD was not highly motivated to press the issue; they already had enough on their plates. Only the insurance company had a vested interest in knowing, and their interest was primarily in recovering the necklace, not in who had perpetrated the crime.

The entire experience left Brian with a bad taste. Although he understood Alan's rationale for keeping him out of the loop, Brian was more concerned about how separated he and his brother had become. This wasn't the first time that Alan had done something without including Brian. Brian knew that he would never have been able to do something like this without first running it by Alan. They had always been a team, and now they were separating.

*Perhaps that's a good thing*, Brian thought. *And we have over a million bucks in our bank account. But why doesn't it feel good?*

# CHAPTER FIFTEEN

# Going Legit

## *2006*

Alan and Brian continued having their strategy sessions. They had decided to move ahead with the money-lending business. They obtained a license to be private money lenders, but many of their loans went way beyond the usury rate, which in California was ten percent per year.

They kept two sets of books for the company: one that was made public for auditors, and on which they paid taxes, and another set that was kept for their own purposes. They knew they were in the loan-sharking business and that it was illegal, but for Alan at least, the return was worth the risk. They expanded the business using the increased capital obtained from the sale of the necklace, and also through inviting friends and associates to invest in the loan operation by offering guaranteed, fixed returns of ten to twelve percent annually. They took a page out of Bernie Madoff's playbook: people wouldn't question the type of investment so long as their returns were consistently high.

In the middle of one of their sessions, Brian was lost in thought.

"Hey, bro, where'd you go?" asked Alan. "You seemed to be in outer space."

Startled, Brian replied, "I don't mind being a grifter or in bending the law, but I don't want to spend time in prison. We—you—pulled off that necklace con, but I don't want to go anywhere near that again … And I want to find a girlfriend and even get married and have children. So, if we're going to be partners, I guess, we're going to have to come up with a new business that could make us both happy—or at least, find a legitimate business that makes big bucks."

"I hear you, bro, but you gotta admit it was a pretty good hustle, no?" said Alan with a broad smile.

Brian returned the smile. "So, are you good with that—going totally legit?"

Alan nodded. Brian looked at his brother, not quite believing the nod of acceptance.

Alan and Brian eventually agreed to continue building their internet gray-market business, as well as the Genuine Imitations division for selling knockoffs. They would also continue expanding their money-lending operation, but in a legitimate way. They developed an independent corporation for giving short-term loans with high interest rates when there was no collateral on the loans and lower interest rates for loans with collateral. They used an attorney to draw up the paperwork.

In addition to these three lucrative businesses, they developed another business that capitalized on the theme of "party central." Hip, Slick, and Cool Enterprises was becoming a conglomerate with multiple income streams.

Rather than having monthly parties at their apartment, they began holding parties at various venues throughout Los Angeles. They connected with real estate brokers who had high-end homes for sale and worked out an arrangement between the broker and the homeowner to allow them to hold a party in the vacated home for one or more of the weekends during which the home was on the market. The home had to be large enough to accommodate one hundred to one hundred fifty people, have a large yard, be relatively private to avoid complaints from neighbors, and have ample street parking.

The twins would stage the home, hire caterers, and charge an admission fee. In addition, they contracted with vendors to sell alcohol at the parties, charging a fee to the vendor plus receiving a percentage of the gross receipts. They worked out a similar deal with the valet-parking company.

Despite Brian's misgivings, they connected with drug dealers to supply quality cocaine and other stimulants, charging a high upfront fee to the vendors for the privilege of selling their goods at these high-end parties. Alan and Brian hired security guards to ensure nothing got out of hand. They also installed wireless video cameras throughout the venue with a multiscreen monitor that allowed them to personally oversee activities throughout the party. Their out-of-pocket costs were carefully controlled: the venue, the catering, staging, security, and setup and cleanup. Anything above these fixed costs was profit, amounting to over fifty thousand dollars per party.

Essentially, they had developed a pop-up Party Central business plan modeled after the pop-up stores—short-term, week-to-week, or month-to-month leasing arrangements—that were appearing throughout the area. News about the parties spread through word of mouth and social media; they had even developed an underground Party Central app where people who knew about it could find out where the next party was being held.

Party Central became a significant source of Brian's and Alan's incomes. And, other than permitting the sale of illicit drugs on the premises, it was all legitimate. Sort of.

At thirty years old, the twins were earning solid seven-figure incomes. They had purchased a large Hollywood home which they shared and decorated in a high-tech style, with a separate guest house they used as an office from which they ran their four businesses.

Alan had given up using drugs, but continued being the consummate player and living the high life.

Brian continued the therapy with Dr. Albertson and was becoming more accepting of who he was and how different he was than Alan. He had learned a lot about himself and how his early childhood of abuse had affected his development. Brian recognized that he had always been more fearful than his brother who, he had learned from his mother during one of their dinners, even as a preemie, had been slightly more robust since birth than himself. This, in addition to his being more of an introvert while Alan leaned toward being an extrovert, would account for why Brian tended to follow Alan's lead.

While they were developing Party Central, Brian reconnected with Linda, whom he hadn't seen or talked to since Alan had overdosed. He found her phone number and called to set up a coffee date. He wanted to come clean with her.

They arranged to meet at a deli in Westwood. Brian wore the disguise he had used while going to college. He arrived at the restaurant before Linda and waited. Linda walked in and craned her neck in search of Brian.

When Brian saw her, he stood up. Linda did a double take.

"Brad? What are you—?"

"Hi, Linda," said Brian. "How are you?"

"I'm supposed to be meeting someone here," she replied, continuing to look around the deli.

"I know," said Brian.

"You know? What do you mean?" she replied, obviously confused.

"Please, sit," said Brian.

Linda hesitated, but then tentatively slid into the booth without moving her wide-open, questioning eyes from Brian.

Brian sat down and slowly removed his eyeglasses and wig. Linda's jaw dropped as Brian removed the contact lenses, revealing his green eyes.

"Brian? What the—?" she exclaimed.

"I'll explain," said Brian with a friendly smile. "When Alan and I started UCLA, we decided that it would be better for us to avoid being known as 'the twins.' We had had enough of that in high school and thought it was time for us to develop separate identities. So, I wore the disguise. And that's when we literally bumped into each other." He chuckled as he remembered their run in.

At first, Linda smiled, but then she became serious. "All that time we were having lunch on campus and even went on that one date, you knew I was the girl your brother insulted at the Vibe? You deceived me!" she hissed.

Brian nodded. "You have every right to be angry," he said.

"Damn right, I do!" she said, her eyes flashing in anger. Linda was about to leave but stopped short. She actually liked Brian and did not want to write him off.

"I'm sorry," said Brian. "And you have walked out on me twice and were just about ready to do it again now." His green eyes searched her face for some sign of forgiveness.

"I don't know whether I should laugh or smack you," said Linda, suppressing a smile. "That was quite a scam—four years pretending that you were someone else. How did you do it?"

Brian relaxed. "Practice. Lots of practice," he said.

Linda couldn't help herself. She laughed.

Brian felt a weight lifted off his shoulders. He liked Linda, only not in a romantic way. He enjoyed her forthrightness, her honesty. Though he was not about to tell Linda everything about his life and the things that he and his brother had done, he wanted them to become friends. This was the first time Brian had a female friend.

"Why did you decide to come clean with me?" asked Linda.

"I guess I'm getting tired of all the lies," he replied. "Especially lying to you. I like you. I liked you when I first met you, and I liked you when we were in school. I didn't like hurting you. And though I didn't like the things you said about me, they were true. They made me think about who I was becoming."

He told her that he was in therapy with Dr. Albertson and was learning a lot about himself.

Linda smiled. "I guess, it's working. You seem different."

"I am different, or at least I am trying to be. People can change," said Brian.

"Well, we'll see," she said. "Remember, I'm from Missouri—the show-me state—you'll have to show me."

Linda had earned her master's degree in social work and was focused on becoming a psychotherapist. Brian had always found Linda intriguing. He found her Midwestern wholesomeness refreshing. She had no airs about her, and he didn't have to work to impress her. Their obviously different life experiences and way of viewing the world both challenged and appealed to him. And now, because of his own experience in psychotherapy with Dr. Albertson, they had found common ground. Brian brought a business perspective to helping Linda set up her practice, and Linda gave him a female perspective on understanding male–female relationships.

Just like when they were college students together, they began meeting for breakfast or lunch on a regular basis.

One afternoon over a cup of coffee, Linda told Brian, "I was attracted to you since we were freshmen at UCLA. But not because of your looks—not that you're not a handsome man—but because of what I sensed behind your persona, a vulnerability that I found appealing."

Brian sat with his eyebrows raised, surprised by Linda's disclosure.

"My vulnerability?" Brian was puzzled.

"Yeah, your vulnerability," continued Linda. "I sensed that there was a sensitive part of you that you seemed to work hard at hiding. I felt it was there, but I couldn't access it. The hard exterior that you put out there to the world, the machismo, I didn't find particularly appealing at all. In fact, I found it off-putting."

Brian grimaced, shaking his head. "I worked hard at being that hard-ass."

"I saw the bravado even at the party where your brother overdosed," said Linda. "I sensed it was an act, but you became the take-charge guy with no feelings. Totally cut off emotionally."

"This is blowing me away," said Brian. "I always thought chicks, I mean women, liked the macho image, the bad boy. I thought they would consider vulnerability a weakness."

"Maybe that's true for some women, but certainly not for all women," said Linda. "And definitely not me." She smiled. Linda enjoyed seeing her friend Brian struggling with issues and opening himself to self-reflection. She felt good about herself, thinking that she was helping him grow.

Brian's head was reeling. He couldn't wrap his mind around the concept that some women could find vulnerability attractive.

*Dr. A said that vulnerability was necessary when it came to developing intimacy,* thought Brian. *He even called it a strength. Now Linda is saying that she found it attractive, and that while women may be attracted to bad boys when just looking to fool around, when it comes to a long-term relationship, vulnerability is what matters. Fuck!*

Brian thought about what Dr. Albertson had said about television shows and characters having been where Brian had learned everything about what it meant to be a man—and television was fiction.

*I've been basing my beliefs and personality on fiction! And what's worse, I've been modeling myself after really fucked up guys. Jason was struggling to find his identity, Tony had serious mommy issues, Harry was ... who knows what!*

# CHAPTER SIXTEEN

# A Big Decision

## *2011*

Alan and Brian continued to grow their businesses and hustle women, but Brian was becoming increasingly dissatisfied with the life he was leading. Alan, on the other hand, loved it. He loved the nightlife, the glitz, the action, and of course, the ladies. Brian continued to want to settle down and have a family. He also wanted out of the internet business, as well as the money-lending operation. He was having thoughts of reinventing himself as a totally legitimate business man. Life in Los Angeles was getting to him. He wanted to do something different.

*I wonder if Linda's Midwestern attitude is rubbing off on me!*

The people around Brian and Alan were moving on with their lives. Martina had remarried and moved to San Diego. Lucas Suarez had got himself in trouble with the law and ended up in jail on forgery charges trying to bring illegal aliens into the U.S. from Mexico using counterfeit documents. Rose Schwartz, who had taught Brian acting, had died, and Nick Pomeranz had developed late-onset Alzheimer's disease.

He was well past ninety years old and did not recognize either Alan or Brian when they visited him in the nursing home.

It was time for Brian to have a conversation with Alan about the future.

"Ya know, bro, I've been thinking," began Brian at one of their strategy sessions. "I think it's time for us to branch out in a different direction."

Alan encouraged his brother to continue. "What did you have in mind?"

Brian hesitated for a moment before making his pitch. Finally, he looked up and said, "We've banked several million dollars each, but I know that you and I have different long-term goals. You want to continue to hustle and enjoy the single, party lifestyle. I want to find a woman, get married, have children, and become a straight businessman. I think I figured out how we can have both."

Alan listened.

"I think we should open an office in another state," continued Brian. "I think it would be a good opportunity for us to create a legitimate, regular business in a separate city, like Chicago, where no one knows us. We could both manage it, capitalizing on being identical twins. No one in Chicago would have known we're twins. We could alternate weeks: one week I'm there and one week you're there. What do think? We'd get to know the businesses in both cities."

Alan sat slack-jawed, obviously surprised. "Wow, bro, as usual, you've been doing some major thinking," he declared. "What brought this on?"

"Yeah, well, I know that we've been moving in different directions," replied Brian. "You like the action, the screwing around, the danger, all of that. And I want something more traditional. We may be identical twins, but we are different. I figure that in a new city where no one knows me, I can be known as just, well, me. Not part of a brand and not as a twin.

Just as Brian. As far as anyone in Chicago would know, the business there would be a sole proprietorship." Brian chuckled. "But in the meantime, this plan would still allow me to fool around in LA every other week until I get settled in Chicago. I don't want to go cold turkey."

Alan smiled and nodded his head in understanding. "I feel you. I can get that," he said. "But what would we, uh, you do there once you're settled? I mean, our internet business can be run from anywhere. We could even find some connections for picking up merchandise in the Chicago area. But what about the rest? Are you thinking of running Party Central in Chicago? That might be cool."

Brian smiled. He felt relieved that his brother was not giving him grief about the idea. "Yeah, we could branch out with the parties into Chicago," said Brian. "I imagine they have a pretty heavy-duty nightlife there, and I imagine the Midwestern millennia crowd likes to party. But I know for sure that I don't want to do the drug stuff at parties, and I am not interested in developing the money-lending operation. I've had my fill of that." He gave Alan a knowing look. "In other words, I want to go totally legitimate, one hundred percent. Catered, pop-up parties work. I was even thinking that we could get into real estate. We have met our goal of becoming millionaires. We have saved a bunch of money, and it's just sitting there. We could invest it. We could even buy an already existing business in Chicago and grow it. I don't know what kind of business, but I figure once we're there, we will be able to do our due diligence and find something to sink our teeth into."

"And what about Linda?" asked Alan. "I thought you and she were an item."

"Nah, we're just very good friends," replied Brian. "She's developing her practice. And she has a boyfriend. With Mom in San Diego and our father in jail, you're the only attachment for me in Los Angeles. And I'm thinking that it's time for us to see what it's like to live apart. In the beginning, we could do the every-other-week thing, like I said, but after a while, word would get out that we have a new business in Chicago, and I'll manage it. It would make for a pretty easy transition. Eventually, I would live full-time in Chicago and run our legitimate businesses from there."

Alan smiled. "Okay, then. It sounds like we have a new plan. When do you think we should begin?"

Now it was Brian's turn to be surprised. He hadn't expected his brother to be so agreeable and willing to embrace the idea of being apart. "I guess, the first thing would be to come up with a more concrete plan, do some homework on the internet, and for me to spend some time visiting Chicago. I've never been there. The only thing I know is that it gets freeze-your-ass-off cold in the winter time. Just the thought of it makes me shiver."

They both laughed.

"Why not choose someplace like Hawaii where it's warm, bro?" asked Alan.

"Too much beach," replied Brian. "Cold winters make young people want to go inside and hibernate. Parties will go over big in Chicago, especially if we bring the LA style to the Midwest: air-conditioned in the summer and warm in the winter. And the Hip, Slick, and Cool flair. Can't miss."

Alan nodded. "On the weeks you're in LA, you're gonna have to play being me, bro. Do you think you can do it? I mean, can you dance on tables?" He laughed at the thought.

Brian smiled. "It'll be a stretch, but yeah, I think I can play the part of being my womb-mate. It's only a week at a time."

Two weeks later, Brian was on a first-class flight to O'Hare Airport. He sat back in his seat, ordered a Scotch on the rocks from the male flight attendant who had welcomed him aboard, and thought about the adventure ahead. This was the biggest moment of his life so far. He had never lived apart from his brother, and now he was planning to live in a separate state altogether.

He felt excited and a bit anxious about his prospects. He and Alan had agreed that they would Skype daily and continue to strategize, but Brian knew that it wouldn't be the same as sitting in their home office face-to-face live. He also knew that once he found a place to live in Chicago, he wouldn't be returning to Los Angeles on a permanent basis. During the every-other-week arrangement, he would be playing a role in LA: he would be Alan. Even that part would be short-lived. Eventually, he would make Chicago his home.

Another flight attendant, a very attractive, caramel-complexioned young woman with a dazzling smile approached his seat carrying a tray with his drink and a bowl of warmed, salted nuts. She gave him a disarming smile as she leaned over to place the drink and warm nuts on the armrest. Brian returned the smile and took a sip of his drink.

"Is Chicago your final destination, Mr. Suarez?" asked the flight attendant.

It always pleased Brian when travelling first-class that the flight attendants knew the names of the passengers. He smiled and nodded, glancing at the attendant's name tag—Natalee Washington.

"Yes, Natalee, it is. Never been there before."

"Oh, it's my hometown," she said. "Are you going for business or pleasure?"

Brian thought for a moment. "A little of both. I am thinking of opening a branch of my business in the windy city. So, I have to get familiar with both the fun stuff and the business climate." Brian gave her a flirtatious smile. "Perhaps you could show me around, Natalee."

Natalee raised one eyebrow. She gave him a knowing smile before moving down the aisle to attend to the other passengers on the plane.

Brian settled into the large leather seat, nursing his drink and musing over his tentative plan for the next few weeks. Instead of booking a hotel, as was his practice for vacations and business trips, this time he had booked a stay through AirBnB. He found an apartment in a high-rise building on North Shore Drive, the northern end of Chicago's main, high-end Miracle Mile commercial district, facing Lake Michigan. He wanted to embed himself in the area in which he intended to live.

Given the infamous Chicago winters, he wanted to also be near where he might find an office space to open HS&C's Midwestern base of operations. His plan was to look around, get a feel for the area, find an apartment, then an office, and begin making connections with brokers and real estate agents who would be open to finding party venues. He figured that once he began connecting with real estate agents, they would soon realize that he would also be on the market to buy an apartment and be ready to negotiate with him. He had a list of agents in the area provided to him by the ones he and Alan had been using in Los Angeles, so he wouldn't have to cold-call.

He knew he wouldn't be able to complete everything on this first trip, but he felt confident that he could make a good beginning and would be happy to just make a few connections. He smiled to himself as he finished his drink, pleased with his plan and looking forward to executing it.

"Care for a refill?" asked Natalee glancing at Brian's empty glass.

"Sure," said Brian. She took his glass, turned, and left.

A few minutes later, she returned with a fresh tumbler of scotch and more nuts. She placed a cocktail napkin on the armrest and slowly placed his drink on it, smiling all the while.

Brian watched her every move. He looked down at his drink and noticed some writing on the napkin. He lifted his glass and saw *Natalee Washington 312-874-9386* and a happy face. He looked up at her and gave her his best and broadest smile. She returned the smile with a wink and moved on. Brian continued to receive a little extra attention from Natalee throughout the flight.

The plane touched down at O'Hare at around 3 p.m. Brian deplaned, mouthing the words "I'll call you" to Natalee as he left.

Standing by the luggage carousel, he saw a tall, sixty-something-year-old gentleman dressed in a black suit and open-collar white shirt holding a sign with the name "Suarez" written on it.

Brian glanced at the napkin Natalee had given him, thought for a moment, and tossed it into the trash as he approached the man with the sign. Brian knew that Natalee, as pretty and as available as she was, would not bring him any closer to finding a girlfriend with whom he could build a future. A hook up with a flight attendant was a part of his old life. Chicago was the beginning of his new life.

Brian smiled and introduced himself to the limo driver. Within a few minutes, Brian's luggage arrived, and they left the terminal. The Cadillac Escalade was illegally parked curbside. Brian smiled. He had found a guy who was willing to take chances.

"Nice wheels," said Brian. "Yours?"

"Yeah," said the driver. "The company requires that you own your own wheels to work for them."

"You must be doing pretty good to have this ride," said Brian.

"I do all right," replied the driver. "But I bought this when I was working at a real job before I retired. Decided to drive because I was bored not having a job. Gives me something to do."

Brian inquired, "What did you do before?"

"I was a cop," he replied. "Chicago PD."

The driver glanced in the rearview mirror. He found it amusing to see how his passengers reacted when he told them he had been a cop.

Brian didn't react. "What made you decide to drive instead of going into security like a lot of cops do?"

"I wanted to be my own boss and make my own hours," he replied. "You here on a visit or is this home?"

"I'm thinking of making it home," answered Brian. "Kinda scouting it out. Needed a change from LA."

The driver chuckled. "You'll find Chi-town a lot different than LA, especially the weather."

Brian smiled and nodded. "That's what I heard."

The driver pulled into the circular driveway of the 1930s built, forty-story building located in the famed Gold Coast area of Lake Shore Drive. Many of the buildings there were considered architectural masterpieces and could be visited on tours. This was one of them. It was quite impressive, Brian thought, not at all like the modern buildings that were being built in Los Angeles.

The doorman hurried to the vehicle and opened the door. Brian stepped out, looked about, and scanned the lake. He nodded in approval. The driver opened the trunk of the Escalade, and the doorman lifted out Brian's luggage.

"Welcome to Chicago, sir," said the doorman.

"Thank you," replied Brian. "I am looking for apartment 3800."

Brian gave the driver a thumbs-up.

The doorman ushered Brian into the building and went behind a desk where he retrieved an envelope with Brian's name written on it.

"Here you are, Mr. Suarez," he said. "It contains two keys, one to the apartment and the other for the elevator. The larger key is for the apartment. I believe you will also find a letter of instructions from the owners. I understand you will be staying with us for two weeks, is that correct?"

Brian nodded. "Yes."

"My name is Lloyd," said the doorman. "The night doorman is Edwin. If you need anything or if we can be of any assistance, do not hesitate to ask us."

"Thank you, Lloyd," said Brian.

"The elevator is right over there, Mr. Suarez," said Lloyd. "Just put the smaller key into the keypad and press number thirty-eight."

Brian took hold of his suitcase handle and rolled it across the marble floor to the elevator. He pressed the button and the door opened. Once inside the elevator, he opened the envelope and found two keys. He followed Lloyd's instructions.

When the elevator opened on the thirty-eighth floor, there were four apartments; number 3800 was directly in front of him. He unlocked the door, let himself in, and found himself in a small foyer facing a huge living room with windows that spanned the entire wall. Brian walked over to the windows where he could see Lake Michigan, the beach, and down toward The Loop, the famous commercial area along Michigan Avenue with its skyscrapers and high-end shopping.

It was quite a different view than what he had been accustomed to in LA. The interior of the apartment was decorated in a combination of classic and modern styles with all the amenities, including an upscale kitchen. Brian unpacked his suitcase, turned on the seventy-inch flat-screen television, and made himself comfortable.

# CHAPTER SEVENTEEN

# New Beginnings

B rian spent the next two weeks making appointments with realtors who showed him condos for sale and apartments for rent. They drove him around the most desirable living spaces in the downtown area, including the fabled brownstones, the more classic buildings like the one he was renting, and the new, modern luxury units.

They all had their appeal for Brian, but he leaned toward the modern units because they were hip, slick, and cool. He also knew that Alan would like them. They fit more with his image.

Driving around Chicago with the real estate agents gave Brian an opportunity to get a sense of the city. The agents were more than willing to function as tour guides and give him the benefit of their knowledge, knowing that he would also be looking for office space, which meant additional commissions.

They told him about the nightlife in Chicago, the in places to eat and drink, and gave him pointers on life in the Midwest. He learned that though Chicago looked a lot like New York or Boston, it had its own style, and Midwestern values were different than either East or West Coast values. Despite

Chicago's notorious history, it was still fundamentally a low-key town.

Brian and Alan had decided that while they were going to rebrand themselves in Chicago as conservative businessmen, they also wanted to be recognized as young, cutting-edge entrepreneurs. They saw their niche as somewhere between staid businessmen and the high-end investment banker types. They joined several business organizations in Chicago, including the Young Presidents Organization and the Chamber of Commerce, where they practiced meeting and greeting other entrepreneurs.

This was a major step for them, especially for Brian, who had always been reserved, even awkward, in social settings. But he pushed himself. When Alan was in Chicago, he found it easier to play the role of Brian than Brian found playing him when in Los Angeles.

By the time three months had passed, the twins had individually settled into the Chicago scene during their alternate weeks in the city. They had bought a condo on Michigan Avenue, rented an office in one of the high-rise buildings in the Loop, and had connected with many of the movers and shakers in the business community.

The realtors were especially helpful in getting their pop-up-parties business off the ground. There were many people in the downtown area who owned apartments but vacated them during the frigid winter months for their second homes in warmer climates, and they were more than willing to rent them out for special events. The moneyed people in Chicago were anxious to leave once the subfreezing temperatures of winter blustered into the windy city. This worked out perfectly for the twins. The winter was the best time to have a party. People wanted to hunker down while still having a good time.

And Brian and Alan knew how to throw a party. Since these venues were private and the events were exclusive, they were not under the same restrictions as the public clubs. They were governed by the same rules as any private party rather than those of a commercial enterprise. They hired bartenders, caterers, and musicians. They even contracted with Uber-like services so that they could send drunken guests home with a designated driver.

The Hip, Slick, and Cool parties soon became all the rage, especially among the millennial crowd. Everything was done in an upscale way, bringing back a feel from the high-society days a la *The Great Gatsby* rather than rave-type clubs featuring heavy metal, grunge, and sweat. It was a classy operation with a LA vibe.

Brian and Alan sold a limited number of tickets to control the crowd and create a climate of exclusivity. Scoring a ticket to one of these events was a prize. The twins knew that making the events feel exclusive and in limited supply would become a big draw for this demographic. It was similar in feel and style to the A-list parties given by and for celebrities who hosted private events, but more affordable and without the requirement of having to be a celebrity. Food was included in the ticket price, but alcohol was purchased through an electronic ticket, similar to a prepaid debit card, which the guests could buy when inside the party. Guests could also purchase a membership to receive advance notification of upcoming parties and assurance of admission and invitations to ultra-exclusive events, such as parties on yachts.

A live band provided the music. All venues were large enough to accommodate a dance area. The entire feeling of the parties was of attending a high-end gala at someone's luxury apartment in a high-rise overlooking the city lights of downtown Chicago. It was a class act and introduced affluent, young adults to something unique. It became an opportunity for people to hook up, create business deals, and feel that they were part of an in-crowd.

Brian and Alan knew how to appeal to egos and snobbery. And they made a lot of money in the process.

As planned, Alan and Brian alternated weeks in Chicago, which gave them both an opportunity to host one of their parties. Since they had decided to be one person rather than twins, they used Brian's name when in Chicago and Alan's name in Los Angeles.

It was at one of these events that Brian met Cynthia Bonaventura, an exotic-looking, tall, athletic-bodied, black-haired young real estate broker. Her eyes were as dark as her hair, and her smile lit up the room. Within the first few minutes of her arrival, she sought Brian out.

"Hi, you're Brian Suarez, right?" Her dark eyes locked on his as she flashed a wide smile, showing her perfectly aligned white teeth.

"Yeah, that's right, I'm Brian," he replied, feeling his pulse elevate.

"I'm Cynthia Bonaventura. Here's my card," she said. "I've heard quite a bit about you and Party Central. You've done business with some of my colleagues."

Brian glanced at her embossed metallic business card and smiled. "Ah, Cynthia Bonaventura, you're a realtor. I imagine you would like some of my business, yes?"

"That's true," she replied, "but mostly I wanted to meet the person who actually thought of this brilliant idea of doing top-of-the-line parties for the well-heeled millennials. Brilliant!"

Cynthia smiled with her eyes as well as her mouth, flipping her hair with a subtle movement of her head.

Brian was flattered. Cynthia was strikingly beautiful, and judging from how she dressed and the accessories she wore, she was obviously successful in her work.

*Smart and gorgeous, what a combo*, he thought.

"I'm glad you like the party, and thanks for the compliment," said Brian, giving her his most gracious smile. "You could probably make a lot of connections here for your business. It's a great networking opportunity, especially in real estate. There are a lot of people here who are up and coming."

Cynthia looked around the room. There must have been a hundred people, all talking and drinking, snagging hors d'oeuvres from servers as they passed through the crowd.

"May I get you a drink, Cynthia?" asked Brian.

"That would be lovely," she responded.

Brian made a slight motion with his hand. As if by magic a smiling server brought two glasses of champagne on a tray. Cynthia, impressed, raised an eyebrow and smiled as Brian handed her a glass and took the other for himself. The server disappeared.

"Are you originally from Chicago?" she asked. "You don't sound like a native."

"You're right," he replied. "I'm from Los Angeles. Home of the Dodgers."

"I thought so. What made you leave the land of sunshine and palm trees?" asked Cynthia, taking a sip of the champagne. "Ever experienced a Chicago winter?"

Brian chuckled. "No, but I've been told about them. It seems that weather is a big topic of conversation here."

"You'll understand why soon enough," she said. "Chicago is a city of weather extremes. Summers are hot and sticky, and winters are frigid. Spring and fall are not so bad. Rather nice, actually. So, why did you leave LA?"

"I was looking for something different," replied Brian. "An adventure. I was born and raised in Los Angeles and thought it might be time for a change."

"I hope you find the adventure here," said Cynthia, giving him a devilish look. "Chicago has a long history. It may seem like a big city, but Illinois is mostly rural; it's farm country. People in the city are different than people outside of the metropolitan area."

"You seem to know a lot about Chicago," said Brian, taking in her flirtatious demeanor. "Is this your home?"

"It's my home now, but I am more of a child of the world," she said, laughing. She tossed her head back as she spoke. "I've lived all over. My father was a career army officer, so we moved around a lot."

"Sounds exciting," said Brian as he casually examined her business card. It was a slick, obviously expensive card with a glossy headshot. Brian smiled. "Perhaps we can have dinner sometime, and you can tell me all about Chicago and your world travels."

"That would be lovely," replied Cynthia. She pointed to her card. "You have my number."

"Yes, I do, um, have your number," said Brian grinning with one eyebrow raised. "And right now, you'll have to excuse me. I must circulate, and you should, too."

And with that, Brian walked off and merged into the crowd.

*** 

As was their custom, during their next Skype call, Brian told Alan about Cynthia. He filled him in on all the pertinent details, keeping him apprised of developments over the weeks ahead.

Brian continued to see Cynthia when he was in Chicago and gave Alan a blow-by-blow account of their interactions. In his previous life, he would have had no problem sharing Cynthia with Alan. They were used to dating the same woman ever since high school. But he was aware that he was becoming more possessive of Cynthia than he had been with other women. He found her intelligent and funny, not to mention beautiful. They enjoyed the same movies and TV shows, which was a first. He had never met a woman who had shared an interest in action drama and shows featuring conmen. She even liked the Jason Bourne movies and was addicted to *Breaking Bad*, both of which had become among Brian's favorites.

Up until this point, Alan had shown no particular interest in meeting Cynthia during his week in Chicago. This had pleased Brian. But when Brian told Alan that he wanted to change their every-other-week schedule to once a month, with Brian visiting LA for only a week each month, Alan became more curious. He sensed that Brian was becoming more involved with Cynthia than he let on.

Alan indicated that the next time he was in Chicago he wanted to call Cynthia and get to know her first-hand. On hearing this, Brian felt something he had never felt before: he felt jealous. He did not want to share Cynthia with his brother.

When he told his brother how he felt, Alan laughed. "Hey, bro, are you fallin' in love?" Alan teased.

Brian blushed. "Love? Me? I don't even know what that means."

But Brian was obviously uncomfortable. He stared at the computer monitor, feeling the perspiration beginning to form on his palms.

"Yeah, you," said Alan, pointing his finger at the monitor. "You're in love!"

Brian didn't know how to respond. He just sat there.

"Bro, it's okay," said Alan. "No problemo. You don't want me bedding her, I won't. But I do want to meet her. So, how about I put on one of our disguises, and you introduce me as a business associate? That way I get to at least meet her, and you get to date her."

Brian looked at his brother. "Cool," he finally said with a smile. "I'm down with that."

They gave each other a virtual fist bump.

"Thanks, bro," said Brian.

***

The next time Alan was scheduled to go to Chicago, he and Brian arranged for him to meet Cynthia at one of Party Central's events.

Not wanting to reveal that they were twins, Alan adopted the style and dress of an uber-successful investment banker. He arrived looking about ten to fifteen years older, graying slightly at the temples, with a short-clipped, black beard and mustache, wearing frameless glasses covering dark-brown eyes, and longish black hair. He wore a dark, pinstriped Armani suit with a red silk pocket square, open-collared custom-fitted white shirt showing just the right amount of cuff, and polished Ferragamo shoes with lifts inserted to add about an inch to his height.

The entire ensemble gave him a sophisticated, urbane look. They had decided in advance that Alan would be Charles Franco, an investor from California Brian had known for several years, who was interested in investing with Brian in Chicago.

Despite the disguise, Brian recognized him immediately. He glided over to where Alan was ordering a drink from the bartender and stood directly behind him. He leaned over Alan's shoulder and whispered, "Hey, bro, lookin' good!"

Alan took the drink offered by the bartender and slowly turned around.

"Well, hello, Brian," said *Charles*, affecting the deep baritone voice he had been practicing. "So nice to see you again."

Brian smiled. "Charles, I am so glad you could make it to this little soiree," he said. "How long will you be in town?"

"I expect to be here for a few days, and then I'm off to New York," replied *Charles*.

"Wonderful. I'd be happy to show you around," said Brian, trying to remain casual and following his brother's lead.

Brian scanned the room and spotted Cynthia. He nodded in her direction. "There's someone I would like you to meet, Charles."

Cynthia joined them.

"Cynthia, I'd like you to meet an old friend and business associate of mine, Charles Franco," said Brian. "Charles, this is Cynthia Bonaventura."

"I'm so pleased to meet you, Charles," said Cynthia, smiling as she extended her hand.

"The pleasure is mine," said *Charles*, giving her a warm handshake and his most dazzling smile. "Brian tells me you are in real estate. Residential or commercial?"

"Both," replied Cynthia, handing him her business card. "If I can help you with anything, please don't hesitate to give me a call."

CHAPTER EIGHTEEN

# Who's Conning Who?

There was something about Cynthia that didn't feel right to Alan. He wondered whether he was just being hyper-suspicious because this was the first time his brother had expressed an interest in someone enough to want a relationship that didn't include sharing. Perhaps he felt threatened. Or just jealous. He knew that if either one of them got into a relationship, it certainly would affect their relationship as brothers.

Once Alan returned to LA, he decided to do some investigating on his own.

Meanwhile, in Chicago, Brian's feelings toward Cynthia continued to grow. They spent several evenings a week together and even managed to squeeze in a few lunches. They enjoyed the same movies, found the same scenes funny, and appreciated good food. Cynthia introduced him to many of the fine restaurants Chicago had to offer. For the first time since Linda, Brian felt comfortable with a woman without having to play a role. With Cynthia, he felt that he was simply being himself.

In Los Angeles, Alan was busy vetting private investigators. He had narrowed his search down to three and eventually settled on Nate Liebowitz, a retired LAPD sergeant who was recommended to him by HS&C's lawyer. Liebowitz had also spent time on the Chicago police force which added to his credibility.

Liebowitz looked like a holdover from the days of *Columbo*, complete with rumpled hair, a wrinkled raincoat, raspy voice, and a half-smoked cigar planted firmly between his teeth. It seemed like he slept in his clothes. Alan liked him and thought that he was cast perfectly for the part. He gave Liebowitz all the information he had on Cynthia Bonaventura, including a picture that Brian had sent him.

"Ya have anything else on her?" asked Liebowitz.

"Like what?" replied Alan.

"A name isn't much to go on, ya know," said Liebowitz. "We don't even know if it is real—or if it's hers. I can check out whether someone with that name holds a real estate license, but it doesn't give a positive ID."

"Do you mean DNA or fingerprints?" asked Alan.

"Either of those would be great," said Liebowitz.

Alan thought for a few minutes and then remembered. He reached into his wallet and carefully retrieved Cynthia's business card. Holding only the edges, he handed it to Liebowitz.

"Do you think this would work?" Alan asked. "Her prints may be on it, but so are mine."

Liebowitz looked at the card, but before taking it, he pulled out a handkerchief from his pocket. Alan dropped the card onto the handkerchief.

Liebowitz nodded. "Yeah, that could work. I'll let you know."

Three weeks later, Liebowitz met with Alan to deliver the report of his investigation. He reported that Cynthia had an unconventional history. She had worked many a con with an uncle who had become her guardian when she was eight years old after her parents were killed in an auto accident.

The uncle was a longtime grifter, who had taught her the tricks of the trade. She had lived her life as a grifter, conning people, developing scams, picking pockets, and other unconventional activities. Liebowitz told Alan that Cynthia had a rap sheet, mostly consisting of small-time offenses. Other than her uncle, she was attached to no one.

Alan gave Liebowitz the go-ahead to find Cynthia's uncle and, if necessary, get some help to convince the uncle to reveal what kind of scam Cynthia and he had cooked up.

Liebowitz took two beefy associates with him and was able to find Cynthia's uncle. The mere presence of the two associates made it so Liebowitz had no difficulty persuading the uncle to reveal the information about Cynthia. He told Liebowitz that Cynthia was looking for a bigger score than the penny-ante stuff she had been doing. And she wanted to do it without the uncle. She wanted to hook up with a wealthy man who could introduce her to more well-to-do clientele, whom she could scam. She figured that if she could seduce a well-connected guy to give her credibility and be her ticket of admission, she could then come up with a scam that would set her up for life.

Cynthia was ambitious and was thinking about her future. Instead of petty cons, her uncle told them, she wanted to enter society where the pickings were bigger, better, and greener. According to her uncle, she viewed Brian, a successful businessman, as her entree into the upscale world of the affluent Chicagoans. Brian was Cynthia's mark.

The uncle told Liebowitz that he was pissed at her because she did not intend to include him in on the con. She was cutting him out of a potentially big score, and he resented it.

Liebowitz reported all of this to Alan who, protective of his brother, instantly became angry. He knew he had to tell Brian, and the sooner the better.

"Hey, bro," said Alan as he stared at Brian's face on his laptop monitor. "How's it going?"

"Great," replied Brian with a grin. "Life is good, my brother. Better than good. Wassup?"

Brian knew his brother better than anyone else in the world and could immediately sense that something was amiss.

"I got something to tell you that you're not going to like, bro," said a sober-faced Alan. "It has to do with Cynthia."

"Cynthia? What?" replied Brian, feeling his stomach tighten.

"She's not who she appears to be, bro," said Alan. "I hired a PI—"

"You did what?" exclaimed Brian.

"A private investigator," said Alan. "I was worried about you. You've been seeing a lot of her, I know. But something didn't feel right to me. So, I—"

"So, you hired someone to spy on her? What the fuck!" yelled Brian, his spittle hitting his monitor.

"Not exactly spying, but just looking into her background, checking her out," replied Alan. "And I was right, bro. She's not who she says she is. She's playing you."

Brian went dead silent. Alan could see the anguish in his brother's eyes as he struggled between anger and curiosity. He knew Brian was falling in love with Cynthia and thought of her as "the one." Now he had to shatter that bubble.

Brian felt stunned, both by his brother's deception in hiring a PI without telling him and on hearing that Cynthia might have been playing him. He finally pulled himself together.

"I'm pissed that you went behind my back to hire a PI and didn't tell me about it," said Brian glaring at his brother.

"I got your back, bro, not behind your back," replied Alan. "If I had told you about it, you would have tried to stop me. You're so smitten with this chick that you can't see straight. Now do you want to hear what I found out, or do you still want to rant about it?"

Brian took a deep breath. "Tell me."

"First of all," began Alan, speaking in a matter-of-fact tone, "her name isn't Cynthia Bonaventura. It's Cynthia Malenovich. She's never been out of the United States. Everything she knows about Europe came from the internet. Her parents died in an auto accident when she was eight, and her father's brother, Josef Malenovich, became her legal guardian. Malenovich is a small-time con and grifter. He taught Cynthia everything, and together, they went from town to town around the country scamming people, picking pockets, you name it. She's spent a fair amount of time in juvenile detention. As an adult, she was busted on a bunch of stuff, mostly misdemeanors, but she was always able to either plea-bargain or talk herself out of the situation. You may have noticed she can be quite charming."

He paused to give his brother time to absorb what he had been saying.

"You with me, bro?" he asked.

Brian nodded. "I hear you. Tell me the rest." By this time Brian was in bad-assed-twins-in-black mode. "How'd you get all of this intel?"

"The PI, Nate Liebowitz—former LAPD and Chicago PD—was able to trace Cynthia through her fingerprints lifted from those fancy metallic business cards she hands out," replied Alan. "He located her uncle and with the help of a couple of goons was able to extract the entire story from Malenovich.

"Cynthia and Malenovich had a falling out when Cynthia decided she was going out on her own, cutting Malenovich out. According to Malenovich, she thought of herself as too upscale for the small-time scams they had been doing and wanted to become a society grifter. She believed that she could do better on her own; she saw Malenovich as more of a burden than as an asset. He told Liebowitz that Cynthia was looking for a high-end mark to hook up with and who could introduce her to a wealthy Chicago crowd and greener pastures. Guess who's her mark?"

Accepting that he had been played, Brian was furious. Rather than being angry at his brother, he was furious with Cynthia.

"That bitch!" he exclaimed. "I'll clip her tonight! Done! Finito! Adios! Sayonara, baby!" He glared at the screen, his eyes flashing.

Alan gave him a crooked smile without saying anything.

After a few moments, Brian broke the silence. "What? What are you smiling about?"

"I've been thinking," replied Alan. "What's better than clipping her? Sweeter? She fucked with you. She messed with your head."

Brian thought for a moment. Then a smile began to spread across his face. "Vendetta!" he said.

Alan nodded slowly. "Revenge. You got it. We should come up with a plan to take her down. No one out hustles the twins! Fuck us once, we fuck you double! Game on!"

They gave each other a virtual high five.

CHAPTER NINETEEN

# The Setup

Brian continued to see Cynthia, but now it was different. Now he was in HS&C mode; he was emotionally closed down in true Jason Bourne style, while playing the role of a charming boyfriend.

He and Alan had decided that if they were going to take Cynthia down, they would have to first see what she was up to. She would have to reveal her hand, and then they could figure out how to use her plan against her. Having this common mission brought Brian and Alan back into alignment. Despite their differences, they were back to being *the twins* and having their weekly strategy sessions just as before Brian moved to Chicago.

It didn't take long for Brian to forgive Alan for going behind his back by hiring Liebowitz. He knew that Alan was looking after him. But he also knew that Alan was thinking of himself, as he always had. He knew that Alan wanted to be in control and that Cynthia was a threat to that control. But Brian was willing to accept that part of his brother; it was more important that they stay connected. Ironically, rather than driving them apart, Cynthia was bringing them together. She had become the common enemy. Having a common adversary became the mainstay of their bond.

While Alan and Brian continued to strategize, Alan kept in contact with Liebowitz, who continued to dig into Cynthia's past.

Brian sustained his relationship with Cynthia, though it was a struggle for him. On the one hand, he remembered how much he liked her and enjoyed her company; on the other hand, he saw her as the enemy, the woman he knew was working him for her own ends, against whom he wanted to exact revenge. He found himself flip-flopping from one extreme to the other, working hard to maintain his focus on the mission: take down the bitch.

Alan had no problem maintaining focus. He was enjoying fantasizing all sorts of scenarios where he and his brother one-upped Cynthia. He was Rocky Balboa knocking out Apollo Creed. He had little compassion for Brian and the struggle he was going through. For Alan, just knowing that Cynthia was playing his brother and, by association, him was enough reason for him to believe that Brian should be able to simply clip her from his heart. But for Brian, it wasn't that easy.

In the meantime, Cynthia was busy with her own agenda. While she enjoyed her time with Brian, in addition to her real estate business, she was passionate about her newest project, developing a nonprofit charity to benefit animals that were on the Endangered Species List. She hired people to set up a website as well as a social media presence, making sure that the nonprofit had all the appearances of both legitimacy and longevity.

The site described the plight of animals from all over the world that were on the verge of extinction. It included National Geographic–quality photographs and videos of the animals and their habitats. She paid people to write articles about the charity along with interviews and testimonials showing her dedication to the cause. Her computer people were quite good at what they did, giving her a presence and authenticity that only the most sophisticated computer experts could determine were fake.

Brian and Cynthia got together a couple of times a week for dinner. One evening, Cynthia suggested that they try an Argentinian restaurant she had heard about where servers would bring various cuts of meat to each table, slicing off portions for patrons. It was an all-you-can-eat type of place.

While the meat courses were served tableside, salads and vegetables were served at a buffet. Located on each table was a half-red and half-green statuette which the patrons would turn to indicate they were ready to be served. Green indicated service requested, and red indicated no service. It was a very popular venue with lots of activity and an upbeat vibe with people milling about retrieving their food and wait-servers rolling carts of lamb, beef, pork, and chicken, slicing portions as requested.

Brian and Cynthia were shown to their table where their cocktail order was immediately taken. They each ordered a martini, Cynthia preferring Grey Goose vodka and Brian requesting Bombay Sapphire gin.

This was not the type of restaurant that Brian typically would choose. He preferred upscale dining, where servers catered to his preferences. Though he could enjoy a hamburger and French fries from a food truck for lunch, when it came to dinner, he preferred to be served. Why Cynthia would choose this place both surprised and confused him. When she decided to choose the restaurant, he assumed she would select one of the many high-end Chicago eateries. Part of him liked the fact that she chose an ethnic, family-style restaurant. It didn't fit with his perception of her as a gold-digging con artist, looking to take advantage of him. And he felt drawn to her.

Their martinis arrived, hers with a lemon twist and his with olives. They clinked glasses and took a sip.

"Perfect," said Brian with satisfaction. "I didn't expect it."

Cynthia raised her eyebrows. "Why's that?" she asked.

"I guess, I only expect really good drinks in high-end places," he replied.

Cynthia smiled. "You're a snob, ya know."

Brian paused, giving thought to what she said. "I suppose you're right," he replied, nodding. "I guess I am."

"I thought you might like a typical Argentinian restaurant given that it is, after all, part of your culture, no?" said Cynthia, smiling as she took a sip of her drink.

That she remembered his heritage touched Brian. *She's good*, he thought.

A moment later, a woman, carrying a plate of salad from the buffet stopped by their table. She was stylishly dressed and well-coifed, with a large diamond glittering on her finger.

"Cynthia!" she exclaimed. "Fancy meeting you here. How are you?"

Cynthia looked up, surprised to see Mary Edgewater standing there smiling down on her and holding a plate of salad.

"Mary, I never would have expected to find you in this type of place," said Cynthia. "What, are you just trying to see how the other half lives?"

"Actually, this is one of my husband's and my favorite places," replied Mary. "We love Argentinian cooking. Ever since we spent some time in Buenos Aires, it has become our go-to place."

Mary glanced at Brian waiting to be introduced.

"Oh, excuse me," said Cynthia, a bit flustered. "I was so, well, surprised that I … Anyway, Mary, I'd like you to meet my friend, Brian Suarez. Brian, I'd like you to meet Mary Edgewater. Mary owns an art gallery here in town."

Brian stood and extended his hand. Mary switched her salad from her right hand to her left in order to shake Brian's hand. "It's a pleasure to meet you, Mary," said Brian.

"The pleasure is mine, Brian," said Mary with a smile.

As Brian sat back down, Mary turned to Cynthia. "I am so glad to run into you. I've been meaning to contact you. I've got something for you. Give me a minute. I'll be right back."

Mary left for her table. Brian looked at Cynthia questioningly. Cynthia shrugged.

Within a minute, Mary was back with her checkbook and pen in hand. "Ever since your last email telling about the jaguars, I've been meaning to send you a contribution." She hastily wrote out a check and handed it to Cynthia. "Now I feel better," she said. "It was a pleasure meeting you, Brian. Enjoy the food."

And with that, she was gone.

"Jaguars?" asked Brian. "What's up with that?"

Cynthia explained, "I have a nonprofit charity that raises funds for preserving, rescuing, and sheltering animals that are on the verge of extinction, especially large animals like jaguars, elephants, and apes."

"Really?" said Brian, shaking his head in disbelief. "You never cease to amaze me. Where are these animals and what made you decide to do this?"

Cynthia smiled. "The animals are all over the world. The people in these countries want to save the animals. They have secured refuges but don't have the funds to either support them or to guard them. Poachers continue to raid the sanctuaries, killing the animals for their pelts or capturing them for private parties. I saw a documentary on the subject and was so moved that I decided to do something."

"That's so cool," said Brian. It was difficult for him to believe that this woman, interested in saving animals, was somehow going to scam him. "Why didn't you tell me about it and ask for a contribution?"

Cynthia's eyes sparkled as she stared at him. "I didn't want you to think that I was dating you for your money," she said. "I know a lot of people are interested in you just for what you can do for them. This happens to all people with wealth. You never know whether people actually like you or just want to use you for their own ends. I didn't want to be in that category."

Brian reached across the table and placed his hand on hers. "I appreciate that, Cynthia. And I would like to help. It sounds like a great charity."

Cynthia smiled in appreciation.

"Tell you what," said Brian, "I'll match whatever amount Mary just gave you."

"But you don't even know how much it is for," said Cynthia in surprise.

"No matter," said Brian, giving her a wide grin.

Cynthia showed Brian the check. Brian glanced at the amount as well as the name of the charity: International Wild Animal Preservation Foundation.

"Ten thousand dollars. Done."

He reached into his jacket and retrieved his leather-bound checkbook from one breast pocket and his Montblanc pen from the other. He quickly wrote out a check and handed it to her.

"I don't know what to say, Brian," said Cynthia, her eyes welling up in appreciation. "That's very generous of you."

"If there is anything else I can do, please don't hesitate to ask me," said Brian.

Cynthia nodded as she folded the check and placed it in her handbag.

Brian glanced in the direction of Mary Edgewater's table. She, too, was glancing their way. She smiled and nodded. Brian returned the nod.

He and Cynthia continued their meal, tasting each of the cuts of meat as the servers brought them to their table. Brian ordered a bottle of Cabernet Sauvignon to pair with the various meats.

Brian enjoyed Cynthia's company and found it difficult to reconcile what he knew about her and how he felt towards her. He kept switching between being Jason Bourne and being himself. He looked forward to talking with both his brother and Dr. Albertson. He wanted to share what he had learned about Cynthia's charity with Alan and talk to his therapist about his confused feelings.

# CHAPTER TWENTY

# The Big Con

The next day, Brian connected with his brother. He explained how Cynthia was running an international charity for helping protect endangered animals around the globe. He told him about his contribution and having visited the charity website.

Alan pulled it up on his screen while they were Skyping. He, too, was impressed.

"It sure looks legit, bro," said Alan. "Very impressive. Must have cost a small fortune just to set it up, especially with the video clips of the animals. I'll have our PI guy look into it. There are all sorts of regulations governing nonprofit organizations."

Brian felt his stomach churn. He wanted the charity to be legit. He didn't want to believe Cynthia was not as sincerely into him as he was into her. He didn't mind that she was a grifter; he only minded being her mark.

"You said that someone stopped by the table and gave Cynthia a check," said Alan. "What was her name?"

"Her name?" asked Brian. "What, you think she might have been a plant?"

"Maybe," said Alan.

"Uh, Mary Edgewater," replied Brian. "I think she's an art dealer. I seem to remember Cynthia mentioning that Mary and her husband own a gallery."

"I'm gonna get right on this," said Alan, signing off.

Brian continued to stare at his monitor.

He thought, *One day I feel great, and the next, I feel like a total sucker. I'd better get my act together.*

He noticed his hands were sweating.

***

A new email popped up on his screen that caught his attention. Dr. Albertson had replied to Brian's email requesting an urgently needed appointment. He was available in an hour. Brian smiled as he replied with his confirmation.

*Doc always comes through*, he thought.

"Hello, Brian," said Dr. Albertson. "It's nice to see you again. How can I be of help?"

While not perfect, the virtual sessions worked well, especially when there was a good internet connection. And Skyping made getting appointments easier for both of them despite the two-hour time difference.

"Hi, Doc," said Brian. "I'm glad you could see me today. I've got a real problem that's confusing the hell out of me."

"What's up, Brian?"

"I've been dating this girl here in Chicago," began Brian. "And I really like her. But I just found out from my brother that she is not who she says she is. She's kinda like me; she's a hustler, a con artist."

Dr. Albertson chuckled. "How did you find that out, Brian?"

"What's so funny, Doc?" asked Brian.

"Of all the people in the world to be attracted to, you were able to find someone who's a grifter. I find that amusing," said Dr. Albertson. He wasn't judging. He was just being honest.

"I guess. But it doesn't feel funny on this end," said Brian. "When I told my brother about her a few weeks ago, he decided to hire a private detective to do a background check on her and found out that she had a rap sheet and was using a false name. It's a long story. Bottom line—we think she's trying to pull a con with me as the mark. In the meantime, I learned that she is running a nonprofit charity trying to save wild animals. So, it confuses me. I really like being with her, but I am also concerned that she may be pulling a fast one on me."

"I can understand why it would be confusing," said Dr. Albertson. "You enjoy being with her, and the two of you have a lot in common. You find yourself liking her in spite of the information you've collected suggesting that she may be taking you for a ride. And your liking her may be getting in the way of your judgment. Is that it?"

"You got it, Doc," said Brian. "If she was just a grifter, it wouldn't bother me. But if she's hustling me, well, that just pisses me off. I think it's the deception that really gets to me, and the fact that I didn't see it coming."

"The fact that you didn't see it coming, that she was able to deceive you, really gets to you, right?" asked the doctor.

"Yeah. I guess, it's an ego thing," replied Brian. "And I really like her. I thought she was into me, too."

"And it hurts, I'll bet," added Dr. Albertson.

"Yeah, and it hurts," acknowledged Brian.

"The good news is that you met someone with whom you feel connected and somewhat attached," said Dr. Albertson. "And you let yourself feel something for someone. And not just about sex."

"I guess. But if it turns out that she is conning me, that'll be the end of that," said Brian.

"All people have a light and a dark side, Brian," said Dr. Albertson. "Even you. Sure, this woman may be playing you. And you can still feel connected to her even if she is scamming you. You connect to her light side. The good part of her."

"Yeah, but if she's hustling me, I want revenge!" exclaimed Brian emphatically.

"And exactly what would revenge get you?" asked Dr. Albertson.

"Satisfaction!" replied Brian.

"But if you find out that in fact she is planning to hustle you, then you've discovered her intention," pointed out Dr. Albertson. "You can simply confront her with what you've learned and be done with her. Why do you need to exact revenge? You could just cut her loose. Why wouldn't that be enough?"

"Fuck us once, we fuck you double," said Brian.

"Excuse me? What does that mean?" asked Dr. Albertson.

"It's something my brother and I say," replied Brian. "If someone screws us, we screw them back, only worse."

"I see. But where does that get you?" asked Dr. Albertson. "Other than making you feel good for a moment, where does revenge get you?"

Brian left the session still feeling agitated. He didn't like the idea that someone was running a scam on him, and he didn't want to find out that Cynthia was just playing him; he couldn't believe that all the good times they had together were merely part of a setup. He liked her and that made it hurt all the more.

*Nobody fucks with the twins,* he thought. *Revenge is payback. She's got to be shown who's the boss. I'm not got gonna be her bitch!*

A few days later, Alan told him Liebowitz had learned that the International Wild Animal Preservation Foundation was a bogus charity with an offshore bank account in the Cayman Islands. All funds given to the charity ended up in that account, with none of it leaving. Online contributions went directly into this account, along with all checks and other contributions. There were no papers filed registering the International Wild Animal Preservation Foundation as a nonprofit charitable organization, nor were there any articles of incorporation filed in the U.S. Everything was bogus.

Despite knowing for certain that Cynthia was setting up a con, they still didn't know when, or how, she was setting it up. Brian and Alan simply waited for her to make the first move. Their strategy would depend on what she did; they would then figure out a way to turn the tables on her.

A dark cloud settled over Brian. He really liked Cynthia, and despite the evidence, he did not want to believe that she was betraying him. Each time he thought about it, he felt like a sucker. The only relief he felt came when he contemplated his vendetta. Anger made him feel strong.

One evening, while Brian and Cynthia were having dinner at their favorite steakhouse, Cynthia looked over at Brian and said, "Remember when you told me that you would like to help my International Wild Animal Preservation Foundation?"

Brian nodded.

"Well, I've been thinking about doing a major fund-raising event," continued Cynthia. "You know, some kind of a gala event, maybe even a formal dinner dance. I was thinking that I could have some animal preservationist speak, maybe even have a comedian to liven things up, and a silent auction where people could bid on items donated by both individuals and vendors. Something like that. What do you think?"

Brian looked across the table; he could feel his heart accelerating.

*This is it,* he thought, *this is the con. I gotta remain cool.*

He took a sip of his drink and began to nod. "Sounds like a good idea," he said. "I've been to several of those types of events. They are usually a lot of fun, and people spend money knowing it is all going to charity." He smiled. "How can I help?"

Cynthia gave him one of her warmest smiles. "Oh, I am so glad you like the idea. I was thinking that since you have all sorts of connections with venues for parties, perhaps you could help me find a good place to hold the event." She paused. "And, of course, if you would be willing to invite your rich friends and business associates, that would also help. High rollers and big spenders who are willing to support the animals with their generosity."

*The bitch is good*, he thought. *I gotta give her that!*

Brian's brain was already engaged. He knew that once Cynthia needed something from him, he could then set up his own con. This was the type of situation that he and Alan had trained themselves for: the art of the hustle.

"I'd be happy to help, my love," he said with a smile as he reached across the table and placed his hand on top of hers. "Just tell me what you need. Perhaps I can be your assistant. After all, I do know something about setting up events."

Cynthia squeezed his hand. "Oh, thank you. That would be great. And it could be fun for us to be doing something together."

Cynthia was clearly excited. She was effusive in her appreciation. Brian too was excited, but for entirely different reasons. He knew that he and Alan had to be clever if they were to out-con the con. The thought of it excited him. He was going to exact his revenge. While Cynthia thought she was using him, he knew he was going to turn the tables on her. He was not going to be her mark. She was his.

He could hardly wait to leave the restaurant, call his brother, and begin their familiar strategy sessions. He knew he would have to stay close to Cynthia and work with her in the planning of the event, while at the same time continue to work with Alan in making their own plans to take her down.

Back in his condo, Brian immediately set up a video call with Alan. He told his brother about his conversation with Cynthia and how he was going to help her set up a gala fund-raising event at one of their party venues.

"We gotta be careful, bro," said Alan. "Remember, she's a pro. If she detects anything, we're dead meat. One of the worst things we can do is to become too cocky."

"She may be good, but we're better," replied Brian. "But you're right. Nick always said that one of the most difficult operations is to outcon a con. But he also said that when done right, it can be the most satisfying."

"Right now, we have the advantage," said Alan. "We know she's trying to con us, but she doesn't know we know and that she's our mark. We gotta keep it that way. Remember, we gotta keep the home-court advantage. She's playing in our backyard."

They both grinned.

"If we're gonna put together a major event, we're gonna need some help," stated Brian. "We need to have our people keeping an eye on things. And, of course, we know that she will have her people there as well. It would be nice to know who they are beforehand."

"You'll have an inside track since you'll be working with her as her assistant," said Alan. "You gotta keep her thinking that she's running the show. You have to remember to play along as the mark, while at the same time gently leaning on her to move in a direction that we want her to go. This has to be your Oscar-winning performance, bro."

# CHAPTER TWENTY-ONE

# The Gala

As the weeks passed, Cynthia and Brian made plans for the charity event to be held at one of Chicago's most prestigious addresses. The home was for sale at around twelve million dollars and was currently vacant. Brian knew the broker and was able to work out a deal where the home could be rented for a charitable cause.

The home was an electrical substation built in 1929 that had been converted to become a mega-mansion with fifteen thousand square feet of living space and a spacious outdoor garden. A perfect venue for a spring affair that could make use of both the indoor ballroom and the outdoor gardens.

Cynthia had decided that she wanted the gala to be a black-tie event with an air of glamour reminiscent of the speakeasy days of the 1920s. Similar to Brian, she was intrigued with the old style of the period when everything seemed very opulent. Brian helped her create the buzz, presenting the gala as the charitable event of the season, where tickets were available for a thousand dollars each. A table of eight could be bought for seventy-five hundred.

Brian's reputation for throwing classy, opulent parties insured that the buzz made this a must-attend event. He knew that words such as "exclusive," "private," and "elite" would make snagging a ticket or two highly desirable by affluent people suffering from FOMO, fear of missing out.

Promoting the affair as a charitable event gave an added incentive for people to spend big. It assuaged their class-conscious righteousness to be donating to charity, not to mention that they would be able to list their expenses as a tax deduction for income tax purposes. Rich people knew how to game the system. They could have a good time at Uncle Sam's expense. With twenty-five tables, Cynthia's charity would rake in a minimum of two hundred thousand dollars just on ticket sales.

The silent auction included vacations at exotic locations, courtside tickets to basketball games, box seats at baseball games, fifty-yard line at football games, and coveted theater and concert tickets. Bottles of rare whiskeys and high-end wines along with gift certificates for dining in the finest, most exclusive restaurants were also available to the highest bidder.

There was a Jet Ski available as well as jewelry, paintings, sculptures, and an assortment of other sought-after items. One of major raffles was for a private jet trip for eight people to Las Vegas with a four-day stay at one of the luxury hotels on the strip.

But the big-ticket items were the people. Brian and Cynthia knew that hobnobbing with the rich and famous in the hopes of striking a deal or snagging a selfie was a big motivator for the attendees.

Part of Cynthia's responsibility was to get people to write big checks for the charity. She had a knack for working a room; she knew how to manipulate people, motivate them, seduce them, and in the end, make them reach for their checkbooks.

She introduced Brian to her team of very attractive women and men who were specifically trained to encourage people to both bid high at the auction and write individual checks to the charity. They also served as escorts and as Cynthia's eyes and ears on the ground, picking up bits of information and reporting them directly to Cynthia.

She presented her team to Brian and the guests as people who came from the countries where the animals were the most endangered. She explained that they were gifted in the art of presenting the charity to guests in such a way that they couldn't resist making a sizable donation.

Unbeknownst to Cynthia, Brian had hired several security guards who reported directly to him. Not only were they to maintain security for the guests and facility, but they were to keep an eye on Cynthia and her associates as well.

Cynthia had prepared a short documentary about the charity that was to be shown while dinner was being served. The video included photos of the animals, the wildlife preserves, the sanctuary, and the personnel. She told Brian that her associates would be introduced to the guests as resources to be able to answer questions about the charity and the animals they were trying to help.

Brian told Alan about Cynthia's plans and how the event was progressing. When he told his brother about her team, Alan suggested that they find out more about them and how they might be influenced to switch loyalties.

"Money talks," said Brian. "I have no doubt that they are all a bunch of small-time grifters for hire. We just have to find out who they are and where they are. The rest is easy."

Alan agreed, "I think I should pay a visit to Cynthia's uncle. He should at least know who many of them are and where they could be found; they could then roll over on the rest. Grifters are all about the money. And remember, there's no love lost between Cynthia and her uncle since she cut him out of her plans for entering high society." Alan grinned.

It turned out that Malenovich, Cynthia's uncle, not only could give them a list of Cynthia's associates, but he was also happy to play a part in taking her down. He, too, enjoyed revenge.

Alan contacted Liebowitz who, in turn, located Cynthia's team. It didn't take nearly as much convincing as he thought it would to turn them to work for the twins. Cynthia's associates had no great loyalty to her. Like most grifters, Cynthia and her associates did not attach to people. They merely went where the opportunities to make a buck led them. Liebowitz simply brought them all together, asked them what the maximum was they could expect to earn for their night's work, and doubled it. He also intimated that if they crossed him, he would do them serious physical damage. He put together a short dossier on each of them, along with photos. He gave these to the twins so that they would know the cast of characters.

On the date of the event, Brian and Cynthia spent the day at the venue insuring that everything was exactly the way Cynthia had envisioned it. The party planner she had hired to work with Brian to oversee and coordinate the event was busy running around making calls and checking things off on a clipboard she clutched in her hand at all times.

By the time evening rolled around, everything was totally under control. Nothing was left to chance; every detail was thought through, from the floral arrangements on each of the tables to the dinner plates to the colors and the types of wine being served and the glasses in which they were served. This was similar to putting together a very high-end wedding. Cynthia was looking to score big.

There were many rooms in this fifteen-thousand-square-foot mansion, several for entertainment purposes. There was a combination bar and billiard room which, with a few adjustments, was decorated to resemble a speakeasy complete with vintage glassware, stools, and other artifacts of the 1920s. When the lights were dimmed, attendees would think they were transported to the gangster days of downtown Chicago.

Another room was set up for the auction. There were long tables on which the various donated items were on display. People could sign their name on a pad indicating the amount they were bidding for the item. In addition, there was to be a live auction for the more expensive pieces such as the Jet Ski, some of the jewelry, and a few of the paintings. Several of these pieces were on consignment and would be returned if the minimum reserve price was not met during the auction. There were also a few items, including a trip by private jet to Las Vegas, that were to be raffled off with raffle tickets being sold at one hundred dollars each.

There was another room reserved for gaming tables: high-end poker and black jack and even baccarat. Another "exclusive" room was for the ultra-high rollers. Cynthia knew people loved to gamble, and the more they drank, the more they spent … and lost.

The grand ballroom was set up for dinner and a dance floor with a live jazz band providing the music.

The stage was set. It was showtime.

Limos, UberSELECT vehicles, and luxury cars began to arrive. The valets, dressed in tails, graciously opened doors and discharged guests in their evening gowns and tuxedos, and whisked the cars off to be parked.

When the guests entered the venue, they were awed, swept into a world reserved for another time, another era. Champagne servers poured Cristal as guests entered the large foyer and were directed toward the various rooms. Other servers carried trays of hors d'oeuvres among the guests.

Cynthia looked radiant. She was wearing a Christine D'Or gown, diamond teardrop earrings, and Christian Louboutin shoes. Tasteful, elegant, and understated.

Brian looked equally elegant in his Armani custom-cut tuxedo and his antique Patek Philippe watch.

It didn't take long for the atmosphere to feel festive. The bar was doing brisk business. The bartenders were pouring specialized cocktails and brand-name beverages, keeping the guests buzzed, but insuring that no one became unruly. The motive was to keep the guests loose enough and sober enough to spend freely. If anyone became obnoxious, sick, or in any way troublesome, they were immediately reported to Cynthia or Brian, or at the security guards discretion, they were escorted to a separate room to sober up or were asked to leave.

Brian and Cynthia mingled with the guests, shaking hands and introducing themselves to many of the unknown attendees. Brian introduced Cynthia to the wealthiest of the guests whom he had invited, letting her know a bit about each of them as they approached or during his gracious introduction.

It was common and expected at charitable events to extol the financial successes of the guests. The guests knew that they were there to donate to the cause and expected to be nudged to write a check or bid high at the auctions. Everyone was made to feel that they had a stake in the success of the event. And they could tell from the opulence all around them that this was not a budget event.

Alan was an early arrival. He was disguised as Charles Franco, the investment banker Brian had introduced to Cynthia early on in their relationship. Cynthia recognized him immediately.

"Hello, Charles, it's so nice to see you again," she said, kissing him on both cheeks. "I hope you have an enjoyable time at this event. And of course, I hope you brought your checkbook. The animals can use all the help they can get."

*Charles* smiled. "Indeed, I did," he replied. "I've been looking forward to this event ever since Brian told me about it. I'm very impressed with what you are trying to do and want to be as much help as I can be."

"Have you seen Brian yet?" asked Cynthia.

"No, I haven't," replied *Charles*, helping himself to a glass of champagne off a tray being carried by one of the wait staff. "I just arrived and was going surprise him."

"I'm sure he'll be happy to see you," said Cynthia.

"There he is," said *Charles*, looking over Cynthia's head. He waved his hand.

Brian gave his old friend a hug. "Charles, it's so nice to see you. I wasn't sure you were going to make it."

*Charles* lifted his glass to Brian and said, "I wouldn't miss this for the world. I was telling Cynthia just a moment ago that I've been looking forward to this event ever since you told me about it."

Brian smiled. "Well, I hope you have a good time. Right now, Cynthia and I have a lot of hands to shake. So, if you'll excuse us, we must circulate. We'll catch up later. There's a gaming room off to the side of the bar if you're interested in trying your luck. Keep in mind, it's not about winning, it's about charity. Have fun."

And with that, he and Cynthia slipped into the crowd.

While Brian was mingling, he felt a hand on his shoulder. He turned and found himself looking at another guest he had invited, a handsome, sophisticated gentleman by the name of Michael Shore.

Michael stood a little taller than Brian and had brown eyes, a bit of premature graying at the temples, and a thin mustache. His tuxedo was obviously custom-made, making him look trim and fit as though he had arrived on the red carpet for the Oscars. Next to him, Brian always felt a bit disheveled.

"Michael," said Brian. "I am so glad you were able to come to our little soiree. What brings you to the windy city?"

Before Michael could answer, Brian turned to Cynthia.

"Cynthia, this is Michael Shore. Michael is one of the largest real estate developers on the West Coast, with corporate offices in Los Angeles."

He turned toward Michael. "Michael, may I introduce Cynthia Bonaventura, the founder of International Wild Animal Preservation Foundation? She will be your hostess this evening."

Cynthia extended her hand. Michael took it in both of his, nodding and smiling broadly.

"It is a pleasure to meet you, Cynthia," he said. "I am very interested in talking with you about your work. It is terrible how hunters are permitted to kill off the large animals, only to have them stuffed and used as trophies."

Cynthia smiled. "It would be my pleasure," she said. "Perhaps we could talk a bit a little later after dinner or—"

"Or perhaps we could meet for dinner tomorrow before I return to Los Angeles?" Michael gave her his most charming smile.

"Perhaps," replied Cynthia, giving him a demure smile in return. "But right now, I must mingle."

Both men watched as Cynthia glided off into the crowd. No sooner had she left than one of the security team approached Brian.

"There is a matter that needs your attention, Mr. Suarez," he said.

Brian turned to Michael. "We'll catch up later," he said as he followed the security agent into the gaming room.

The agent pointed toward a heavyset, boisterous man in his mid-thirties at the blackjack table. "He's been harassing the dealer, trying to get her to give him a private tour of the premises. Says he's a friend of yours."

Brian looked in the direction of the table. He didn't recognize anyone sitting there. He walked over to the table and introduced himself to the players.

"Is everyone having a good time? Anything I can do for you to help loosen your wallets and checkbooks for the animals?"

The heavyset man looked over at Brian. "Yeah, you can instruct this young thing to give me a tour of this place, and I'll write a ten-thousand-dollar check to the International Wild Animal Preservation Foundation!"

The man was obviously drunk and getting a bit out of control. Brian walked over to him and placed his arm around his shoulder.

"That's quite generous of you, my friend," said Brian, maintaining control of both the man and the situation. "For that kind of donation, you deserve more than a dealer giving you a tour. I bet I could get Cynthia Bonaventura herself to take you on a tour."

The man's face lit up. "Really? Cynthia B herself?"

Brian smiled and nodded. "The lady herself. Deal?"

"Deal!" the man replied.

"What's your name?" asked Brian.

"Don't you remember me, Brian?" replied the man. "Dominic Angelino, from Los Angeles. We met when you and your brother were running parties in West LA, but I never could keep up. Now things are different. I've made it and made it big!"

"That's great, Dominic," said Brian enthusiastically, covering a sense of foreboding. "I'm thrilled for you!"

*This guy could totally fuck things up!*

Brian leaned over to the security agent and asked him to locate Cynthia. The agent whispered into his walky-talky, and within a few moments, Cynthia made her appearance. She was accompanied by *Charles*, who immediately recognized Dominic. He quickly sized up the situation, sensing his brother's concern, and was prepared to step in if necessary. He gave his brother a two-finger salute, acknowledging he understood the situation.

Brian introduced Cynthia to Dominic.

"Cynthia, this is Dominic Angelino," he said. "Dominic and I go way back. He wants to donate ten large to the foundation in exchange for a private tour of our lovely home." He gave her a wink. "I told him you'd be delighted to show him around."

Cynthia gave Dominic a wide, flirtatious smile.

"I'd be pleased to be his personal tour guide," she said extending her hand. He took her hand, stood up, stumbled a bit, and he and Cynthia walked off, the security agent a few steps behind.

Brian followed them with his eyes. He knew that Cynthia was perfectly able to fend for herself in these types of situations. And if she needed help, the agent would be close at hand. But it worried him that Dominic claimed to know him and Alan from Los Angeles.

*What if she asks him how he knows us? What if he tells her that I have a twin brother?*

Alan sensed what Brian was thinking.

"Not to worry. Bro," he whispered. "I've got you covered. But somehow, I think she's got things under control."

As Cynthia was walking off with the man, she was thinking about her options. On the one hand, she could simply escort the man out of the building and have the agent, whom she knew was close at hand, send him on his way. On the other hand, she did not want to pass up the ten-thousand-dollar donation.

"What would you like to see first, Dominic?" she asked, giving him a sultry glance.

She could feel him salivating. He gave her a salacious look, letting his eyes go up and down her body. "How about the bedrooms?" he asked, grinning. He was trying to maintain his balance and sucking in his gut.

"I don't think they are on the ten-thousand-dollar tour, Dominic." she replied, holding his eyes with hers.

Dominic reached into his jacket pocket and retrieved his checkbook and a gold Montblanc pen. "How about a nice round twenty-five-thousand for a *complete*, all-inclusive, personal and private tour with, uh, a happy ending?"

He scribbled out the check and handed it to her. Cynthia quickly tucked the check in her cleavage and gave Dominic a kiss on the cheek.

"That's very generous of you, Dominic," she said. "Let me get us a couple of drinks, and I'll take you upstairs. Don't go anywhere. I'll be right back."

She gave him another kiss on his cheek as she left.

Within a few moments, she returned with two martinis. She handed one to Dominic as they ascended the circular staircase leading to the upstairs portion of the mansion. Dominic, excited by his own expectations of what would be forthcoming, gulped the martini in two swallows. Cynthia simply smiled at his impetuousness.

Together they climbed the stairs, Dominic stumbling on his way up. Just as they were about to reach the landing, Cynthia feigned tripping on the last step. Dominic made a grab for Cynthia in an awkward attempt to help her. She suddenly pulled back, avoiding his lunge. Dominic lost his balance and tumbled down the stairs, arms flailing, grasping for the banister as he fell.

He yelled out in pain as he came to a halt, legs twisted, toward the bottom of the stairs. Cynthia ran down to help him up, but both his girth and his already swelling ankle made it impossible for her to be of assistance. The security guard was already there.

Several people gathered around as Cynthia called out for help. Two more security agents along with Brian and Michael Shore, who happened to be walking by, quickly helped Dominic to his feet. He appeared dazed, unsteady, and in pain, but maintained that salacious grin plastered on his face.

"I guess, you could say I really fell for you," he said to Cynthia. His speech was slurred, and it was difficult for him to stand, let alone walk.

Cynthia chuckled at his pun. "I am so sorry, Dominic," she replied sympathetically. "It looks like our tour will have to wait for another time. Right now, I think you ought to have a doctor take a look at your ankle."

"I'll be fine," Dominic slurred. "Jus' call me a limo."

He was more disappointed about his missed opportunity to be with Cynthia than concerned about his swelling ankle.

Brian whipped out his cell phone and made the call. The security agents placed Dominic in a chair to wait, where he promptly passed out.

"Make sure he gets into the car," said Brian to the agents. "And be sure that he gives the driver his address." He then turned to Cynthia. "Are you okay?" he asked. "What happened?"

"I'm fine, Brian," she replied. "I was just going to give Dominic a private tour. We were going upstairs, when he stumbled and fell. I guess he had way too much to drink. But he did give me this." She reached into her dress and pulled out the check Dominic had given her.

Brian looked at the check, raising his eyebrows in surprise at the amount. "How convenient that he gave you the check before completing the, uh, tour. He probably won't even remember giving it to you until he sees the cancelled check."

Cynthia gave him a knowing smile. "Yes, very convenient."

Brian gave her a puzzled look, but mostly, he couldn't help but feel a sense of relief in the wake of Dominic's accident.

Seeing Michael, Brian said, "Michael, would you mind escorting Cynthia into the dining room. It's time for dinner to be served and the rest of the evening's entertainment to begin. After she offers some welcoming remarks, it might also give the two of you a chance to talk more about the foundation. In the meantime, I can take care of Dominic."

"It would be my pleasure," replied Michael, graciously offering his arm to Cynthia.

Brian stayed behind, assuring the few guests who had gathered around that everything was under control.

"Hey, folks, we're all good here. The gentleman just had a bit too much of the bubbly. Please enjoy yourselves, have some fun, and of course, be generous," he said, imitating his brother's wide smile and outgoing demeanor.

He waited until the limo driver arrived, not wanting to leave Dominic unattended.

# CHAPTER TWENTY-TWO

# The Vendetta

Cynthia was excited to get to know Michael better and to figure out a way to entice him to make a sizable contribution to her foundation. Earlier in the evening, she had asked her associates to vet Michael to verify whether he was actually as successful a real estate developer from Los Angeles as suggested by Brian. They had reported back that indeed Michael was a very successful, very wealthy, and well-connected player in Los Angeles and throughout the west coast.

They chatted on and off throughout the dinner and beyond. Cynthia learned that Michael was developing another business that had the potential of giving investors a forty to fifty percent return on their investment within six months. He had made arrangements to purchase large blocks of tickets to A-list concerts given by such celebrities as Beyoncé, Taylor Swift, Pink, and others.

"There are a limited number of prime tickets available for these major concerts," explained Michael. "The best tickets are bought up long before the tickets go on sale to the general public. Such places like Ticketmaster, The Hub, and Ticket City get first dibs on large blocks of tickets. Then there are the scalpers who buy whatever they can and hope to make a profit on resale; the closer to the event, the higher the price, especially if the concert is sold out. Through various contacts I have developed over the years, I have been able to arrange to buy blocks of the best and most sought-after tickets for the most must-see concerts. I buy them and sell them for at least double the price; more often than not, I can get triple or more. Therefore, I can guarantee investors at least a fifty percent return on their money."

"Why do you need investors?" asked Cynthia.

"If I am going to buy two hundred tickets for, let's say a Pink concert, at around eight hundred per ticket, it becomes expensive and risky," explained Michael. "And if there is more than one concert going on in different parts of the country, the cost is even greater. It is much more convenient to use OPM—other people's money. And since I know that all the tickets will eventually be sold, I can guarantee as least no one will lose money."

"That sounds great, and it must be a lot of fun as well as a chance to make a killing," replied Cynthia. "Do you get to see the concerts as well?"

Michael chuckled. "Yeah, that's one of the perks. I can choose the best of the best for myself."

"Where do you find investors?" said Cynthia. She could feel her pulse quicken. This seemed like a great way to make some serious money, especially if she could do more than one concert. She knew that concerts were happening all over the country, especially in big cities like Chicago, New York, and Los Angeles. Big-name musicians were always going on tour.

"I have a small group of trusted people, a pretty exclusive lot, who are willing to buy up everything I can find," replied Michael. "They come up with about fifty thousand dollars each or more to bankroll the purchases. Then I can sell the tickets through various online venues using a very sophisticated computer program at whatever the market will pay. Price is determined by demand."

"I wish I had a group like that for my foundation," said Cynthia. "Do you think your group would be interested in giving away some of their returns to charity?"

"I'd be happy to ask them," replied Michael. "Maybe they would want to become a sponsor for your foundation by creating a fund to make regular donations."

Cynthia's face lit up. "That would be awesome!" she declared. She was already seeing dollar signs in her head.

"Is the documentary that you showed here tonight on your website?" asked Michael. "It would be great if they could actually see the amazing work you are doing for those animals."

"I can make that happen," said Cynthia. She paused. "By the way, do you think I could become an investor in your group? In fact, it might be a good investment opportunity for the foundation, especially since it sounds like a no-lose proposition. I wouldn't want to gamble with the foundation money. I have a fiduciary responsibility."

"Hmmm," murmured Michael. "Are you sure you'd want to invest the foundation money? It's still a pretty risky proposition. You know, concerts get canceled, people get sick, a lot can happen."

"I know," replied Cynthia, "but where else can I get a potential fifty percent return with no downside? Just think how much good I could do for the animals."

"How much would you be thinking of investing?" asked Michael.

"Well, based on what I've seen so far, tonight should net about a two-hundred-fifty-thousand-dollar profit to the foundation," replied Cynthia.

"And how much of that would you want to invest?" asked Michael.

Cynthia thought for a moment. "I might be willing to go for broke. Plus, I have a little of my own money that I might want to add to the deal. Maybe another fifty."

"I see. So, you're thinking about three hundred thousand altogether, eh?" asked Michael, nodding as he spoke. "That's like six positions at fifty thou each?"

"Sounds about right," said Cynthia, trying to stay calm. "Am I in?"

"I'll have to think about it," he replied. "That's a substantial amount for one person. I'd have to think about whether to limit others whom I have known for a while or whether to expand." He hesitated. "I'll let you know by tomorrow. By the way, if I say yes, I'll need either cash or a bank check, not a personal check. No offense, but—"

"No problem," said Cynthia. "Now what about a donation to the International Wild Animal Preservation Foundation?" She playfully punched him on the shoulder.

Michael chuckled. "Absolutely." Michael withdrew his checkbook from his inside jacket pocket. Cynthia handed him a pen with the IWAPF logo on it that had been placed on each dinner table. Michael wrote a fifty-thousand-dollar check and slid it across the table.

Cynthia glanced at it and said with a satisfied grin, "Perhaps now I can invest three hundred FIFTY thousand." She gave Michael a wide smile.

CHAPTER TWENTY-THREE

# Busted

The following day, Michael emailed Cynthia to let her know that he had decided to include her in his group of investors. In the email, he included a contract spelling out the terms of the investment. He suggested that they meet at Brian's condo to close the deal since Brian too had decided to invest. They could all meet together to sign the contracts.

Cynthia was ecstatic. Not only was she able to solicit a major contribution to the nonexistent charity, but she was also going to be able to double down and significantly increase her bank account. She felt very self-satisfied and looked forward to the meeting.

Cynthia gave Robert, the doorman at Brian's condo, a cheery greeting as he escorted her to the elevator and used his key to open the door for her. Cynthia was almost giddy with excitement. This was her biggest score ever.

Brian was waiting for her as she approached the door to his apartment. He gave her a warm hug and a kiss. Michael was already inside waiting for her. The dining room table held a bottle of champagne as well as a light snack. The contracts were laid out on the table for both Cynthia and Brian to sign.

Michael greeted Cynthia with a friendly smile and a hug, kissing her lightly on both cheeks.

"Are you ready to begin our new partnership," Michael said, smiling.

"Absolutely," replied Cynthia. "I am so happy that you decided to include me in your venture."

"Did you bring the money?" asked Michael, looking at both Cynthia and Brian.

Brian pulled a cashier's check from his pocket and placed it on the table.

Cynthia took her cashier's check out of her purse, placing it next to the contract that had been prepared with her name printed on it.

"Great," said Michael, picking up both checks and placing them in his pocket. "Now both of you sign, and it will be official."

Cynthia and Brian looked at each other.

Brian gave her a wink. "Now we'll officially be partners," he said. "I am looking forward to the next chapter."

Once the signing was complete, Michael uncorked the bottle of champagne and filled their glasses. He lifted his in a toast. They all stood up.

"To a fulfilling future filled with good fortune and adventure."

They clinked their glasses and sipped the bubbly.

"Now if you'll excuse me," said Michael, "I must use the facilities." He smiled and turned, leaving Brian and Cynthia to enjoy their drinks.

"How long have you known Michael?" Cynthia asked Brian. "I've invested quite a bit of the foundation's money and a bit of my own with him."

"I've known him for quite a long time, and I trust him completely," said Brian. "Like a brother."

Cynthia smiled. "I am so glad to hear that. I had my people look into him, but it's nice to know you have confidence in him as well. I probably should have asked you sooner, but things were so hectic last night that I just didn't get around to it. I hope you don't mind?"

"Hey, no problem," said Brian. "You're a big girl. You can make your own decisions. I know you. And I know you are quite capable and quite astute as a business woman."

At that moment, Michael returned.

Cynthia's jaw dropped, and the champagne glass slipped from her fingers, crashing onto the floor. Standing in front of her was not Michael, but a duplicate Brian. Her head snapped back and forth between the two of them. Her knees felt weak. She held onto one of the chairs for support.

"Wha-what, who ..." The color drained from her face.

"Cynthia, I'd like you to meet my brother, Alan."

Alan smiled and gave a small bow. "Perhaps you should sit down. You look a little pale."

Cynthia sat.

Brian walked over and stood next to Alan.

"One thing you should know, Cynthia," began Brian.

In unison, Brian and Alan exclaimed, "You should never fuck with the twins!"

"You know?" said Cynthia, trying to recover her composure.

"Everything," said Brian. "We know about your uncle Josef, and your real name is Malenovich."

"And we know that Brian was your mark," said Alan. "And that was a mistake. We've been hustling since the day we were born. Nobody, but nobody, outcons us."

"We gotta give you credit though," said Brian. "It was a pretty clever idea to put together a phony nonprofit charity with offshore accounts. Impressive even." He tipped his glass toward her in a quick toast.

"So, what happens now, Brian?" asked Cynthia. "I am fond of you, and we did have some fun together."

"I think it's time for you to pack up your stuff and say goodbye," said Brian, pointing toward the door. "Consider yourself lucky that we only out-scammed you, and unlike poor Dominic, you can still walk."

Cynthia had regained her self-control. "Win some, lose some," she mused, trying to appear nonchalant. She walked toward the door, paused, and turned around.

"I have one more question. Who is Charles Franco? I rather liked him."

Brian and Alan looked at one another.

Alan took a deep bow.

Cynthia smiled, turned, and left.

The twins gave each other a high five.

As she rode down the elevator, Cynthia found herself feeling something she hadn't felt in years—sad. Not about losing the money; that was part of doing business, especially in her business.

*I'm going to miss Brian*, she thought. *I liked him. First time in a long time that I really liked a guy. It was fun hanging out with him, planning the party, like having a partner. I've never felt lonely before. It was always just me and my uncle, and then only me and the work.*

Now, thinking of not seeing Brian ever again, Cynthia felt a lump in her throat.

She shook her head trying to get away from her thoughts. But she couldn't stop the tear that slid down her cheek.

As she left the elevator, Cynthia waved goodbye to Robert, the doorman, and walked out onto Michigan Avenue.

# CHAPTER TWENTY-FOUR

# Wait, There's More

As the adrenalin rush of outconning Cynthia drained from his system, Brian realized that he actually missed her. The feelings confused him. How could he miss someone who had tried to take advantage of him, someone who had betrayed him?

Each time he thought of Cynthia, rather than being angry, he found himself smiling. He would wake up in the morning with an urge to call her. And in the evening, he would think of the good times they'd had chatting over dinner.

He thought about how similar they were to one another. They both distrusted people in general and had difficulty attaching to others. Neither of them had been in a long-term relationship. They had both learned early in life to rely mostly upon their own wits to survive in a competitive world. They had a lot in common, including liking the same TV shows, similar business interests, and just enjoyed each other's company. That combination was hard to find.

Brian found himself feeling sorry for Cynthia. Her parents had died when she was young. She was raised by her uncle who had used her as a shill in his cons. She had moved around a lot, didn't have any friends, and had to grow up fast. She was pretty, she was sharp, and she was clever. He liked her, but could he forgive her? Could he ever trust her?

When Brian told Alan in their next strategy session about his thoughts about Cynthia, predictably, Alan thought Brian was being irrational.

"Are you fuckin' kidding me!" exclaimed Alan. "That bitch tried to con you, bro! You should be happy she's out of your life."

"Yeah, I know," replied Brian, shaking his head from side to side. "I know you're right, but still, I liked her, really liked her."

"Are you getting soft?" asked Alan in disbelief. "How can you like someone who tried to screw you?"

"She was just doing what we've been doing all our lives," said Brian, "trying to make a buck. She's a hustler. And you gotta admit, she was pretty cool about it. Very slick. She's like us: hip, slick, and cool."

Brian smiled at the thought.

Alan stared at his brother for a long moment. "Who are you? I don't fucking know you anymore."

"Yeah, well, sometimes I don't know me anymore either," said Brian. "It seems the more human I become, the more hard-ass you become. Where's your compassion, bro? Your humanity?"

"Compassion? Humanity? What the fuck?" replied Alan. "Remember, bro, there are two types of people in this world, winners and losers. And right now, you sound like a loser. The only thing good about this chick was that we walked away with a cool three-hundred-thou. And she walked away with nothing."

Brian looked at his brother once again, realizing that they were going down diametrically opposite paths. The more human Brian was becoming, the more robotic his brother was becoming. Brian wanted to reach out to Cynthia to see whether they could find a way to reconnect. He knew he needed to talk with Dr. Albertson.

"Let me see if I understand what you've been telling me," said Dr. Albertson, gazing intently at Brian's face on his computer screen. "The last time we chatted, you were hell-bent on getting your revenge, a vendetta, I think you called it. And now, after following through with her scam on you, and you and Alan reversing the situation by using your being identical twins to hustle her to the tune of three hundred thousand dollars, you still find yourself liking her to the point of entertaining the notion of reconnecting with her and perhaps even forgiving her. Is that about right?"

Brian thought for a moment. "Yeah, that about sums it up," he said. "It confuses me that I could want anything to do with her at all, much less want to remain friends with her."

"Is that what you want, Brian, friendship?" asked Dr. Albertson.

"Huh, yeah. Why? What's wrong with that?" asked Brian.

Dr. Albertson gave him a wistful smile. "Maybe it's more than just friendship you feel toward her?"

Brian didn't know what to say. It was not easy for him to articulate his feelings or even identify them. He knew that he felt annoyed when Alan called her a bitch, despite what she had tried to do to him.

"I think I feel protective of her," said Brian, feeling a bit sheepish.

"Interesting," said Dr. Albertson. "Why do you think you feel protective?"

"I suppose beneath her self-sufficient, hard exterior, I can sense a, I don't know, vulnerability? Isn't that what you call it, Doc?"

"Yes, could be vulnerability," replied Dr. Albertson. "A lot of people put up a façade of toughness to mask their vulnerability. They see sensitivity and vulnerability as weakness. Can you relate to that, Brian?"

"Sounds a little like me, huh?" he replied with a smile. "Maybe that's why I feel connected to her. She reminds me of me. She grew up without parents and with an uncle who used her. At least I had my brother; she had nobody."

"So, you feel attached to her, connected, eh?" asked Dr. Albertson. "Maybe that's why she was able to hurt you. Maybe hurt was underneath the initial anger. People we care about can hurt us."

"I suppose so," replied Brian. "But how could I ever forgive her for what she tried to do? I've always believed nobody fucks with me and gets away with it."

"But did she get away with it?" said Dr. Albertson. "I thought you profited from it to the tune of over a quarter-million dollars. Isn't that enough of a vendetta?"

"But the point is, she tried to scam me," replied Brian.

"True. But at the time you and she were not going with each other. There was no commitment," said Dr. Albertson. "It seems to me that now you are considering going down a different path with her. Maybe something more intimate. Upping your game. But to do that, you would have to be at least open to the possibility of forgiving her."

"I don't know if I can do that, Doc," said Brian. "And besides, my brother would never forgive me. If I forgive Cynthia, I might lose Alan."

"Weren't you already on your way to separating from your brother and following your own path?" asked Dr. Albertson. "You and Alan seem to be growing apart, no longer identical in every way. You have described him as being a lot darker than you, more capable of doing things without feeling. Being more of a robot than yourself."

"So, what are you saying?" replied Brian. "That I should decide for myself whether I want to get back together with Cynthia regardless of how Alan feels? Is that it?"

"At the end of the day, Brian, it is your life, isn't it?" replied Dr. Albertson.

When the session ended and Brian got back in his car, he sat quietly for a while just thinking about what Dr. Albertson had said about it being his life. He knew that he and his brother had always said that forgiveness was for losers. People only got one chance to prove themselves worthy of trust. If they blew it, they got clipped. Now, he wanted to forgive, something he had never done with anyone but his brother. He also knew that there was something special about the way he felt toward Cynthia. The only other woman he had ever felt close to was Linda, his friend from college. His feelings toward Linda, however, were different than those he was developing toward Cynthia.

More than a month had passed. Brian decided to reach out to Cynthia. He figured that at the very least he could find out if she was interested in seeing whether they could repair their relationship and perhaps move forward. He stared at his cell phone for several minutes looking at the text he had written: *How about meeting me at 6 for a drink at our usual place? B.*

He finally hit the send button. The reply came seconds later: *C U there.*

Brian smiled. He was happy to see that she was still in Chicago. Grifters were notorious for moving on.

Brian arrived early and was sitting in a booth across from the bar when Cynthia walked in. She was wearing jeans, an off-the-shoulder top, and an effervescent smile. Brian felt immediately drawn to her. She seemed confident yet accessible, perhaps a little fragile.

He knew her dark side, but was captivated by her nevertheless. He recalled how Dominic's accident had raised questions in his mind as he watched her being more focused on the twenty-five-thousand-dollar check than on his well-being. He smiled as he thought about his own reaction at the time; he had been more relieved than concerned. He also recalled suspecting that Cynthia might have had something to do with the accident. They were so similar. Perhaps that was part of the attraction.

"Hi, Brian," said Cynthia, her smile radiant and her dark eyes sparkling. She felt a bit uncertain. "How've you been? I was surprised to hear from you."

Brian returned the smile, motioning for her to take a seat. "I surprised myself as well," he replied. "I was really pissed for a long time. But the truth is I've missed you."

Cynthia's features softened. "I've missed you, too," she said.

"I must admit, you pulled a great con, very impressive," said Brian with a grin.

"Thanks, but where did I go wrong; what was the tell that gave me away?" she asked.

"No tell. You just picked the wrong guy as a mark," said Brian. "My brother and I have been hustling since the day we were born. Nobody fucks with the twins; that's been our motto since forever. We were born to hustle. It's like in our DNA."

"Your brother is still pissed, right?" she asked.

"Yeah, he'll never trust you again," said Brian. "We decided a long time ago, we don't give second chances. Fuck us once, and it's all over, no second chances."

"And yet here you are," she said, holding his green eyes with a steady gaze of her own. "What's up with that?"

Brian blushed a bit. "I dunno. I guess, I like you more than I am angry or even hurt." He realized that this was the first time he ever admitted to being hurt by someone. It caused him to pause for a long moment before continuing. "When I realized I was … hurt by what you did, I knew that I must care about you more than I imagined."

"You care about me?" Cynthia's eyes welled up.

"Yeah, I do … a lot," said Brian, reaching across the table and placing his hand on hers.

"I-I care about you, too, Brian," said Cynthia as a tear rolled down her cheek. "I'm glad you reached out. I wanted to contact you so many times, but I was afraid you'd either not respond or tell me to fuck off."

Brian nodded. "I get that. We are a lot alike. Neither of us trusts people. We're both afraid of too much intimacy. We tend to be loners, except I've always had my brother. And we both love the art of the con."

They both chuckled at that.

"You're right about all of that," said Cynthia. "How'd you figure all of that out? No one has gotten me so well."

"First of all, you should know that we did a complete background check on you, so I probably know a lot more about you than you know about me," acknowledged Brian. "I know about your parents, your uncle, and your rap sheet. You've had a rough life. You're a survivor."

Cynthia was not surprised.

"And second," continued Brian, "I've been doing a lot of personal work, trying to figure out who I am and where I am going. The more I understand about my own motivations, the more I am able to figure out other people and what makes them tick."

"Now that's impressive," said Cynthia. "Is your brother as introspective as you? Is that a twin thing?"

Brian laughed. "No, not a twin thing. Alan could care less about self-examination. He's a Jason Bourne kind of guy. No feelings. No psychology. Just power and money and, of course, himself. He is far better at hustling than I am. As hard as I tried, and I really tried, I could never completely turn off my feelings. Alan has become a robot."

"So, what happens now? I mean between us?" asked Cynthia, her eyes wide in anticipation.

Brian remained quiet for a moment before saying, "I would like to give us a shot. What about you?"

Cynthia smiled. "I'd like that."

They stayed in the restaurant through dinner and beyond, talking.

Brian told Cynthia about growing up as a twin and how, until he moved to Chicago, he and Alan had never been apart. He explained how he found himself and Alan moving in different directions, with Alan enjoying the party life, being single, and life in the fast lane, while he wanted to live a quieter life, be in a relationship, and maybe even have a family. While he enjoyed the art of the hustle, he did not want people hurt. He told her he would rather hustle people who deserved to be hustled because they took advantage of others. Instead of being Tony Soprano, he could be Robin Hood.

Cynthia listened as Brian shared more about his background and what he wanted from life. She was deeply affected.

"Until I met you," she began, "I never thought of being in a relationship. I certainly never thought I could be really honest with someone. But now, with you knowing everything about who I've been, and even being my mark, and liking me anyway ..." Her words drifted off. She looked away, trying to hide the tears building in her eyes. After a moment, she continued, "Now I have nothing else to hide. It's a strange feeling to be known by someone and be liked anyway, ya know?"

Brian nodded. He reached across the table and held her hand and her gaze. "Yeah, baby, I know exactly what you mean."

By the time the evening ended, they had decided to give living together in Chicago a shot. He didn't know if the relationship with Cynthia would lead to marriage. But he wanted to give it try.

He thought about Alan saying, "No risk, no gain." Brian also recognized that his brother would not be happy about him living with Cynthia, and he might never embrace Cynthia, but as Dr. Albertson had said, it was his life.

He gave his head a good scratch and smiled.

# Note to Readers

Developing a sense of personal or individual identity begins early in life, most notably during puberty and throughout adolescence. It goes hand in hand with developing character and in defining one's personality; the two combined—character and personality—gives us our sense of self. Our early experiences growing up can either facilitate the development of a sense of self—that sense that tells us who we are and how we are different from others—or make it difficult for us to figure out who we are and find our place in the world.

Some cultures and families believe that we should subordinate our individual identity in the service of a group identity. People who grow up in this type of culture are discouraged from thinking about an individual self, but instead develop a sense of being part of a group identity. The group defines who they are and dictates what is expected of the individual. Developing a sense of independence and individuality is suppressed.

Western culture encourages individuality and independence. However, even in a culture such as this, developing a sense of individual identity can be made extremely challenging by several external or circumstantial pressures. For example, certain cultural and ethnic groups try to maintain the cultural ethos of group identity where the individual is placed in a situation trying to adapt to conflicting pressures—that of the dominant culture as well as their particular subculture. Sometimes the two cultures are contradictory, pulling the individual in opposite directions and forcing him/her to choose one over the other. Some people find it easier than others to shift from one set of norms to another, depending on the circumstances.

There are other circumstances that also make developing one's own sense of identity challenging. For example, being the child of celebrity parents presents a unique challenge. Being the offspring of a famous parent often leaves a child being identified solely as "the son or daughter of Mr. or Ms. Celebrity, as though that were integral to the child's identity. In my more than half-century experience as a practicing clinical psychologist, I have seen firsthand how difficult it is for these children to find their own identity outside of the shadow of their famous parent. The child is seldom seen as an individual, but only as the offspring of the celebrity. In addition, there are multiple expectations placed on these children to live up the status of their illustrious parent, not to mention the pressure to be as successful. Such external pressures make it difficult for the child to answer the question: "Who am I if not the son/daughter of—?"

Identical twins (aka "idents") are another group that struggles with identity development. They are often referred to as "the twins." They look alike, are dressed alike, and are frequently treated as though they were a single entity rather than as unique, separate individuals. Not only are they viewed this way by their parents—who often cannot tell them apart—but other family members, friends, and teachers treat them similarly.

There are several ways identical twins deal with the issue of differentiating themselves from one another when the entire world expects them to be identical in every way. Some continue imitating each other and fail to develop a sense of individuality. Others become polar opposites—one good twin and one bad twin, one athletic and one a coach potato, etc. Others try to find ways in which they are different from one another and develop an identity around those differences.

They use their differences to differentiate themselves, for example, "I'm the talkative one, he's the quiet one."

As adults, some idents will remain living in the same town with one another, doing everything together just as they did as children. They may even continue to dress alike into their adulthood and live next door to one another, if not under the same roof, while other idents move to different cities or states where they feel freer to develop a separate identity and life from their counterpart.

It is not my intent to offer in these pages a treatise on identity development. Rather, I wanted to set the stage for understanding the struggle confronted by the twins being introduced in this book. Identity development is challenging under the best of circumstances. But when placed in the context of a dysfunctional family and the absence of community support, identity development is even more vexing. Survival becomes the focus.

# About the Author

During the course of fifty-plus years as a practicing psychologist, I have been privileged to enter the lives of countless people as their psychotherapist. Their lives and struggles revealed profound truths about the human condition. After having written five nonfiction books, when I turned seventy-five I decided to turn my attention to writing psychological fiction based on my years as a practicing clinical psychologist. Many of the stories I heard in my practice have provided themes for my books. Often a common issue rather than a particular individual stimulated the stories.

Everyone has a story to be told. Usually, we get so caught up in living our life that we fail to see the extraordinary embedded in the ordinary. We look at our lives as just putting one foot in front of the other, trying the best we can to live our lives in a meaningful, productive way. For some of us, the task is merely to survive in the world in which we find ourselves. Sometimes it takes an outsider to tell the story.

As a psychologist I have tried to help people make sense of their life experience, come to terms with their inner demons, and find greater fulfillment. As a writer, I try to tell their story in a way that might help others find meaning, purpose, and fulfillment. A recurrent theme in my writing is the exploration of the light and dark sides inherent in all of us. I hope to encourage people to embrace both sides, learn to integrate them, and thereby experience a greater sense of wholeness and fulfillment.

More than once, their stories resonated with my own life and helped me to gain clarity and perspective. I am profoundly grateful for the insights provided by those who trusted me with their stories and permitted me to join them on their journey of self-discovery.

I was born and raised in The Bronx in New York City, attended City College of New York, and earned a Ph.D. in Clinical Psychology from the University of Kansas. Before retiring to write fiction, I practiced as a clinical psychologist for more than fifty years in the Los Angeles area. I have been married to my wife, Barbara, for over thirty years, have three grown children, five grandchildren, and two pooches named Charlie and Benji. My hobbies include vegan cooking, photography, woodworking, and physical fitness. Lastly, I am active with nonprofit agencies that serve children, youth, and families. All profits from the sales of my books go to these charities.